PSYCHOLOGICAL THRILLER
STALKER ROMANCE

SNOWMAN

A.EM.

Copyright © 2024 by A.eM. Snowman
All rights reserved.

This book, including its title (Snowman), characters, locations, scenes, and content, is a work of fiction. Any resemblance to actual persons, living or dead, events, or locales is purely coincidental.

No part of this book may be reproduced, distributed, or transmitted in any form or by any means, including photocopying, recording, or other electronic or mechanical methods, without the prior written permission of the author, except in the case of brief quotations used in reviews or other non-commercial purposes.

For permissions, inquiries, or other information, contact: a.em.author00@gmail.com

ISBN: 9798305922356

First Edition: January, 2025.

Cover and interior book design by A.eM.

SNOWMAN

A.EM.

TO ME

"TO THE MONSTERS WHO
TAUGHT ME TO DANCE IN THE
SHADOWS."

TO YOU

"TO THE GIRLS WHO READ THE
TRIGGER WARNINGS AND SAW
A STORY WORTH SURVIVING."

TO ELIZABETH

WHO GAVE ME THE DREAM OF A MAN WITH AN AXE.
WHO WAS ON SPEED DIAL WHEN NO ONE ELSE WAS.
WHO TRIED HER BEST WHEN I HAD GIVEN UP.
THANK YOU, MY FRIEND, FOR MORE BLOODY SCENES LIKE THIS ONE.
ENJOY THE CHAOS BETWEEN THESE CRAZY-ASS LINES.

TO MOLLY

WHO TOOK MY MADNESS AND
CALLED IT MAGIC.
WHO BELIEVED IN MY WILDEST
IDEAS—EVEN WHEN I DIDN'T.
WHO SAW THE MESS AND
CALLED IT ART.
WHO STOOD BY ME WHEN I WAS
SELLING DELUSIONS AND
SIMPLY SAID, "WRITE IT DOWN."
I COULDN'T HAVE PAINTED
SNOWMAN WITHOUT YOU.
THANK YOU FOR BEING THERE
FOR ALL MY DELULUS.
THANK YOU, MY FRIEND, FOR
SIMPLY BEING YOU.
ENJOY THAT SIX-PACK WITH AN
AXE AND THE CHASE THROUGH
THESE BLOODY LINES.

PLAYLIST

YOU WANT IT DARKER - LEONARD COHEN
HURT - JOHNNY CASH
CREEP - RADIOHEAD
MAD WORLD - GARY JULES, MICHAEL ANDREWS
CONTROL - ZOE WEES
SNOWMAN - SIA
FADE INTO YOU - MAZZY STAR
KISS ME - SIXPENCE NONE THE RICHER
SILVER SOUL - BEACH HOUSE
APOCALYPSE - CIGARETTES AFTER SEX
RUN - JOJI
SAME OLD ENERGY - KIKI ROCKWELL
ARSONIST'S LULLABYE - HOZIER
THE KILLING MOON - ECHO & THE BUNNYMEN
LULLABIES - YUNA
ICE ICE BABY - VANILLA ICE
RING OF FIRE - JOHNNY CASH
FOLSOM PRISON BLUES - JOHNNY CASH
DON'T DREAM IT'S OVER - CROWDED HOUSE
I THINK WE'RE ALONE NOW - TIFFANY
IRIS - THE GOO GOO DOLLS
PEOPLE HELP THE PEOPLE - BIRDY

SCAN FOR MORE

TRIGGER WARNINGS

AS THIS IS A DARK PSYCHOLOGICAL THRILLER AND STALKER ROMANCE, THIS BOOK MAY BE TRIGGERING FOR SOME READERS. FOR THIS REASON, PLEASE REVIEW THE FULL LIST OF TRIGGER WARNINGS (100+) ON MY WEBSITE BY SCANNING THE QR CODE.

BELOW IS A BRIEF SUMMARY OF SOME KEY WARNINGS:
- PARENTAL NEGLECT
- ABDUCTION
- VIOLENCE
- TORTURE
- STALKING
- SERIAL KILLER
- CORRUPTED AUTHORITY
- ABUSE
- EXPLICIT SEXUAL CONTENT (18+)

PLEASE PROCEED WITH CAUTION AND PRIORITIZE YOUR MENTAL HEALTH WHILE READING.

PART ONE

PROLOGUE

BREE

IF I COULD TELL you how a beginning turned into an end, I would. But in this story, the end wasn't really an end; it was just a beginning. Just as it started, it ended, and nothing was as it seemed. This is the story of a man, someone who was as cold as snow, his heart frozen, yet he decided to melt for one person. Me.

"Bree!"

The shout pulled me from my thoughts. I looked up, pushing my blonde hair off my shoulder as I peered around the coffee machine. My coworker Nea was wrestling with a basket full of coffee bean bags, having wrapped her arms around it as if it weighed a ton. Her voice pitches higher with urgency as she yells again, "Bree! A little help here?"

I hurried over, sliding around the counter. Her face was scrunched with effort, and the basket wobbled precariously in her grip. Before she could cry out again, I grabbed one side. Together, we wrestled it onto the bar. It hit the surface with a dull thud, and Nea let out an exaggerated groan, her hands flying to her hips as she stood straight.

"You know," I teased, brushing my hands off, "you could've asked for help earlier."

"It's six in the morning," she said, fighting off a yawn. "I'm half-asleep."

"Clearly," I said, raising an eyebrow.

She gave me a saucy wink. "Besides, I forgot you were here."

"Nea," I laughed, shaking my head as I walked back to the coffee machine. "Sometimes I swear you've got early-onset dementia."

She laughed loudly, the kind of laugh that could wake the birds. She tapped the side of her head with mock seriousness. "You're probably right. I should check on my last two brain cells before they die."

I tossed a cleaning cloth at her, smirking. "Oh, stop it."

The loud tick of the clock announced six a.m. sharp. The sun had not been bold enough yet to cast its light upon us, and the café was wrapped in the darkness. This was my haven-mornings like this. All the nightmares that haunted my nights felt so small under the glowing lights of this warm café. And when sleep at least decided to be a foe, I knew I would be in peace here.

The jingle above the door yanked me back to the here and now. Cold air swirled in, touching my skin, and on its heels came the scent of winter: sharp, clear cold and the earthly, homelike smell of wood.

I turned toward the sound of the door, my gaze rising from the counter to the man who'd just walked in. A black coat clung to the lines of his tall frame. The quiet intensity came with him into the air, like a whispered promise, as he turned toward me. Café light caught against his face, and my breath hitched. His eyes, as icy as the frost, locked onto mine, piercing, freezing me in my spot. His gaze was sharp, hard to forget, and my heart stumbled in my chest as recognition struck.

"Bree?" he whispered low and raspy as if wrenched from him. He seemed to look as shocked as I felt; his exhalation froze in the cold air between us.

It had been far too long, far too bloody long since I'd last seen him. Even through a cold swirl stirring around, I felt the warmth inside melt something frozen in me that had been there for far too long. And it was suddenly back, just in his eyes, in the tone of his voice, how the air around me felt when he was there. Suddenly, it was all there, and a torrent of memories came over me, memories of a time far away, of another me.

And I was back in the year 2016.

ONE

BREE

NOVEMBER, 2016

> "Leaves fall,
> Snow melts,
> Everything ends,
> to begin,
> Again."
> — Unknown

THE FIRST SNOW HAD fallen, that kind of snow that covered the world in silent stillness, muffling the chaos of the city. Years had passed since I had seen such snow, and its beauty took my breath away. Each flake seemed to dance before settling on the ground, adding to the white expanse that stretched as far as my eyes could see.

I sat on a worn-out wooden bench, with peeling paint and creaky slats, holding in my hands a steaming cup of coffee. Heat seeped through the frozen fingers as the biting chill clung to the air. With my legs crossed over, I exhaled strongly, my breath rolling upwards into the air in curled wreaths before it broke. Closing my eyes for just that moment, allowing icy silence to wrap me up. When I opened them again, motion, like a different life, unfolded before my eyes.

People were hurrying, scarves and coats wrapped high, the sound of footsteps crunching through the snow. A woman slipped, flailing her arms, catching herself with a nervous laugh. Children shrieked, their laughter carrying through the stillness. Two girls crouched by a snowman, their cheeks red with cold.

The older one yanked a striking scarf from her sister's head and threw it around the snowman's neck. The tiny one giggled, pushed askew a bright hat upon her head, and positioned it on the top. The little gloved hand fixed in a wayward smile on the grim iced face of the picture; two twig arms rubbed on either side into their frosty giant. I couldn't help but smile. At that moment, it was almost as if the world had condensed itself into something so pure and simple. And I almost envied the children who bring joy to their world, untouched by the weight that obscures it. I shut my eyes again, trying to catch my memories, but they all slipped away, melting like snow. My childhood is a blur, hazy at best; pieces missing, edges frayed. Who was I? Some shell, a shadow of the person that I once wanted to be yet could no longer remember.

I opened my eyes, and they fell upon the cup of coffee cradled in my hands. The dark liquid rippled where my fingers had slightly moved. My eyes dropped down to my wrists, where old scars carved across like faded whispers of a pain I wanted to bury.

Two parallel lines, remind me of nights when the darkness had promised to swallow me whole. A lump rose in my throat, and unwanted tears spilled out, running down my cheeks and the sudden warmth shocking my cold skin. Memories washing over me.

I set the cup carefully down on the bench which groaned under the weight of the cup, and I tugged at my sleeves to cover the scars, as if to hide them from everyone. My hands rose to my face and rubbed off the tears that clung to my chin.

"I'll be fine," I whispered, my voice trembling. "I promise."

I reached into my handbag and pulled out my notebook, its leather cover smooth to the touch from a thousand moments like this one. Its earthy, brown surface seemed to stare back at me as if it held secrets I was yet to write. My fingers were trembling, flipping it open to a blank page. The cool paper felt fragile under my palm.

A tear broke free, unnoticed until it splashed onto the corner of the page, oozing outward in a small, uneven stain. The date spilled from my lips in a whisper, anchoring me.

"November 6th."

The pen hovered over the page before pressing down. My handwriting, shaking, carved through the silence around me.

Date: November 6th.
Mood: Fine.
Thankful: For life.

I slapped the notebook shut, the leather spine softly snapping in the air. I pushed it into my purse and mashed the flap down like I was sealing away what was inside.

My hands clasped together, fingers lacing, thumbs pressed side by side. I bit my lower lip, the sting grounding me, my thumbnail digging into the soft skin of my other hand. The faint pain distracted me but wasn't enough to block the tide of nightmares and memories that crept in.

"I am fine," I muttered to myself.

The words left my lips like a mantra, though my chest tightened with the fog of flashbacks. Fragmented and fleeting faces that I could not name, voices humming just beyond recognition; impossible to discern which were nightmares and which scenes from real life that I had elected to forget.

Then, the touch on my shoulder, when I least expected it. I opened my eyes, my breath caught in my throat.

A voice came, soft and familiar, though distant. "Bree, are you ready?"

I blinked at her, my mouth opening but no sound coming out. Then, as if drawn by instinct, I whispered, "Mom?"

She smiled a small, hesitant smile, the sort that carried more questions than answers.

"Yes," she said simply, her fingers slipping into mine.

"Why did you change your hair?"

She blinked, startled, and then chuckled low. Her hair was deep, almost jet black, not the golden blonde I was used to and had grown up seeing every day. It was pulled back into a high ponytail. The contrast made her look like a version of herself I didn't know.

She stared at me, her face searching, like I'd struck upon some secret she'd never intended to reveal. Her fingers toyed with a stray lock of hair, twirling it over and over.

"You don't like it?" she asked, her tone casual, yet hesitant.

I didn't want to deflate her, not when she already seemed so unsure of herself. Forcing a smile, I softened my tone. "I do like it. I just... have to get used to it."

A small, relieved smile curved her lips and she squeezed my shoulders reassuringly. "Yeah, me too."

We walked across the parking lot together, the thin snow crunching beneath our steps. A car came into view, Dad sitting in the driver's seat, his red baseball cap tilted low as he fiddled with the radio. In the back, my sister sat silently, her head turned out the window, watching something outside in the world.

"You two done chatting?" Dad called out as we approached. His tone was sharp, impatient. "Get in. We're late."

Mom hesitated, then leaned closer to me, her voice a whisper that carried more weight than I was prepared for. "Maybe we can all start over," she said. Her eyes, dark and hopeful, lingered on mine.

I nodded, unsure of what else to say. "It'll be fine."

Fine. That one word had become my shield, my answer to everything. When nothing was fine, I said it anyway, hoping repetition would make it true. Maybe if I said it enough, I could trick myself into believing it, into feeling whole. Maybe then I'd be enough. Maybe they'd care. But we all had our masks. From the outside, every town we moved to, every dinner table we gathered around, painted the picture of a perfect family. Inside, we were splintered, each of us silently searching for ways to escape—through tears, through alcohol, through others—but never truly leaving. We were trapped in the illusion of perfection, our four walls painted in lies and cracks no one dared to acknowledge.

We were far from perfect. We were fucked up. And we knew it.

I opened the car door and slid into the back seat, crossing my arms over my chest to lean against the cold window. My eyes strayed into the rearview mirror and locked with Dad's. He shook his head slightly, small but with tons of unspoken emotion attached to the gesture. I could feel his disappointment, which came from him in heavy waves.

My sister sat next to me, still watching the world blur past outside. She didn't speak, hadn't, not since the accident. Her silence hung in the air between us like a weight. For a long time after, I hadn't spoken much either. But where I'd found my voice again, hers remained lost, stuck somewhere in the past, playing the same day on an endless loop.

I reached over and let my hand drop onto hers. I squeezed it gently, silently promising, "I'm here. I'll stay. For both of us."

That's why I didn't run; that's why, when the urge to leave seared through me like a fire, I hadn't left. I couldn't leave her behind.

With the humming noise of the car and nothing but silence between us, I watched as the world changed through the window: snow dusted hills and tall trees gave way to small towns and their dimly lit streets with shadows passing.

Two hours in and the fog thickened over the road, settling heavy like a veil. Darkness closed in and the landscape darkened as if trying to swallow the car into the trees that leaned near. It was gloomy outside, and the heaviness in us was mirrored by the heavy shadows of all that we would carry.

I felt the weakness pulling me down, the darkness closing over me and luring me into sleep, until I saw the light again. It cut across the void so brightly that it stung, and I raised my hand to shield my eyes, the glow flickering across my face.

"Come," the voice whispered, soft and far away, pulling at something deep inside me. A small hand reached out to grab mine, tugging me forward. I had dreamt of this before. A woman, her eyes as endless as the sea, her hair white like freshly fallen snow, spun me in circles, her laughter ringing through the air. She whirled and danced, her hand gripping mine, pulling me into a world that was nothing but the sound of children's joy and the shimmer of golden light.

I had no idea who she was, or who the little girl was whom she spun so effortlessly in her arms. All I knew was, that in those dreams, I was happy. And somehow, I never wanted to wake up.

But dreams are not life. They are illusions, glimpses of the world the way we wish it could have been. I am a dreamer, clinging to shadow, refusing to accept life, colder and harder than that. Yet, in my dreams, I was alive somehow, in a way I would have no words for.

The light shifted, pulling me back, the sun knifed through fog sharp and gold, and my eyes flew open. Turning my head to the window, I watched the car speed past a small, wooden sign, letters worn, but still readable; Írafoss, Iceland.

The GPS voice finally spoke in a low hum: "You will reach your destination in forty-three minutes".

Forty-three minutes was all that remained until it started all over again: a new town, a new life; another mask to wear, another set of lies to tell. Another perfect picture to paint over the fractured reality we carried with us. I wasn't ready. Not yet.

TWO

BREE

The car rumbled to a stop in front of an older house, isolated from the neat rows of homes we had passed on the way. Its weathered façade loomed against the gray sky, the place that seemed to hold its breath in the silence of winter. Dad was the first to step out; his boots crunched against the snow as he moved toward the trunk. He stopped, looking now at the door through which an old woman stood patiently waiting for him.

The dim porch light framed her, the gray of her hair spilling over her shoulders in loose, uneven braids, its strands flashing dull silver. Deep lines wrinkled her face, tracing years she had left so long behind her. She let her thin hand rise, shaking, in a slow wave to greet our approach.

Dad opened the door for Mom, movements brisk, and she went out, elegant, as if smoothing her coat could shield her against the slicing wind. She moved toward this woman, hand extended. Their fingers clung a moment before the two turned into the house.

I stayed in the car for a moment longer, staring out at the house. Its blackened bricks looked scorched, weather-beaten, and tired. Two large, dark windows flanked the front door, gleaming faintly with reflections of the snow-covered yard. Pine trees with sparse, twinkling lights stood on either side of the path leading to the door, their needles catching flakes that drifted lazily down from the overcast sky. The roof was sharp and stark against the dull backdrop, its edges outlined by a thick blanket of snow.

I finally reached out and grasped the handle of the car door, easing it open so I wouldn't make a sound I didn't need to. My boots bit the snow with a silent crunch. Snowflakes swirled down in tangles around me, catching in my hair and lashes. I tilted my head up for a moment, and let the cold flakes kiss my skin. Despite everything, it wasn't hateable.

The sound of the trunk slamming brought me back to the moment. Dad was wrestling with something, the metallic scrape of iron on paint setting my teeth on edge. He was dragging out the wheelchair for Mel, his movements sharp, irritated. He unfolded it with a violent snap, his face darkened by the shallow scratch he'd made on the car.

It was as if he valued the paint job on his car more than the fact his daughter couldn't walk.

He wheeled the chair to the left side of the car and yanked the door open. Wordlessly, he dragged her out of the seat, hoisting her like a sack of grain. Mel's body was limp but compliant, her head canting slightly as he plopped her into the chair.

"Would you fucking mind?" he barked, his voice sharp enough to make me flinch. Then he muttered under his breath, just loud enough for me to catch, "One's a plant, the other's dumb."

The words stung across my face, far harder than I cared to admit. One tear had escaped my eye before I could manage to check it. Heart racing, I hurried over to Mel's side, shaky hands grasping for the grips of the wheelchair. She doesn't turn to me; instead, her eyes are fixed somewhere, as always.

She sat straight, her posture impossibly perfect, but she didn't move, not even a twitch.

Her dark blonde hair framed her face, soft curls falling to either side like a halo. Her pale skin was flecked with freckles, dancing across the bridge of her nose. Her lips were delicate and bow-shaped, giving her an uncanny perfection, like a porcelain doll. Yet, it was her eyes that held me, deep brown, almost the color of cognac, too wise for someone only sixteen. Even now, stuck in that state, she seemed more mature than me. I wiped away the tears welling up in my eyes and leaned forward, speaking softly, pretending she could hear.

"Maybe we'll get you a room with a view of the lake," I said, forcing a smile. "Or the mountains. You'd like that, wouldn't you?"

Behind us, Dad scoffed, the sound sharp, slicing the air. "Why does she keep pretending Mel can hear a damn thing she says?"

I kept my eyes ahead, fingers tightening on the handles of the wheelchair, knuckles white to the black rubber. The air froze thick between us, the kind of silence nobody wanted to break.

I just didn't get the hate. Never did. Even more so, I didn't understand why Mom let it happen, why she never spoke up, never told him to stop, why her silence made her complicit in this quiet erosion of everything we were supposed to be. But I knew one thing, as I pushed Mel toward the old house, snow crunching under the wheels: for her and for me, I wouldn't stay silent.

We reached the front door, and as I pushed Mel inside, I leaned in toward her and whispered, "We don't deserve you, Mel."

The house wrapped itself around us like a heavy blanket, in extreme contrast to the icy grasp of the world outside. There was a roaring fireplace, alive with life; it cast flickering shadows around the walls.

The chill clinging to my skin seemed to recede slowly, melting in the heat. There was a faint scent of wood smoke in the room and of something old, faintly musty as if the house had stood silent for years, waiting.

I looked around, trying to find a place to retreat into and hide in. The house's structure was strange, though, and with one hand still on the cold iron of the wheelchair and the other lightly resting on Mel's shoulder, I just felt kind of exposed, standing here.

Mom stood beside the older woman; her voice was soft, questioning. "Is there anything else we should know?"

The woman nodded.

She spoke, her hands slightly trembling. "Yes. There's a lockdown in the town. Two weeks, starting in December." Her voice was even but had a hint of unease in it. "Dark times. No one goes out."

"Interesting," Dad muttered, a grin tugging the corner of his lip sideways as he turned to Mom.

The woman's eyes flickered in his direction before she looked back at Mom.

"A lot of police patrols," she said, as if sharing a secret, her voice going low. "Ever since that poor woman disappeared. They're everywhere."

"What woman?" I replied, breaking the tension because I had to face her directly.

She stiffened, her gaze avoiding mine as she brushed past me, her lips moving in a near whisper. "You're just his type."

These few incoherent words sent a cold chill down my spine. Frozen, I turned towards Mom and Dad. It went so silent in the room that the sound of the door clicking shut behind her sounded deafening.

"Don't you guys wanna know what's going on?" I asked.

"No," Dad barked, his tone final.

"Joe, please," Mom said softly, trying to temper the sharpness in his tone. Then she turned to me, her eyes calm but weary.

"Every family has secrets," she said. "Maybe that woman has her own. Let's not rush to conclusions."

"Ridiculous," Dad muttered, turning right into the kitchen, his heavy boots making a lot of noise on the wooden floorboards. I watched him cast a sideways glance out the kitchen window and the frozen fields beyond it.

"Mom," I whispered, my voice low so that Dad wouldn't hear me, "I don't like this place." I wrapped my arms around myself as goosebumps prickled along my skin. "It gives me chills."

"Every place we go gives you chills," she replied with a sigh. "We're spending a year here, and we have to adjust," she said, sharp before softening slightly as her eyes flicked to Mel. "Please, for once, just try."

"Fine," I muttered, brushing her off. "Where's the bedroom?"

"Yours and Mel's is through the living room, on the left." Her fingers pointed to the only open door. "Dad and I will be upstairs." The hand motion indicated back in the general direction of battered stairs with scratches etching lines into the wooden handrail. "The bathroom's next to the kitchen.

I nodded wordlessly and reached for the grips of Mel's wheelchair, wheeling her toward the bedroom door. One more backward glance, then I pushed her inside.

It was a basic room, but it was much larger than I'd imagined. At the far end of the room stood a huge window, stretching from floor to ceiling. It overlooked the woods; their branches dusted with snow, dancing in the soft breeze, and behind them, a hill draped in white. I wheeled Mel closer to the window so she could see the snowflakes falling softly against the glass.

"Oh, Mel," I said, dropping down beside her, my voice cracking. "I'm so, so sorry."

My head fell into her lap, her stillness was a comfort and a grief I couldn't shake.

I lifted my eyes to the window again, following the way the breeze teased the branches, their movements calm. For a moment, it was almost meditative, something you'd watch in a loop to quiet your mind. But just as the calm began to settle in, a known feeling crept up my spine.

Someone is watching.

My eyes leaped towards the shadow of a tree standing at the edge of the woods. For a moment it seemed to be some great animal, crouched low, its horns curling upwards. Its fur was as thick as the wool of a sheep. Then it moved. Slowly, it rose, and my heart plunged. It was a man.

He was tall, with his face hidden behind the mask from a deer's skull. The antlers cut upwards, ragged and sharp, while the empty sockets in the skull seemed to cut through the glass of my window and fasten on mine. His body was wrapped in something heavy, like fur.

He was watching me.

My breath caught as his eyes locked onto mine. My heart thundered in my chest, and I found myself frozen, unable to look away as he tilted his head to one side, studying me.

Slowly, I sat up, my face pale, my voice barely above a whisper. "Mel, do you see him?"

But Mel's eyes remained on the snow, unseeingly, as if there were nothing out of the ordinary there at all.

I was frozen. My lungs burned, refusing to draw in air as my entire body locked in terror. My eyes followed the tilt of his head, left then right, like some sort of predator sizing up his prey. It wasn't just his eyes that were on me; it felt like his gaze pierced through me, through the walls of the house, to every nook and cranny in our lives that was vulnerable.

And then, like a gasp breaking a dam, I screamed. The sound ripped from my throat, raw and primal, shattering the icy stillness. My eyes squeezed shut, and the image of the man seared into my vision. Footsteps thundered toward me, but when I dared to open my eyes again, he was gone. The window reflected nothing but the still, snowy woods, serene and empty, as if he had never been there at all.

Mom crouched beside me, her face white, her lips uttering some hurried whispers, but I couldn't hear her. The sound was muffled like I was underwater, her voice just a vibration in the air. My hand was shaking while I pointed towards the woods, willing her to see what I had seen. Her gaze followed my finger, but her expression didn't change; her eyes scanned the trees without recognition.

"I knew it," Dad's voice cut through the fog as he stomped into the room. His face twisted up in exasperation. "That shrink shouldn't have taken her off the meds. She's fucking insane."

Mom turned towards him shaking her head. She turned to look at me, as if silently pleading, wondering if she could truly believe what I was telling her. Her confusion betrayed her, her eyes went back searching in mine to outline the bits she could not understand.

"I... I saw...," I whispered, my voice trembling, my lips parched from forcing the words out.

"What?" Dad sneered, stepping closer. "A monkey?"

"No." My voice was more steady now. "There was someone."

"Oh, sure," he sneered. "It's the woods. You know what's out there? Beasts. It's called wildlife." He chuckled darkly, shaking his head. "You probably saw a bear."

"I know what I saw," I snapped, glaring at him. "It wasn't a bear, there was someone."

Dad leaned down, yanking me to my feet, his fingers not light on my arm. "Quit acting," he hissed in a low, corrosive voice. "You're embarrassing yourself."

"Joe," Mom said sharply, stepping between us. She pushed his arm away and spoke in a low but firm tone, "Let her be."

He held the look a beat longer, his expression hard, judgmental, then his shoulders shrugged, and he left the room. Mom followed, casting a backward look at me, closing the door softly behind her.

I stood there, my knees trembling, my mind racing. A tear welled in the corner of my eye but refused to fall. I clutched my wrist in my hand, gripping tightly, as if grounding myself in the moment could prevent breaking.

"I am fine," I whispered, over and over. "I am fine."

But I wasn't fine. Not even close.

I looked at my palms and willed my breathing to steady up until suddenly a loud **thud** of a snowball at the window got the air huffed out. My head snapped toward the window, and there it was, a small snowman in the yard.

The snowman was not there before.

Three spheres of snow stacked irregularly atop of each other; its arms made of crooked tree branches, its face a rough smile, with coal-black eyes. But there was something wrong. Like it was missing something.

My chest stiffened as I stared at it, a lump welling in my throat. Whoever the man was, whatever mask he wore, it was more real than the one I forced myself to wear every day.

The snowman was a message, I knew that, even if no one else would see it that way. To them, it was just snow. But to me, it was a warning.

Mom's voice cut into my thoughts as she reentered the room, a folded blanket draped over her arm. "We can hang up curtains," she offered, soft.

"Thanks," I said, forcing a smile. "That would be great."

Blocking the view was a relief. As much as I loved the sight of the snow-covered woods, the idea of being watched made my skin crawl. I could leave one side open for Mel, let her watch the snowflakes drift peacefully, and close the other for myself, shutting out whatever lurked beyond.

"Great," she said with a slight smile, her tone light but rushed as if wanting to flee the tension. "It's a deal."

Then she turned and left the room, the door softly creaking shut. I stood there a moment longer, glancing between Mel and the snowman outside. I wanted to look away, but my eyes kept drifting back to the snowman in the yard.

Late afternoon brought with it a creeping chill that slithered into the bedroom, seeping through the walls and settling in the corners. The sun was slipping behind the mountains, casting long shadows that stretched across the room like ghostly fingers. I sat stiffly on the edge of the bed, body taut, eyes not blinking. Every time I attempted to close them, even for a second, his mask would appear, an animal skull with sockets, and twisted horns. It was not the sight of him that froze my blood, but this question, gnawing inside of me; Who was the man behind the mask?

   I looked over to Mel. Laying in her bed on the left side of the room, her small form was cocooned in blankets. She had closed her eyes, and her face relaxed softly, as if she floated far away, folded in some quiet dreamland. She lay so quiet, unaware of the horrors that racked my brain. She made me ache. I'd lost the ability to dream anymore.

Dreams were turning into nightmares fractured echoes of fear clawing even at daylight.

I stood, my legs unsteady, and walked to the window.

Beyond the pane of glass, the woods had changed in ways so dramatic that the fading light made an unfamiliar world. It seemed much deeper, darker. The shifting shadows here lived as trees breathed and changed with shifting shades of dark on their own. I misted the glass as I looked without taking any notice of anything; Could he be out there somewhere watching me?

The woods seemed to be calling to me, daring me to find him or to let him find me. I turned finally, my bare feet cold against the wooden floor as I padded back to the bed.

Lying down, I pulled the covers over me, the weight of them doing little to still the pounding in my chest. Closing my eyes felt like a risk, but exhaustion tugged at my mind. I tried counting. Numbers came slowly at first, my mind resisting the monotony. By the time I reached ten, I could feel my body begin to relax. At twenty-three, the weight of being awake began to lift, pulling me deeper into the stillness, and I was falling asleep.

THREE

SNOWMAN

MIDNIGHT HAD STRUCK, AND the faintest tick of the second hand echoed within the kitchen's silence. I watched the cigarette pinched between my fingers, its smoke tail curling lazily. Its glowing pulsed with every jolty breath I took, while, hunched against the table rim, felt its corners dig deep into my palms.

I almost got caught. I almost fucking got caught.

The thought clawed at my mind, refusing to let go. My teeth sank into the inside of my cheek, the sharp sting grounding me momentarily. Years—years—of discipline, of keeping everything contained, nearly undone because of a single glance. Because of her.

Fuck.

The image of her was seared into my brain. Those eyes, so limpid, so knowing, stripped me bare in an instant. She was beautiful. Too beautiful. The kind of beautiful that could see through a person entirely.

I inhaled again, the smoke heavy, hot, and acrid in my lungs. It coated my tongue with a bitter film, but it wasn't enough to drown her out; wasn't enough to push the thoughts away.

"Fuck!"

The word exploded from me, loud and raw, into the fragile silence.

I slammed the cigarette into the ashtray, grinding it out with unnecessary anger. The filter crumbled under my thumb, and I watched as the ember died, its light turning out. Just like I had to turn every reckless thought about her. But I couldn't turn away. Her face haunts me, like a ghost that I didn't want to let go of. She saw me, not the surface, not the mask.

I could tell by the way she looked at me. She saw the cracks. She saw what I worked so hard to bury. And that terrified me more than anything else.

I paced to the center of the living room, the hollow creak of the floorboards cutting through the suffocating silence. The room was scant, just as it always would be. A couch sagged in the middle. Scratched coffee table that could tell a thousand stories of careless use. A single lamp that seemed to cast shadows against the peeling paper on the wall. Never had much, and never asked for more than I needed. And yet with so little, I carried so much. This was my curse, my birthright.

My mind filled with the picture of my father, a man whose sins had been passed on to me like heirlooms, polished and sharpened through years of handling. I was eleven years old when it all came to light.

I was eleven when he showed me what lived in the blood that coursed through my veins. He hadn't taught me to fight it—no, he'd nurtured it, made it a part of me, made it—me.

And my mother? She hadn't saved me. She hadn't even tried. She'd turned a blind eye, her silence complicit, her inaction deafening. And now, here I was, a living, breathing manifestation of everything they'd left behind. A monster dressed in their sins.

I hated it. Hated me.

By day, I played the part. Just another person, blending into the crowd, invisible. But by night, as soon as dark fell, the truth surged to the surface. The memories. The urges. The visions of blood. They swallowed me. I couldn't escape them, no matter how hard I tried.

I blamed my father for planting this sickness inside me. I blamed my mother for letting it take root. And I blamed myself for not being strong enough to cut it out, for not being able to stop it.

My fists clenched at my sides, standing in the middle of the room as my chest rose and fell with each uneven breath. The compulsion seared under my skin, restless and insistent. It whispered to me, tempting me, promising release. I knew the cost. I'd seen it play out a hundred times before. But it was still there. And I knew that no matter how tightly I tried to hold myself together, the cracks would keep spreading. The curse was part of me now, as undeniable as the blood in my veins. I was ill. I knew it. And there wasn't a damn thing I could do about it.

The only sound in the room beneath my boots was the soft hum of the radio above. The red carpet, worn and frayed from years of use, hid the weight of secrets. I crouched, my fingers curling into the edge of the rug, pulling it to one side. The old fabric bunched against the sofa as I folded it away, revealing the carved square of wood beneath. The edges of the hidden door had been a bit rough, but it had served well. In the middle, it glittered with a round iron handle and dimmed light. I grasped the handle, my palm feeling the coolness of the metal, and pulled.

I lifted it and swung it to the side, the wooden lid creaking with the weight of what was beneath. Before me yawned the opening, a passage framed by rough wooden stairs leading down. I stood and placed the cigarette between my lips. As I lit it, the cherry-red tip of it seemed to glow in the dark as I inhaled. Then I stepped down, each creak of the stairs awakening the silence.

The air was heavier down here, thick with the smell of wood, rust, and something more metallic. The walls were close, almost suffocating, and the dim bulb that hung from the ceiling cast long shadows on the dirty floor. Chains swayed gently in the air, dangling like silent sentinels from the beams above. In the center of the room was a wooden table, its surface scarred with years of use.

I walked to it, the cigarette hanging loosely from my lips. The tools were laid out precisely, their sharp edges gleaming faintly under the weak light. Next to the radio was my mask, a plain white one, almost featureless apart from openings for the eyes and small holes for the nose. It was ordinary and that was why it worked. It hid my face, and in doing so, stripped me of anything human.

I stubbed out the cigarette on the table and began to strip to my underwear. The chill in the room immediately pricked my skin. Reaching for the neatly folded black jumpsuit on the table, I slid into it. The nylon clung to my skin, waterproof, erasing the last vestiges of softness from me.

I caught a glimpse of myself in the mirror propped against the wall, and the reflection staring back was my worst nightmare, an avenger, but not the kind to save anybody. No, I was the villain in this story, the bad kind.

I turned to the table that was next to the wall, a tilt in my head so that the woman bound tightly to it could be regarded full on. Against dark wood, her body seemed very pale, her skin bruised, wrists and ankles tied rather tightly by coarse rope. She was nude, bruising, shaking all over. Only her red eyes looked up at me amidst the swelled face, from multiple hours of crying. Her muffled sobs came through with weak strength through the duct tape that was pulled over her mouth.

"Fuck, momma," I rasped, the words dry and hoarse through the mask. I tilted my head, letting the notes of the song Sweet Dreams waft from the radio. "Being a killer is a full-time job."

Her body flinched at my words, trying in vain to pull away. I walked to the tools, selecting a needle and a tube. As I tested the needle's sharpness against the pad of my glove, I turned back to her.

"You know," I said, "when I read your file, I thought, Wow, this poor woman's been through a lot." I chuckled, a sound that echoed off the walls. "But then, I saw him."

Her head was shaking violently, desperate denials muffled behind the tape.

"Little boy," I continued, my voice lowering, "bruises covering a small body. Fearful, wide eyes stared back at me, screaming for help."

I exhaled, "Do you know what he gave as his explanation?" I leaned in closer to hear her whisper, my face inches short of touching hers. "I fall down the stairs."

Her cries grew louder, her head thrashing. I reached for the duct tape, peeling it off in one sharp motion. Her scream ripped through the room, shrill, but my gloved hand clamped down over her mouth before she could finish.

"Tsk, tsk, tsk," I shushed her. "Typical. But no one can hear you, momma. You're eight feet underground."

I let my hand slip away slowly, giving her the chance to speak.

"Now," I said, "if you'll be a good girl and listen, maybe I'll be fast with you. Anything to confess?"

She gasped, her sobs coming in heaving bursts. "Please," she choked out. "Please let me go."

I tilted my head, and my tone dropped to a dangerous whisper. "So, nothing to confess?"

She shuddered and the tears streamed down her cheeks. "I will," she said hastily. "I will... just please... let me go."

My jaw clenched as I leaned in closer.

"I'll think about it," I muttered.

"I..." Her voice was quaking, her body shaking. "Maybe..."

"SPEAK!" I barked, my voice cutting through her hesitation like a blade.

"I pushed him!" she shouted, the words tumbling out in a wild rush. "He wasn't listening, and I just—just exploded! But that doesn't make me a bad mother!"

I froze, tilting my head. "The problem is," I whispered in her ear, "you're not his mother."

"I am!", she cried. "I am!"

"Nah," I said only, stepping back as her sobs grew louder.

She begged, her words incoherent, a tangle of pleas and apologies. But the sound faded into the background as I focused on the task ahead. Her tears fell freely, her voice cracking under the weight of her desperation.

"Please," she whimpered, "please."

"Hmmm. I'm still thinking about it," I muttered, tilting my head to one side as I watched her squirm against the bindings. Her tears streamed freely now, cutting streaks through the grime on her face.

"I took him when he was five," she blurted, her voice shaking. "I never knew he'd be such a pain in the ass, but please—"

A thin, mirthless smile curled around my lips, and I leaned the needle toward her arm. "He is a child, not an animal," I said, ridiculously calm.

Her head thrashed about, desperation etched into every strained movement. "Nooo, please," she screamed, her voice cracking.

"You see," I said, crossing my arms, letting the needle hover just above her skin, "I know you're lying."

Her breathing hitched, the words tumbling from her lips in a frantic rush. "No, I swear! I—"

"You took him when he was a baby," I said, cutting her off. My voice was ice, flat. "From a nursing home." The needle pricked her skin, sliding in gently as I began to draw blood into the tube. It flowed in a slow, crimson stream, dripping into the bucket beneath her.

"They were after you for poisoning those poor little angels. And then when the walls started closing in on you, you took one with you. You stole him—and turned his life into one big misery."

Her sobs grew louder, her head shaking violently. "I was helping him," she said, her voice cracking. "I wanted to make him better!"

I scoffed, my eyes rolling. "Oh, how sweet." Sarcasm oozed out of my voice. "You made him better by breaking bones, pushing him like a dog?" The dark chuckle escaped my lips. "You disgust me."

Her eyes turned hard, flashing defiance, even as her strength ebbed. "You're no better," she spat out. "Monster!"

I laughed, and it sounded hollow in the room. "Yeah," I said; my tone came out sharp and cutting. "I am."

It is people like her that monsters are born of, made by their hands, shaped by their cruelty, and unleashed upon the world. I had no illusions about what I was: no heart, no conscience, just a purpose.

"Killer!" she screamed, the word torn from her, tattered and weak. She spat at me, spittle wetting her lips.

"Yep," I replied, smirking. Her words didn't cut. They didn't even graze.

"Why are you doing this?" she croaked, her voice little more than a whisper now. "What did I ever do to you?"

"You didn't," I said, leaning forward, my voice low even. "But someone else did." I chuckled darkly and shook my head. "And I'll be damned if I let it happen to that boy from anyone else, either."

Her eyes fluttered shut, her body trembling as her strength was drained away.

"Fuck you," she whispered, the words faint and slurred.

"Yeah, bitch," I muttered, leaning down until I was eye-to-eye with her. "Fuck you too."

I straightened, turning to the table as her body stilled behind me. Lighting another cigarette, I inhaled deeply, letting the smoke curl out of my nostrils as I tugged the mask from my face. The cool air kissed my skin, and my reflection in the mirror caught my eye.

The face hiding behind the mask wasn't the monster I wore for the world; it was the broken boy, hurt by all those who were supposed to care for him. The mask made it easier to do what I had to do. Beneath it, though, vulnerable, I still held the scars of a stolen childhood. They had made me this way. And if I was going to hell, I'd make damn sure to take every one of them with me. Monsters aren't born; they're made. And, I'll be damned, I had been a good one.

The space was silent, while the heater hummed softly and blood occasionally dripped into the bucket. I leaned back in a rickety chair, its legs groaning under my weight, and lit another cigarette. The smoke swirled in slow patterns in the hot air while I watched the blood seep steadily into the second bucket.

Draining them made the job neater, and more effective. Once the blood was gone, it was far easier to separate them, piece by piece, less mess, and splatter.

I had prepared the room before sitting, wrapping the space around her in thick plastic curtains that hung from the ceiling. The warmth helped slow the pumping of her heart and made sure the blood flowed at just the right pace. I learned a long time ago, that it was easier this way.

The file sat on the table before me, its edges smeared from weeks of handling. I flipped it open and turned the page over the page of photographs and notes that were in handwriting until I found her name in printing. I read it out loud, "Sigrid Halvorsen."

The name hung in the air like a question.

Her story lay before me, scant as it was: orphaned young. Grew up in a nameless home, her parents unknown. No police record. It would seem that she also had a talent for slipping in and out, leaving no evidence that she was even there. My only picture is the one holding the little boy, the same child now lying beaten and broken in the hospital.

I stared at that photograph, my cigarette burning down to the filter as the memories clawed their way back. In the picture, the boy had such hollow eyes; clinging onto her, screaming at me from the page.

And then, as always, the flashes struck.

I was six years old when my father took me into the woods. He said we were going hunting. I didn't know any better. I thought it was a game, another one of his weird lessons. The hike seemed endless, the trees growing thicker, their shadows darker, until we reached a place where the sunlight no longer broke through.

He spoke coldly, "This is where you will stay. Survive the night. Prove to me you are not weak."

I stared at him, unsure if he was playing, but as he turned and walked away, leaving me in the freezing winter, it became clear this wasn't a game. My breath hung in the air like smoke, my body shaking as I went to find some cave to stay in. I gathered sticks with trembling fingers, scraping stones together until sparks finally caught.

But it was hunger, not the cold, that made me like an animal. And when I saw the deer, I didn't think. I only lunged forward in a wild, desperate lunge and sank my teeth into its flesh. Raw. Bloody. My stomach churned, but hunger won out over disgust.

When my father came back the next morning, all he said was, "I'm glad you're not dead." That's all. No congratulations, no affection, just apathy. He was pleased I had lived—not because I was his son, but because I had proved useful. That night I knew what he wanted me to be.

I tore my gaze from the photo, my chest tight with the anger I hadn't felt in years. Snow had always been a cruel reminder of him, of the life he forced me into. But it also reminded me of my brother.

Only one happy memory...

The snowmen we built together, how we snuck coals and carrots from the kitchen and argued over who could do the better face, and how we laughed, our gloves soaked through, making lumps of snow into something we'd call perfect.

But perfection was not a word for it, not yet. I came to understand that too late. Snowmen don't come alive when buttons are stolen and sticks have been carefully carved, they only begin to breathe when made of human flesh. Human parts. For then, and only then does it fully come into the aspect of chaos that's buried inside.

I stood, walked toward the plastic curtains, and glanced back at the bucket beneath her. Nearly full. The sight didn't bother me. It was just part of the process.

"Call me a monster if you want," I muttered, softer, staring at her lifeless body. "But the monster is just an image I want you to see."

FOUR

BREE

THE LOUD THUD GOT me up from bed, my heart sprinting, as I swiftly sat up. The room was dark except for the thin slice of moonlight that spilled across the other bed. Mel's bed. But it was empty.

"Mel?" I called out softly, my voice barely above a whisper. "Mel?"

I swung my legs over the side of the bed, my feet slapped against the cold wooden floor. The wheelchair was kept alongside her bed, but she was gone. My stomach twisted. Mel hadn't been able to walk for two years... how could she have disappeared? Where would she go?

Another thud beyond the door cut into my thoughts like a knife. I moved as quietly as I could to the door which was slightly ajar. My fingers brushed the edge, and I peeked out. The living room stretched before me, empty and only dimly lit by moonlight that seeped from the window.

I pushed the door open and stepped out, my toes barely making a sound as they hit the floor. I breathed shallowly, every muscle in my body was strung taut as I moved toward the center of the living room. The fireplace still flickered softly, dancing shadows upon the walls. Something was wrong and it felt thick in the air, something I just couldn't put into words.

Then I saw her.

Mel stood at the top of the staircase, her white dress aglow in the soft shine of the fire. My breath caught. She was pale, her lips all but colorless, her face drained of its usual warmth. Her eyes were fixed on the front door, unblinking as if she were waiting for something.

"Mel?" I whispered, my voice shaking.

She didn't answer, didn't make a move. Slowly her hand rose, her sparrow-like fingers extended pointing towards the window.

My eyes followed her motion. There, just beyond the glass, stood the snowman I saw earlier. Its carrot nose glimmered weakly in the moonlight, but something about it made my skin crawl. The snowman was... finished now. It hadn't been before. I didn't know how I knew that, but I just knew it.

I returned to the stairwell, but Mel was no longer there.

"Mel?" I whispered louder, "Where did you go?"

Above, the creak of measured, light footfalls sounded. I made my way up the steps slowly and felt my heart racing strongly inside my body. A door that was slightly open at the far end of the corridor led toward the darkness of the attic.

"Mel?" My voice shook the word out, barely audible.

I pushed the door open, and the narrow staircase leading upwards appeared in the opening. The wood groaned under my steps and seemed deafening while I walked up. Dark from above grew closer and closer, and then, suddenly without a warning, the door banged shut behind me.

Panic surged through me. I turned, ready to scream, but a large hand clamped over my mouth before I could make a sound. Another hand wrapped around my waist, lifting me with ease off the floor. I thrashed, my arms and legs flailing, but the grip was so strong.

"Hello, birdie," a deep, gravelly voice whispered in my ear. "Don't fly away." His voice was low, almost playful, but beneath it lay a menace that froze the blood in my veins.

Every fiber in my body was screaming that this was the man from the woods, the one I had feared might come, and now he was here holding me in his arms.

He lifted me up the last steps like I was nothing but a feather, my struggles barely registering. And as we reached the top, he spun me around to face him.

His hand was still clamped firmly over my mouth, silencing me, while his icy blue eyes bored into mine. They were the only part of his face I could see through the white plastic mask he wore. The mask was plain, a bone-white oval, except for the eyeholes that revealed those piercing eyes. There were no contours for a nose or mouth, just a blank, faceless plastic that hid his face from mine.

There was something in the way he looked at me like he was searching for something, trying to see if I could see through him the way he was seeing through me. The world seemed to fade around us, the room growing silent except for the sound of my ragged breathing.

"I'll let you go if you promise not to scream," he whispered, close to my face.

My heart thundered within my chest, and I wanted to scream, to fight, but I was more afraid of waking my father than anything this stranger might do. So I simply nodded, moving my face gently, slowly.

His grip on my mouth loosened, but his hand remained there, an implied presence ready to return if the promise was broken. For a moment neither of us did anything but breathe; our silence pulled taut as stretched rubber on the verge of snapping, fragile and close to breaking altogether. His eyes never left mine, and for that minute, I knew he was not done with me yet.

"Who are you?" I whispered, shaking, taking a step back, trying to put some distance between us.

"Nobody," he said calmly, almost detached, as he moved closer.

"Why are you here?" My feet instinctively receded another step backward.

"Curiosity," he said simply and took another step closer to me.

"Are you the man from the woods?" I'd not gotten the question out before my back slammed against the wall, stopping me cold.

"Yes," he said, now close enough to dominate the air between us. His hand slammed against the wall beside my head, followed by the other, boxing me in. His arms formed a cage I couldn't flee. Trapped, like a birdie, he called me.

He leaned his head to one side, scanning my face as though he would find something there. His eyes roamed over me, searching for some sort of story my body might tell—scar, mark, clue—but there was nothing. Just pale, plain me. I felt exposed under his body as if he were peeling back layers I didn't know I had.

"Your eyes," he whispered, his voice softer now. His gaze snagged onto mine, and I turned my face away, but his gloved hand caught my jaw. Gently tilted my face back toward him. His eyes locked tirelessly into mine, the ice melting into the ocean.

"What about my eyes?" I asked, trying to veil my fear with defiance.

"Ocean blue," he growled a low whispered rustle of words against my lips. I could feel his breath through the mask. "I found my favorite color."

Goosebumps spread over me, a shiver running down my spine. His words hung in the air, turning them into an emotion I couldn't quite explain, one that touched something deep inside of me. My heart pounded against my chest, with a savage rhythm of fear and something else altogether.

"Let me go," I whispered, the pleading not even audible over the loud hum of my pulse.

"Fine," he said, stepping back. The sudden loss of his proximity was almost dizzying. "I will, birdie. Just for now."

He spun on his heel and began walking toward the stairs slowly, almost carefully. When he reached the middle of the staircase, he paused, his head angling slightly, though he didn't turn back.

"What is your name?" he inquired. His voice carried well in the still air.

"What's yours?" I shot back, surprising myself by the boldness in my tone.

A low rumble of a chuckle escaped him. "I'll let you figure that out," he said, still in amusement as he continued down the stairs.

The moment his footsteps began to fade, I couldn't help it, "Bree," I whispered, the name passing my lips before my better judgment could stop me. "My name is Bree."

He didn't say anything, didn't turn back. He just walked through the door and shut it behind him, as if he had never been there at all.

For a while, I stood, caught by the silence, a load pressed against me. But a deep frustration boiled inside me, and with the palm of my hand, I hit my forehead twice.

"Stupid, stupid, stupid," I muttered under my breath.

Why did I give him my name? How could I be so careless?

"Fuck," I hissed, dropping down the wall until my ass hit the floor. My head dropped into my hands, my fingers digging deep into my scalp.

"Fuck," I whispered again.

I had always done this. Acted on impulse, and dug myself into holes without a second thought. But this was different. This wasn't one of those mistakes I could shrug off.

This man in his mask, his eerie calm, walking into my house as if he owned it as if he belonged here, and the worst of it, the way he made me feel, not just afraid, but deeper, more unsettled. I needed to stop this, whatever this was before it reached the point of no return.

I opened my eyes, and gray was the first color of morning. It filtered through the glass of the window down to me. The familiar outlines of my bedroom surrounded me, the faint smell of dust and wood settling into my senses. For a while, I thought I must have just dreamed it all— noise, Mel standing on the stairs, the stranger up in the attic. That all felt so distant, like any memory seen through frosted glass. But the chill that ran down my spine told me otherwise.

I pushed the blanket off and got up, turning to the woods beyond the window. The trees stood perfectly straight, their limbs bare and brittle against a winter sky. There was nothing to show he had ever been there, nothing to show anything existed. Just silence.

By the time I turned my head in the direction of Mel's bed, she was wide awake, staring in some direction.

"Mel," I whispered, crossing the room to kneel beside her. "You're awake." I brushed a strand of hair away from her face, my fingers trembling slightly.

Her eyes remained fixed on the ceiling, but for a moment, I could have sworn I saw the faintest flicker of recognition in her gaze. I opened my mouth to continue, but the faint hum of voices from the other room caught my attention and drew it away.

I stood and, silently moved toward the door. The whispers were low but distinct enough to outline the edges of their conversation. My parents. There was tension in their voices that churned my stomach.

"She walked last night," my mother said, her voice strained with urgency. "Bree can't find out."

"If she knew." her voice quavered, with almost a begging note to the words.

"Stop it, Laura," my father snapped, his whisper sharp. "I won't let it happen. And stop fucking pretending. I'm sick of it."

There was a silence; then his voice came again, lower but no less harsh. "Bree's nineteen now. We should have gotten rid of her a long time ago."

I reeled back from the door, the words hit like a blow.

Rid of me?

The words cut clear in my head, sharp, cruel. My breath snagged in my throat, and before I knew it a tear slipped down my cheek. They wanted me gone. All this time secrets and hiding things; now this? The overwhelming urge to run grabbed at me, yet it was the thought of leaving Mel behind that glued my feet to the spot. She was the one I wouldn't leave. Not her.

I ran back to Mel's bed and fell onto my knees on the cold floor beside her, my hands clenching her thin shoulders. "Mel?" I whispered urgently. "Mel, can you hear me?"

Her eyes were open, staring blankly at the ceiling, "blink twice if you can, please," I whispered.

My heart sank until, slowly, she blinked once. Then again.

Relief washed over me. She could hear me. She was still there.

"Can you walk?" I whispered, shaking.

Her eyes blinked once.

No?

The words were no sooner out of my mouth than the door flew open, and my head snapped back up. My father filled the frame, his expression neutral, almost too calm. His presence ran ice through my veins.

"Morning," he said, his eyes darting between us.

"Morning," I replied. My voice was flat, my body stiff.

"Laura made you breakfast. Get Mel ready and come eat," he said, his tone almost unnervingly casual. Then, without waiting for a response, he turned and left, the door clicking shut behind him.

As soon as he was gone, I turned back to Mel. Again her eyes moved, blinking twice this time.

"You can walk," I whispered, more statement than question.

Her eyes blinked once, in slow motion.

No? What does she mean?

I sat back on my heels, my mind racing. There was something I wasn't seeing, something they weren't telling me. All my life, I'd been the "crazy one," the one no one believed. I'd learned to play my part, to keep my suspicions hidden behind the mask of the shy girl they thought I was. But now, the cracks in their perfect world were showing. Something was going on, something I couldn't just turn a blind eye to anymore. And this time, I wasn't going to pretend.

FIVE

BREE

The wooden table was rough beneath my fingers, its surface scarred. Plates of golden pancakes sat between us, syrup pooling in sticky puddles around their edges. Strawberries sat piled high in a bowl, ruby-red skin glistening under the morning light next to a jar of honey that glittered like amber. I inched the plate across the table, the porcelain scratching softly against the wood and breaking the quiet. My stomach churned.

"Eat." My father's voice shattered the quiet as though it were a command rather than an invitation.

"I can't." My voice was thin, barely scraping above a whisper. "I'm allergic."

I dared meet his gaze. His eyes were hard, daring me to defy him.

His lips twitched, amusement curling in the corner of his mouth. "Allergic? That's bullshit."

I swallowed hard. "I am."

My hands shook as I grasped the edge of the table.

"Prove it," he barked, shoving the bowl of strawberries toward me.

Strawberries tumbled, one of them rolled out and bruised against the table. His laughter bubbled up, jagged, cutting through the still air.

I flinched as the sound rippled through me. Across the room, Mom stood as still as a shadow. The bruise under her eye had flowered into a deep plum, proving words she couldn't say. Her lips were pressed thin, her expression blank, but her knuckles whitened as she gripped the edge of the counter.

"No!" I sprang up from my chair, which scraped along the floor with a screech.

Dad slammed his palms onto the table, rattling the plates and sending silverware clattering.

"Sit the fuck down!"

The force of his voice struck me like a physical blow. My knees buckled, and I fell back into the chair. My heart thundered in my chest, each beat a desperate plea to be free.

"If I eat this," I whispered, my voice quivering as I reached for the bowl, "I could die."

"Good." The word was low, his eyes seemed to narrow into blackened slits.

My throat tightened, and the words I'd been swallowing finally burst free. "Why do you hate me so much?"

For an instant, his lips parted, the sharp edge of his response poised to cut me down. Then came the knock—loud, insistent, like a hammer striking the front door.

The sudden sound snapped the tension in the room, and his head flinched to the door, his eyes darting to Mom. He dropped the napkin he'd been twisting in his fists and growled out, "This isn't over," as he stormed past me.

Another knock echoed before he reached the door. Two men stood on the threshold when he pulled it open.

The tall one was imposing, a big, burly man clad in a black overcoat strained on his shoulders. His chestnut brown hair flowed behind his head in a loose bun, resting at the nape of his neck, while a short beard, dark with the merest hint of silver shadowing a strong jaw reached the underside of his chin. Beneath his coat, a dark brown turtleneck stretched over a chest that looked as solid as granite.

The man beside him was shorter and leaner, his light brown hair cropped neatly above a face that was all sharp angles and tension. He wore a crisp suit, one of those that spoke 'I might be an important person', with a paper folder tucked under his arm.

The tall man flashed his badge in the air, his deep voice carrying over the threshold.

"May we come in?" His eyes swept around the room, lingering on the table and faces around it.

Dad hesitated, hand stiffening on the doorframe. A sheen of sweat covered his forehead, and as he stepped aside, a hesitation seemed to quiver into his voice.

"Of course."

I sat paralyzed as they entered.

For that one, swift second, the tall man's eyes caught my gaze, furrowed in some kind of recognition. My chest tightened, the air was now too thick to breathe.

Behind me, I heard Mom shift, and when I glanced back, she was smiling faintly. The bruising on her face stood in vivid contrast to the pale pink flush of her cheeks.

I wanted to scream, to rip that smile off, it wasn't real. It was survival.

Dad's throat was clear in that tight, stiff voice. "What's this about?"

The short man glanced at me and then back to Dad. "This may not be appropriate for the children."

"They're not children," Dad snapped, though his voice betrayed a quiver. His hand fidgeted at the back of his neck, fingers scratching at the skin there. "One... well, one can't talk. Or hear. Or walk, for that matter. And the other—"

"We understand," the taller man interrupted smoothly, gesturing toward the sofa. His presence seemed to fill the room, his tone both firm and disarming. "Perhaps we should sit down."

The white sofa facing the fireplace almost looked too innocent for what was about to weigh upon it. Their feet whispered on the rug as they moved across it towards the sofa, before, with a smooth swoop, the taller of the two settled onto it.

The shorter man followed, placing the folder on his lap. "I am Detective Erik Skarsgard," he said, his Scandinavian accent sharp and precise. He inclined his head toward his partner. "This is Detective Thor Karlsson."

Karlsson nodded. "We're here to investigate the disappearance of your neighbor, Sigrid Halvorsen. She lived about two miles from here."

Skarsgard's voice was grave. "We have reason to believe that whoever took her may target this house next."

The words landed like a bomb. Dad paled, his voice stumbling. "What? That's ridiculous. We just moved in—why would anybody—"

Skarsgard raised a hand, silencing him. "Did you notice the snowman in your yard?"

Dad's head whipped toward the window. The snowman stood silently outside, its crooked grin twisting in the dim winter light.

Skarsgard opened the folder, revealing a series of photographs. The first showed a snowman—eerily similar to the one outside. "This was found at Halvorsen's house," he said, sliding the photo across the table.

Dad's hand shook as he turned to the next picture. His breath hitched. Beneath the snowman's photo lay an image of a pale, bruised body sprawled lifeless on the frozen ground.

"My God," he muttered, recoiling as though the photograph had burned him.

"We've seen this before," Karlsson said, leaning forward. "Whoever is behind this leaves the same calling card: a snowman in the yard."

The room seemed to grow colder despite the crackling fire. Mom's fingers dug into the back of my chair. "Dear Lord," she whispered.

"Word of advice," Karlsson said, his tone softer now. "Lock your doors tonight."

Dad shot to his feet. "Is there anything else we can do? Cameras, perhaps? We can install more—"

"We noticed two cameras out front," Skarsgard said. "You might want to check with the property owner for access. They may have caught something."

Mom's voice trembled. "And the backyard? Couldn't you see who built the snowman?"

Skarsgard shook his head. "Unfortunately, the cameras don't cover the backyard. The woods block the view."

Dad rubbed his forehead, sweat glistening under the firelight. "You checked the camera footage? Did it show anything?"

"Nothing suspicious," Karlsson said tightly. "We reviewed it twice."

Silence pressed down on the room like a heavy blanket.

At last, Karlsson snapped the folder shut and stood. "Thank you for your time."

Dad followed them to the door, his movements stiff, his mind elsewhere. "Thank you," he mumbled.

As Karlsson opened the door, the winter wind whistled through the gap. Before stepping out, he turned back, his eyes narrowing.

"One last thing," he said, his voice quieter now. "What happened to your wife's eye?"

Mom straightened beside me. Her answer came too fast, too quick.

"I fell," she said, her voice too bright. "Slipped, actually."

Karlsson didn't say a word at first. He was clenching his teeth and the tendons of his neck stood out.

"Accidents would seem to occur quite a lot here," he finally said, his tone dripping with unsaid meaning.

"Yes, yes," Dad cut in, waving it off. "Thank you again. Good luck with the investigation."

Karlsson's eyes lingered a beat longer before he nodded and stepped out into the cold. His partner followed him and tucked the file back under his arm.

Dad shut the door, the latch clicked, and then it was the perfect silence. A moment he had stood there, still, his back to us, his shoulders rising and falling with the heavy sigh. When he turned, his face calmer than it was.

"Bree," he said, his voice even. "Take Mel to the bedroom. Breakfast is over."

A small, shaky breath escaped my chest as I rose to my feet, moving toward Mel. My fingers wrapped around the cold, metallic handles of her wheelchair. And without a word, I pushed her down the living room floor, my eyes fixed ahead, refusing to glance back—couldn't. The weight in my chest pressed heavier with each step.

We were finally at the room, I shut the door behind us, making sure it clicked softly in the still, quiet air. Mel sat sideways in her wheelchair, her frame seeming even smaller in dim light, her eyes set only on one spot on the wall. I couldn't hold it anymore, it was too much inside.

Kneeling beside her, I closed my eyes. Tears fell in cascades, soaking her jeans as I buried my face in her lap. My shoulders shook hard, the only sound in that room was my cry. Mel's hand slowly moved to rest on the crown of my head. But she didn't speak. Her head didn't turn, her expression was empty, as though she were lost in some place far away from here.

I closed my eyes, and darkness behind my eyelids swallowed me in. Shapes danced in the dark; white, circular flashes, like distant stars.

I was six years old again. My birthday. I could see Mom in the kitchen, smiling as she set a strawberry cake in front of me. Its pink glaze sparkled under the warm kitchen lights. I reached for it in a hurry, pushing a bit into my mouth before Mom could reach me.

Then, everything changed.

My throat constricted while the world seemed to spin into panic, and the muffled sounds of Mom's voice trying to be frantic. The memory suddenly blurred into the fading rush of sirens. And just as I opened my eyes I was already in a car with an unknown world passed by my window. "We're moving," Dad had said simply, his hands clutched to the steering wheel.

He said later that was because Mom was afraid of losing me, but in this bedroom, back with Mel, that sounded wrong.

What was she afraid of?

My eyes flickered open, drawing me back into the here and now. I straightened up in my chair, blinking through welling tears. The sight of Mel's empty stare was right on the edge of my vision, yet my mind would not settle. It gnawed on some strange and hollow feeling inside. I looked down at my hands and then at Mel.

I couldn't remember her birth, not the day, not the moment Mom and Dad brought her home, not even a single hazy image. We were three years apart, but it was like the memory didn't exist at all.

What was wrong with me? Was I starting to forget or was I beginning to remember things I was never supposed to remember?

I couldn't breathe. I needed air, space, clarity.

"I'll be back," I muttered, jumping up and out of the room.

My feet took me into the living room to Mom and Dad on that worn, faded sofa. Whatever conversation they were having stopped mid-sentence as I appeared.

"Can I go out?" My voice was softer than I meant. "I just... need to go out."

Mom's eyes flickered, but she nodded. "Don't go far, okay?"

"Okay," I said, already heading on my way.

When I returned to the bedroom, I tore off my red coat that was hanging over one of the hooks in the wardrobe. Before, it carried a faint, humble smell of fresh rain and wet leaves, gently mixing with the sharp taste of detergent. Now, as I slid its weight over my hunched shoulders, the mass settled heavily around me, smelling of the sweet escape outside.

I caught myself hesitating for just a moment as I passed by Mel. I repeated, "I'm coming back," not particularly sure if she heard me.

In the living room, they barely looked up as I crossed toward the door. Again, their low murmurs resumed, muffled only by the thudding of my heart. None of them asked where and why. It was just like I was invisible, some sort of passing shadow that flickered for a brief moment.

The front door groaned as I opened it; a wave of cold air entered, so sharp, so crisp. I closed my eyes, breathing deeply to fill my lungs with that clean, biting chill. As I exhaled, the tension in me seemed a fraction lighter, as some weight lifted from my chest.

I stepped into the yard, boots crunching on the snow path. The house shrank behind me as I followed the narrow trail leading into the woods. Bare branches stretched overhead, clawing at the gray sky like skeletal fingers. As it was, with every step taken, that tightness inside my chest started to soften.

Breathing had also started to become easy now. Here, with the quiet and the trees around me, I finally felt free. Free to breathe. Free to think.

Thirty minutes must have passed, and the sun was now brighter, its rays bouncing off the snow. Ahead, there was this thick gnarled branch lying on the ground half-submerged in the ice. I walked to it and sat down, feeling the cold right through my coat as I let my breath out in a long sigh.

The woods stretched around me, almost endless, their silence pushing against my ears. I was alone, just a girl in a red coat in a vast expanse of white.

It seeped into me—the stillness. No pretending here, no mask to wear, no lying to myself. Just the void, the loneliness. For a moment, it felt like peace.

But then something moved.

It was subtle, just a flicker in the corner of my eye. My chest tightened and I stood abruptly, my boots crunching the snow. I spun in place, scanning the shadows in between the trees.

"Who's there?" I called, my voice sharper than I expected. The sound echoed into the woods, swallowed quickly by the thick silence.

No one answered but I was not alone—I could sense it. My breathing grew quicker as a wild thought entered my mind.

"Snowman?" I called, half-expecting, half-fearing a response.

And then, laughter. Low and mocking, it rolled from behind me, shearing the air like a knife.

"Guess again," a voice said.

I spun around, the pulse pounding in my ears. The endless woods stretched out in every direction, yet I couldn't pinpoint which direction it came from.

"Who's there?" I called, picking up the branch I'd been sitting on and clenching it above me like a weapon. My hands shook as hard as I clutched it. It was silly, I knew, but that was the best I had.

Another voice joined in, this one more teasing, almost playful. "Are you lost?"

"Show yourself!" I shouted, my throat tightening.

There was a rustling, and then two of them came from behind a sturdy tree trunk. One threw the other a shove for good measure before stepping forward. He seemed tall, about my age, actually, with ginger hair that picked up the sun and wearing a smirk that stretched too wide across his freckled face. His confidence unnerved me.

"You must be the new girl," he said, then put a hand to his chest in mock chivalry and gave a shallow bow. "I'm Vic."

The other figure came closer, shorter and stockier, the beanie yanked low over his head. The jacket was hanging loose over his frame, and the zipper was open despite this cold. He grinned, you could see his breath in the crisp air.

"And I'm Josh, my lady," he said in a voice dripping with sarcasm as he parodied Vic's dramatic gesture.

Vic laughed, but Josh pulled something from his pocket, holding it out to me. A hand-rolled cigarette, crumpled and stained at the tip. "Want a smoke?"

I instinctively stepped back, wrinkling my nose in distaste. "No," I said more firmly than was maybe required. "Thanks."

I turned my back to them, my feet crunching in the snow as I began to walk away. But their laughter followed me, low and insistent, working its way under my skin. I quickened my pace, but so did they.

"Where are you going?" one of them called out. Their footsteps crunched louder, closer.

The knot in my stomach twisted tighter. I didn't need to look back to know they were following me. My pulse thundered in my ears as their chuckles turned to whispers, their tones no longer playful but darker.

I broke into a run.

The snow clung to my boots, slowing me, but I pushed forward, my breaths coming in ragged gasps. The trees blurred around me as my legs pumped harder, my focus narrowing to one thing: escape.

"Hey! Slow down!" one of them said, carrying the tone of his voice laughing. "We're only trying to talk."

My chest was burning, my vision swimming as the cold air sliced into my lungs. But I didn't stop. I couldn't stop.

Then it happened.

I was jogging along when my foot caught on some unseen branch buried in the snow. The world slewed violently as I went tumbling forward, arms flapping. I hit hard, the shock of impact rocking every bone in my body.

The snow was like ice against my cheek, and for a moment, the only sound was my breathing. Behind me, their steps crunched closer. My gut skidded with panic, paralyzing. I tried to push myself up, but my legs just felt heavy, useless. The branch I'd carried lay inches away, but it might as well have been miles.

"Where do you think you're going?" one of them said, mocking, laughing.

But then, the laughter was gone, replaced only by the sound of their feet as they closed the space between us. They lunged after me, then came to a sudden stop. They stood fixed, faces slack with surprise as if the very air around them had crystallized with cold.

Something was wrong.

I heaved myself up, using my shaking arms, to brush away stray tufts of blonde hair from my face. My breaths huffed out in short, panicked hitches, misting the chilled air. Slowly, I peeled my gaze upward and froze.

A few meters in front, something was standing—a snowman, so out of place against the silent woods. But it was different, wrong. Vic reached forward and yanked on my arm, pulling me to my feet. His face was white, his hands hard.

"Let me go!" I shouted, pushing him away. The force sent him stumbling back, but I couldn't stop staring at the snowman.

Because on top of its round, snow-packed body wasn't snowman's head of ice and buttons.

It was a human head.

I screamed, the sound tearing out of me before I could even think. My legs buckled, and I fell backward into the snow, scrambling to get away from it. Vic tripped when I pushed him, landing hard beside me. Both of us crawled away, our hands sinking into the icy ground as we retreated in shared fear.

Behind the snowman, the woods were silent and oppressive. But I could only see two great balls of snow stacked on top of one another, and atop those, the head of a woman, severed from her body. Her hair was braided and neatly combed, although strands were stuck with snow. Her eyes were wide open and glassy, staring at nothing. Her lips were pursed in deep purple, and an eerie stillness was frozen on her face.

The second ball of snow was streaked with the jarring red against the white, like some sort of bloody scarf. The snowman's stick arms reached out, jagged branches that seemed to claw at the air. Coal buttons were arranged on its body with chilling precision, as though someone had made it with sick care.

I squeezed my palms over my eyes, willing the horrific image to disappear. My heartbeat roared in my ears, drowning out everything but the sharp inhale of my breaths.

Josh finally broke the silence, his hand shaking as he dialed the numbers on his phone. With every click, the phone seemed to echo through the stillness. "D-d-dad," he stuttered, voice shaking. "We... we found Sigrid."

Sigrid Halvorsen, the missing woman. I felt the bile rise in my throat as reality crystallized around me. She wasn't only missing. She was here. And she was dead.

Her frozen, lifeless eyes stood silent, guarding the woods, hauntingly empty. It felt as though she was watching us, mocking us, daring us to look away. But I couldn't.

SIX

BREE

SIRENS WAILED IN THE air, their shrill cries mingling with the sharp pulses of blue and red lights dancing across the ground that was heavy with snow. I sat frozen, my body stiff beneath the gray blanket somebody had laid over my shoulders. Outside, the world was moving like a silent movie, shades of people in white nylon suits, the black body bag being zipped up carefully, yellow tape cordoning off trees, and shouting warnings in thick black letters: **DO NOT CROSS.**

But I was not in a position to move, not even if I wanted to.

I looked down at my wrists, instinctively pulling my sleeves over the faint scars marked into my skin. They were reminders of the time when I had thought that I had long since died. That part of me now felt like it was resurfacing and breathing its way back into my chest.

A woman patted my shoulder, her voice muffled and far away. I couldn't make out the words. My eyes didn't leave the men carrying the body away, and I was horrified to find myself wondering if they'd found the rest. All I had seen was the head. My gaze strayed back to the plastic tape, the jarring unnatural yellow slicing through the cold white expanse of the woods.

I heard Josh and Vic talking to the police nearby. Their voices were fragments, pieces of a puzzle that refused to come together. Then, around this chaos, I caught a voice. My stomach clenched, and I scanned the faces around me, my eyes locking with the hope of recognition. But nothing matched. Only strangers.

Until, out of a sudden turn, a man stood before me. The calmness of his face was there, but something in his eyes seemed like an unending weight, never to be light or relieved. His hand had rested gently on my shoulder; his lips moved and spoke words I couldn't hear. He felt so unreal, like a ghost attached to my mind.

"Hey," he said, snapping his fingers in front of me. The sharp sound cut through the fog in my head. "Are you okay?"

My lips parted, but no sound came out. For the first time in my life, I couldn't bring myself to say the automatic lie, to say that everything was fine. My head was shaking weakly, and hot tears spilled over in rivulets against the cold air. For the first time in my life, I allowed myself to be seen.

He knew. I could tell it from his face, in the softening of his eyes. He drew me into his arms gently and his warmth sliced through the chill that clung to me. I didn't protest. My fragile voice managed to break through with one cracked word, "No."

My head fell onto his shoulder, my body quivering, while I wept softly. It was the first time in so very long that I was wrapped in anyone's arms. The first time a man ever had taken me in such a way. There wasn't any judgment in his hug, no expectations, just safety.

"I'm not fine," I whispered, words caught in my throat, harder to admit than it should be, but a truth that felt like its own liberation.

"And that's okay," he said softly, his voice steady, grounding. "You don't have to be okay."

I nodded, clenching my fingers into my sleeves as I retreated a small step. I wiped a hand across my eyes until his gentle face blurred through my crying. His expression was staunch but patient in its kindness in giving me some time for myself.

He drew a small notebook from his pocket and flipped it open. "I really hate having to do this," he said with the slightest smile, trying to lighten the moment. "But I need to ask you a few questions, if that's alright."

I nodded again, my voice still caught somewhere in my chest. His eyes searched mine, not for answers, but for reassurance, like he wanted to be sure I wouldn't break under the weight of the moment.

"Did you see anyone else around?" he asked, poised pen in his hand.

My breath caught and the image of the snowman flashed in my mind. My throat constricted as I whispered, "No." The word felt brittle, breaking apart as it left my lips.

"You know those two?" he asked, tone low, steady. He moved a pen toward Josh and Vic; they stood a short ways off, shifting their weight while talking with another cop.

I hesitated, my throat tightening. "No," I whispered, hardly audible.

"They said you found the..." His voice trailed off as he cast a wary glance in my direction. His words were measured, carefully chosen to avoid further upsetting me. "The snowman?"

"Yes," I said. My voice broke. The memory was flooding back clearly now, as I'd squeezed my eyes shut. "I fell, and..." I tried to find the right words. My chest ached across, each breath jagged. "He," I gagged out, "he somehow... does it make me sound crazy if I think he... completes them? By adding..." Again my voice failed me where the word got stuck in my throat over a hard swallow. "A head?"

The detective's jaw flexed. His eyes narrowed slightly, studying me through a gaze more like concern and less like suspicion. He said nothing right away.

"You think I'm crazy, don't you?" I said, my voice quivering; I brushed stray strands of hair behind my ears. My hands fidgeted nervously in my lap.

His eyes dropped briefly to my wrists, where faint scars traced stories I wished I could erase. My heart sank as I realized. I tugged my sleeves down quickly, pulling my hands into my lap, and pressing them tightly between my thighs.

"No," he said, his voice firm and clear. "You're not crazy."

He stood abruptly, his gaze sweeping around the scene in a slow arc. The snow swathed in blood, the quiet empty woods, the hush of unutterability lingering. He was gathering pieces of a puzzle seen by nobody else into a total picture.

I swallowed the lump in my throat and stammered, "Can I go home?

Softness stirred within his eyes then turned back to me. "Sure," he said much more quietly, "I can take you home."

I nodded, my body trembling as I rose to my feet. He waited patiently, then led the way to his car. I glanced back at the scene one last time—the yellow tape, the distant officers, and the woods that now felt like they would never let me forget. My steps were shaky as I followed him.

The black car stood out against the snowy backdrop, its polished surface gleaming in the light. Somehow, its solid presence calmed me. He opened the passenger door and waited for me to get in before closing it gently behind me. I sank into the seat, clutching the blanket tighter around me, the cold still gnawing at my bones.

Through the windscreen, I watched him wave at another officer—signal, most likely, letting them know he was taking me home. A moment later, he slid into the driver's seat, hands resting lightly on the wheel. He glanced at me briefly before turning the ignition.

"I'm Thor," he said, his voice even as the car burbled to life. "What's your name?"

"Bree," I answered, my voice barely audible, my eyes fixed through the windshield ahead on the snow-misted distance, a vague blur instead of that press in my chest.

"Word of advice," he said, the silence after his voice sounding loud, as he geared the car first. "Those two boys—Josh and Vic—they're trouble."

I nodded slowly, my eyes drifting back to where the two of them stood. Their posture was casual, but something about them felt wrong, like an itch I couldn't scratch.

"I know," I whispered, the words more to myself than to him.

"Good," he said quietly, the corners of his mouth pulling into a tight, approving smile.

Without another word, he tapped the gas, and we began to roll forward down the street. The crunch of the tires on the snowy ground occupied the space between us, without being uncomfortable. For possibly the first time in the last few hours, breathing was easy.

Those ten minutes were the shortest in my life as we pulled up to the house. With every rotation of the tires, it sounded like a drum echoing in my chest, my heart matching the rhythm. As it finally came to a stop, I reached for the door handle, but my eyes didn't leave the screen of the windshield. My body froze, refusing to move. The house sat there before me, a dark shape among the snow, but the real shadow seemed to wait inside.

"We can sit here for a while if you want," Thor said in a soft voice that held calm. "No rush."

I nodded, one tear welling its way down my cheek. It was hot against the cold numbness of my skin.

The silence between us drew out, until he spoke again, softly breaking it. "You fall a lot too?" His eyes flickered to my wrists, the question hovering in the air between us like a fragile thread.

I twisted toward him, now caught under the weight of his question. In my silence, he saw more than most people grasp in a lifetime, a thought of it sent jolts of fear through my spine. My lump was growing low in my throat and swelled now in pain as I shook my head.

I'd never fallen. Not like that. I'd hurt myself only in quiet, cowardly ways that felt somehow like control. Dying had been an escape I wished for when the weight became too much to handle. When I came back, when I saw what it did to Mel, I told myself I would never again be so selfish. Mel had tried, too. And I could never let her do the same to herself.

Thor reached into his coat and pulled out a small scrap of paper. He held it out to me, his hand steady.

"Here," he said. "My number. If you ever... Fall... You can call for help. Asking for help is okay, Bree."

I stared at the paper a moment before reaching out for it, my fingers brushing against his. "Okay," I whispered, folding it carefully and tucking it into my pocket.

I let my gaze dwell on him a moment longer, then reached to open the door. His eyes are chestnut, I said to myself. Brown. Not blue, brown.

And then I said them over and over in my mind, as though trying to burn them into my memory. But beneath that, I was still looking for someone else. For the man who had come into my room last night. The man who had made the snowman. The man who knew now that I had seen something I was never supposed to see.

And suddenly, fear wrapped its icy tendrils around me. A deeper fear than I'd ever known. Because now, I was more afraid than ever to talk, to breathe, to even exist.

It was Thor's voice that brought me back. "Are you sure you told me everything?" The firm tone was soft and his eyes searched mine.

I nodded, forcing a faint smile that didn't reach my eyes. "Yeah."

He nodded back, but his face told another story. I stepped out of the car and shut the door behind me. He remained inside, observing me as I walked to the house. I did not look back; could not. My legs were lead, heavy with a weight that seemed to tug me closer with each step to something I was not prepared to face.

Through the window, I could see Dad. His face was hard, his jaw clenched, and his eyes burned with anger that seemed to radiate even from a distance. My stomach twisted into knots. I wasn't ready for him either.

I stopped in front of the door, my hand shaking, clutched on the handle.

Thirty seconds passed, I counted each and every one with the heavy beating of my heart in my ears. Then I finally pushed the door open and stepped inside. The sound of the car pulling away behind me reached my ears just as I shut the door.

I wanted to call Thor. I wanted to scream out through the phone for him to save me right now. How could he? How was I allowed to be saved when all this time, I did not even believe I was worthy of saving? How could I get help from a person who wants to fight for me when I no longer have hope left in me? My hope was already dying, bit by bit.

Inside, the house was suffocating. Mom was in the kitchen, going through her motions as though she didn't even see me, Mel was in her room quiet and still like she hadn't moved today. And Dad?! Dad was just waiting. His gaze had snapped onto mine like a lock disengaging the instant I crossed over the threshold.

"What were you doing with that cop?" He spat the words like droplets of venom.

I shook my head fast, my back against the door. "I didn't..."

"Don't you fucking lie to me!" he roared, his voice cracking through the air like a whip. Another step closer, and he was towering over me. "You told him something, didn't you?"

"I didn't, I swear!" I stammered, my voice rising in desperation. My hands pressed against the door behind me, searching for a way to push myself further away. "I didn't tell him anything!"

His face twisted in anger as he leaned in. My body was shaking so much I could hardly stand.

"Don't lie to me," he hissed, his hand twitching at his side. I froze, my breath caught in my throat. I wanted to run, but there was nowhere to go.

"You won't fucking leave this house again," he growled as his hand shot out, grabbing a fistful of my hair. Pain exploded across my scalp as he pulled me down, the sharp pull making my head move violently. I clenched my teeth, biting back a scream, but the tears welled in my eyes.

"You will learn," he thundered, dragging me across the room, never letting go, not even once.

My feet stumbled after his as he pulled me up the stairs. Each rise upwards felt like a shock of hurt across my body, but I did not fight back. It was only worse if I resisted.

No one's ever going to save me, I thought, my mind climbing some sort of spiral staircase. No one ever will.

He pushed me onto the floor at the top of the stairs. My body crumpled like a ragdoll, cold wooden planks biting against my skin.

Before I could catch my breath, the tip of his shoe slammed into my ribs. White, hot pain seared through me. A sickening crunch followed, and I knew—something was broken. My ribs throbbed with every shallow breath.

But I stayed silent. I always stayed silent. This wasn't the first blow I'd taken.

Frustrated, he leaned over me. "I swear—"

His fist whacked again, this time finding its mark on my shoulder and shaking through my body while his hand tangled again into my hair, wrenching me down the hallway like a broken toy, scraping my knees along the floor, too weakened in body to oppose him and too beaten in the brain to even think about fighting.

Then, slicing through the chaos like a thin, distant thread, I heard it.

"Daddy?"

The voice was tiny, small. One word, but it stopped him cold.

He went completely still, his breathing harsh, his grip easing. Slowly, he turned his head to face whatever had made the noise, leaving me splayed upon the floor. His boots echoed on the hardwood as he crossed to the glass railing at the far end of the hall. His fingers wrapped around the glass, smudging the clean panes as he leaned forward.

"Mel?" he yelled, his voice a weird combination of shock and disbelief. "You can talk?" He let out a nervous, almost hysterical chuckle. "And walk?"

I tried to push myself up, but my arms folded beneath me. My body felt heavy and unresponsive, not my own. All I could do was lie there, watching helplessly as he ran down the stairs, his mood changing. I could hear him laughing when he reached her.

He was now laughing with Mom, hugging her. It was as if nothing had happened downstairs, as though the man who had unleashed his fury upon me never existed. I was forgotten upstairs, left crumpled on the floor, my face silently streaming with tears.

Why do people have children if they cannot give them the life they deserve? The question burnt in my mind without an answer.

The pain burned through my chest, though it wasn't even nearly as deep as the ache inside. A dark, festering trauma carved into my bones, deeper with each blow, and I walked in fear as though it were my second skin, turning at every step, afraid to trust or love.

Every tiny flicker of hope I'd dared to hold onto had been taken from me, leaving only emptiness.

I heard soft footsteps approaching. Mom.

"Go to the attic," she whispered, her voice low, her eyes darting toward the staircase. "Hide until he feels better."

Until he feels better. What about me? I wasn't better. I wasn't whole. I was broken. Summoning every last bit of strength in my body, I struggled to my feet. My ribs shrieked with every shallow breath, and my knees wobbled beneath my weight while I made ungainly progress toward the attic door. Mom followed along silently behind me.

I came to the door, stopping in front of it. "Mom?" I whispered, looking towards her.

She said nothing. The moment I stepped inside, the door swung shut behind me with a hollow click. The metallic sound of the key turning in the lock followed. My heart fell.

"Mom?" I called out, shaking and pounding on the door. "Mom!"

Her footsteps retreated down the stairs, fading.

I leaned against the door, hands falling limply to my sides as the tears came. They spilled over like waterfalls against my bruised and battered skin. My chest heaved up and down, the pain from my sobs mingling with agony from my injuries.

More than the outside wounds that were bleeding, though, were the inside ones. And these bled memories, regrets, terrors of burdens too hefty to bear.

It was cold and dark in the attic, with only a little bit of light allowed to pass through a round frosted window. I crumpled to the floor, bringing my knees up to my chest and wrapping my arms around them tightly. I had nothing.

SEVEN

Snowman

T̲h̲e̲ ̲l̲a̲t̲e̲ ̲a̲f̲t̲e̲r̲n̲o̲o̲n̲ ̲s̲u̲n̲ cast a warm, golden glow across the horizon as it began its slow escape. The kind of peace I once cared for, felt so far away now, like a distant memory.

Ever since I saw her, peace had become a stranger to me. My mind was tethered to hers, drawn to her like a moth to a flame. She was faint yet vivid, as though she were both a ghost and a dream—something I could see but never touch. Something I could never truly have, not with the life I lived, not with the lies I carried.

I was lying on my bed shirtless, the cool air barely brushing against my skin as I glared at the wooden ceiling over me. The wall lamp flickered once in a while, light throbbing like a pulse as if trying to convey something to me.

She wants to see me again.

Then, I closed my eyes, just for a second, her face disappearing, but everything else sharpening.

She was everything I'd ever imagined perfection to be, yet I knew she'd never see herself the way I saw her. She didn't know the spell she had cast, the way she haunted my every thought. Her long blonde hair, streaked with shades of sunlight and shadow, shone like fresh snow under a winter sky. Her ocean-blue eyes, the deepest and darkest I'd ever seen, were now my favorite color. Blue.

She fitted together so perfectly that she seemed to have been made for some specific purpose. The soft outlines of her face, the slight shine on the tip of her small nose, and her skin were smooth and blemishless. Her lips, full and soft, held a gentle pink that gave them an almost surreal appearance. But it was her eyebrows, curved delicately over those sad, stormy eyes, that stayed with me. They gave her the look of a porcelain doll; fragile, innocent, perfect.

She stirred something in me that I had not felt in years. Her sorrow reached into me, where the cold had taken permanent home, and started to melt the frost. I was a man who rarely felt anything at all, and now I found myself longing for something I wasn't even aware of.

I wanted to see her smiling; I wanted her to smile a lot more.

I rolled onto my side and faced the window. The woods were still and silent, dark silhouettes against the fading light. They reminded me of everything I'd left behind, everything I thought I had escaped. But a sudden knock at the door pulled me from my thoughts, scattering them behind.

I let out a heavy sigh, the weight of the moment settling back over me, and got up. My bare feet hit the cool floor as I made my way out of the bedroom and into the kitchen.

Even before I saw her, the smell of chicken soup greeted me. She was standing near the stove, her grey hair all braided, her back to me. The familiar smell filled the little kitchen, warm and comforting.

"They found her, you know," she said, turning to me now. Her face was more wrinkled than the last time I'd truly set eyes on her.

"I know," I replied, walking into the kitchen island that stood proudly in the middle of the place, its polished wood glowing shyly in the evening light, two chairs up front.

She moved to lift the pot from the stove and set it down on the counter. The lid clanged softly upon being set down, and then she reached for a spoon from the drawer, dipped it into the soup, and brought it to her lips.

"You know Joe's back?" she asked casually before leaning over to taste, her face screwed up and went pale. "Damn, it's hot." She blew on the spoon before setting it on the soup plate[1] and sliding it onto the island beside the pot.

"Yeah, I saw him," I said, standing and going to the cabinet. I pulled out another soup plate, with a silver spoon from the drawer. The kitchen was small, and cozy in a way that sometimes felt suffocating.

I set the soup plate down. She didn't wait but poured soup into it for me, the ladle making soft ripples as it moved through the broth. I walked around the island and sank into the chair across from her.

"Did you see the oldest one?" she asked, blowing softly on her spoon of soup before taking a cautious sip.

"Yeah," I muttered, dipping my own spoon into the soup. The liquid scalded my tongue as I took a hasty sip, but I didn't flinch.

"You know why he brought them here?" she started, her voice laced with curiosity. But before she could continue, my fist came down on the wooden surface

---

1. Soup can be served in both soup plates and soup bowls, and the choice between them depends upon different factors, including the type of soup you serve, the thickness of the soup, the size of the plates, and the presentation you want to display for your guest.

of the island, the sudden, sharp sound cutting through her words.

"Let me stop you right there," I said. My jaw tightened, all the muscles in my face rigid. "Mother."

She threw her hands up in defeat, her face smooth except for the flicker of mirth in her eyes. "Okay, okay," she said much softer now. "All I am saying is, he's different. He barely recognized me. And Laura—" she paused, rolling her eyes "Laura thought I was the housekeeper."

A dry chuckle escaped me, tinged with bitterness. "How rich of her," I said, my tongue clicking against my teeth. "He didn't recognize me either."

"Who would?" she shot back with a smirk, her eyes crinkling. "With that beard?"

I huffed a laugh, the corners of my mouth pulling up briefly before falling flat again.

"What do you think I should do?" I asked, leaning forward as my gaze sharpened. "Let him be? Or should I stop him once and for all?"

She tilted her head, studying me. "He is your father's son," she said, every word a careful choice. "He is no blood of mine, never will be." Her voice gentled and she leaned in and placed her hands like fall leaves on mine. "But he once was your brother."

"Stepbrother," I said, shaking my head. My voice lowered, "And that is no answer."

She stepped back, smoothing the folds on her dress before reaching for the knitted bag which rested in the corner of the table.

"I am off," she said, her tone all at once brisk, all practical, and she walked to the door, suddenly turning to me.

"Oh, and...." she added, one brow rising. "Do you think he is smart enough to figure it out?"

I clicked my tongue again, "Nah."

She hummed and pressed her lips together, weighing my response. Then, without a word more, she turned and left. The door shut with a firm click, bringing a faint breeze in her wake.

I sat down, again, and stared at the bowl of soup in front of me. Steam spiraled upwards in diaphanous curls, then disappeared into the air, just like my focus.

An hour nearly passed, with me still behind the shadows of her window, watching and waiting. Waiting for something, I don't even know; just a simple silhouette of her. Yet, the window remained as empty as when I'd begun. It was the silent stillness that gnawed at my soul.

I had to see her, even from afar, even if it meant risking everything.

The snow crunched beneath my boots as I moved closer, the cold biting through the fabric of my clothes. My coat weighed on me, heavy and restricting, so I pulled it off and buried it in the snow. The sharp chill bit at my skin, but I didn't care.

I pulled my hood over my head, the dark sweatshirt clung to me like armor as I slid a white mask from my pocket. I glanced over my shoulder, scanning for any signs of movement, any eyes upon me. The woods were silent.

Satisfied, I reached back and laid the mask on my face, its cold surface pressing against my skin.

I moved slowly, crouching low as I followed the faint lines of the narrow path leading to the rear of the house.

Leafy branches and thorns acted like a barrier across the yard. Concealed behind them was the rusty creaking of old ladders. At the very top sat this large circular attic window that was always left slightly open, inviting me in. You could easily fit through a gap that narrow yet nobody ever managed to glue it shut. A spare key would be something I had with me, though with a mask looking like this, front doors weren't the best choice.

It was a silent climb, my hands clasping the icy wood of the ladders until I reached the attic window. I eased it open, careful not to make a sound. The glass creaked slightly as I slid through, my feet landing softly on the wooden floor. I knelt, pushing the window back into its usual crooked position.

My heart jumped as I turned.

She was there.

She was kneeling at the far corner in her red coat, her body shaking. Her hair spilled down her shoulders, glowing with that weak light filtering through the cracked window. And she did nothing. Didn't speak. Just sat on and on, her eyes fixed somewhere as if she neither saw me nor cared.

I raised my hand weakly in a small awkward wave. Twice. Really idiotic.

What the hell am I doing? I silently scolded myself.

She glanced at me, then crossed her arms before lying down on the floor, moving slowly, ignoring me. Like I wasn't even there.

"Were you waiting for me?" I asked, my voice breaking the heavy silence. I stepped toward her cautiously, unsure of myself.

"Don't flatter yourself," she snapped out, her voice whetted to a sharp edge though her head remained unlifted. "If you came to kill me, do it."

I froze, the words striking harder than they should have. I crouched beside her, studying her face, her body, for some evidence of fear or even care. But there was nothing. Just emptiness.

I reached out tentatively and brushed a strand of her hair away from her face. Her skin was pale; her lips were chapped. She didn't pull away immediately, but as I whispered, "Why would I do that, birdie?" she threw her head sharply to the side, moving out from my touch.

Her body shuddered, wrapping her arms tighter around herself, and her whole frame shook like a fragile leaf in the middle of a storm. I tilted my head to the side, trying to read her, trying to understand. Something was wrong. I reached for her hand, gently pulling her up, but the moment she moved, she winced, clutching her ribs. My stomach sank.

"What happened?" I asked, my voice low, steady.

"Please," she whispered, her tears spilling down her cheeks. Her voice cracked, as if made of glass, barely holding together. "Just go."

I bit my tongue, knowing I shouldn't be here. This was wrong, everything about it. Yet something in her made it impossible to leave. I needed her. I needed her close to feel alive again, even if only for a moment. I sank to the floor against the wall, pulling her head gently onto my lap.

"Better?" I asked, my fingers threading softly through her hair.

"No," she whispered, her voice cracking with the burden of her pain. A jolting laugh tore from her lips as she choked over the words. "Do you do this to all of them?"

Her gaze fluttered up to me shining with unshed tears. "Before you chop their heads off and turn them into snowmen?"

I chuckled low and sharp. "Not to all of them."

She reacted in an instant, disgusted and furious. She pushed my hand away and turned her face from me, pressing her cheek to the cold floor.

"Disgusting," she spat.

"They were all bad people," I said so casually, as though that somehow excused it, that with one simple justification, the truth should be rewritten.

"I doubt that," she shot back. She pushed herself further away, creating more space between us.

She was a defiant one, and it irritated me, needling under my skin.

I blinked twice, my patience fraying. "I first torture them," I said, my tone growing darker and colder. "Before I cut them to pieces."

Her body went stiff. She turned back to me then, kneeling. Her eyes scanned mine, but I wouldn't meet them, facing instead the window I came in through. I could smell her fear, rising out of her, thickening the air around us. It was an infectious thing, it made me feel the need to keep going; to confess, to lay it all bare.

"It's so good to tell someone," I said, my voice smooth, almost amused. "To finally confess."

"You're mad," she said, her voice trembling as she fell back onto the floor. She crawled away, inching toward the opposite wall, her eyes wide and unblinking.

I moved my head to one side, observing her reaction with detached curiosity.

"No," I whispered, lying through my teeth as a faint smile curled my lips. "I just have a bad reputation."

I knelt again, my palms pressed flat against the floor as I crawled closer to her. The movements were slow.

"You know what I love the most?" I asked, my voice dropping to a near whisper. "When I get in while they're asleep when they're most vulnerable."

Her breathing was in sharp, shallow gasps, her chest rising and falling in quick succession. She did not move, frozen on the spot.

"I take my knife," I said, my fingers brushing the floorboards. "And I place it right here." I reached out, tracing a line along her leg, my touch light but intentional, moving toward her inner thigh.

She swallowed hard, her lips trembling as she pushed my hand away. Her movements were shaky, panicked.

I chuckled, leaning in closer. "You'd like that, wouldn't you, birdie?" I growled lowly, tauntingly, my voice low. "C'mon, admit it."

"Stay back," she stammered, her tone cracking. Her breathing now, frantic, came with a raw fear in each uttered word.

"Imagine," I said, my voice all but dripping with mock seduction as I leaned in closer. My hand moved onto her back, tracing along the line of her spine downwards to the curve at the bottom. "Imagine how it would feel inside of you. The way you'd twitch... but couldn't move."

I took a single, rapid step to pull her all the way into me; falling backward onto the hardwood floor and bringing her down with me. She lay on top of me shaking, my palms planted into her sides, urging her closer into my body.

"Can you imagine it, birdie?" I murmured low against her ear.

But as I shifted, rolling her beneath me, something inside her shifted. Her hand flew to her ribs and her face twisted in a silent scream into her palm. She pushed weakly at me, tears welling up in her eyes. I froze. The tension bled from my body as I stared at her.

Slowly, I rose to my feet, my eyes dark and searching. Her coat was loose on her, the zipper calling my attention. In one swift move, I yanked it down, revealing her shirt underneath. My hands lifted the fabric instinctively. Her skin was a field of bruises, dark and angry, sprawling across her ribs and sides. Faint red marks told the story of her pain and my chest tightened.

"What happened?" I demanded, my voice low but edged with fury.

She shook her head, her trembling hands pulling the shirt back down. Tears were streaked across her face as she whispered, "I fell." I snorted loudly, a harsh, acid sound.

"Aha," I hummed. My fists clenched as I stared at her, my mind racing with possibilities.

I stood, my body rigid as I moved toward the stairs. My blood was boiling in my body, my fists so tightly clenched that my nails dug into my palms. But before I could take a step, her voice stopped me.

"You can't," she said in a weak voice, shaking. "It's locked."

Locked. Beaten, and locked.

The words rang in me like a blow to the chest. My vision blurred with anger.

I will burn this place to the ground.

I pivoted on a dime, walking away toward the window in silence. My hands clutched the edges of the glass, preparing to pull it out of its frame, but before I stepped through, she rose. Barely, but she stood. Her legs trembled under her weight, her ribs rising visibly under every shallow breath.

"Can you kill me?" she whispered, her voice breaking as the words slipped out.

A moment, and I stiffened, my fingers tightening on the sill. The air in the room seemed to thicken, my chest aching, anger and sorrow battling within a storm I couldn't contain. My heart thundered, the heat of my fury threatening to spill over.

He hurt her, and I couldn't bring myself to hurt him—not yet.

I just pushed the words out through my teeth, my voice low and heavy. "Tomorrow," I said. "I can kill you tomorrow."

"Walk to the woods at five. I'll find you."

Her broken figure shook, staring at me, but she said nothing. She didn't need to.

I climbed onto the windowsill, pulling the sliding glass back into its crooked frame. Cold night wind smacked my face once I swung my feet to the ladder and started lowering myself. Every step I took down felt heavier than the last; my mind rewound her whispered plea with every step.

As my boots hit the snow below, I glanced back up at the attic. A dim light seeped through the crack in the window, casting faint shadows inside. My body screamed to go back, to tear the place apart, to take her with me. But I couldn't stay. If I stayed, I would do something I'd regret. Something that wouldn't make her safe but would only make things worse.

So I walked away.

Each step crunching through the snow felt like a fight against myself. My fists clenched with every step I took from that house, my chest constricting as though the air had turned to ice.

Then I saw it.

In the kitchen window, the light was on; the dim light focused on the man, with no shirt, the broad shoulders hunched over. He was plunging into a woman underneath him across a kitchen table, her body arced. The thrusts of the two movements were raw, like two animals.

I froze, my breath catching in my throat. My hands fisted at my sides, the blood roaring in my ears.

It wasn't just any man. It was him. The man raised by my father.

And then the woman turned, just enough for me to see her face. Blonde hair spilling across the table, her lips parted, moaning. It was her, the girl in the wheelchair.

He did it, he did what Father always did.

My stomach twisted in knots as the truth clawed its way to the surface. The taint of my father's sins had spread, like a disease passed down. He had taught this man and shaped him into the monster now inside that house. The same monster now taking her, holding her captive, using her, just like Father had done to my mother, to the others, to the ones who disappeared, one by one.

A part of me, of course, wanted to rush back inside, to rip him off her, to carve into his face the same sort of ruin I had managed with others before. To make him feel the agony he created. But a wiser part of me, a part of me that had learned to play the long game, stood back.

Watched. Learned just how deep the sickness ran before I struck. Because when I did strike, it would not be quick. It would not be merciful. This was far from over.

EIGHT

BREE

Night bled into a day, shadows softening to light, yet I couldn't sleep. I wouldn't let myself. Every time I closed my eyes, the snowman came back. That image, her head perched on top, the blood staining white snow like a crimson halo. And her eyes. Wide, glassy, unseeing yet somehow always watching me. Just me.

Sleep was supposed to be the only place of escape for most, not mine, not anymore. The moment my eyelids shut, the flashes returned, memories I'd tried so hard to bury clawing their way back to the surface. The pain, the shame, all of it circled like vultures. So I kept awake, holding onto hope that as long as I kept my eyes open, they might leave me alone. But they always came back.

I saw him through the faint gray light. Snowman. He moved stealthily, carefully sealing the crack of the attic window with glass and putty. I watched him, my body still, my heart pounding. I knew how to escape if I wanted to. But I also knew that once I did, there would be no coming back.

The sound of footsteps pulled me from my thoughts. I turned, startled, to see Mel standing behind me. She looked small, and fragile in the light, her hands twisting nervously together.

"Bree," she whispered, shaking. "Can we talk?"

Her words caught me by surprise. For a while, I'd resented her silence, the way she'd appeared to pretend everything was all right, locking me out when I could have helped. Yet a part of me was just as relieved she'd stayed silent herself, looking after herself in what little way she knew of. And part of me hated myself for making her go to that place in the first place.

"Yeah," I said softly, turning my gaze back to the window. The glass was cold, fogging slightly with my breath as I tried to calm my racing thoughts.

She moved closer until her palm came to rest ever so lightly on my shoulder as if she needed to fix herself to the floor.

"Two years ago," she began in a watery tone, "do you remember anything?"

"Just pieces," I said, my throat arid. "Pain."

"I remember," she whispered, leaning in closer yet. "And now... I understand."

My chest tightened. I turned to her slowly, "Understand what?"

"What you did," she said softly, it was a dagger to the heart. "Why you did it," her voice broke and her sniffles caused her face to rise toward me. "I wish I did it too."

She slumped against me before a word could escape my lips, her sobs shattering the silence. I drew her close, wrapping my arms around her trembling frame as her tears drenched my shoulder. I could feel her trembling, her pain bleeding into mine.

"I had to," she managed to choke out. "I had to call for him. And if I didn't..." Her words fell away, lost amid the racking sobs shaking her frame.

I drew back, gently, and cupped her tear-streaked face with my bruised hand. "He... last night...?" I asked, my voice shaking, not wanting to know the answer.

She looked up at me with red, swollen eyes. "He did it again," she whispered, her voice cracking. "And I let him."

My heart stopped.

"What happened?" I managed to say, barely more than a breath.

She looked at me, her eyes dark with a truth that stole the air from my lungs. "Joe..." she whispered. "He's not our dad."

The words crashed over me like a wave, pulling me under. He's not our dad.

I was paralyzed, unable to move, or breathe. My arms dropped listlessly at my sides, numbing into oblivion. Everything around me began to blur together, swirling into a gray haze. My mind sought to make sense of it-to piece together the shards of a puzzle I didn't even know existed. But it was too much.

The memory of her arms around me was grounding, but then- footsteps. Heavy, growing louder.

Before I could react, I had felt her being ripped from me. I staggered forward, reaching for her, when I saw him.

Joe.

His dark eyes connected to mine, and not a thing showed in the blankness of his body language. Soulless, empty, blacker than the shadows surrounding him.

"That's enough of you two," he growled, his voice a sharp edge slicing through the air.

Mel screamed as he tugged her away, and I couldn't move, couldn't stop him. My feet were glued onto the floor, my body frozen. Then his attention fell on me. His face contorted in anger as he closed the gap between us. I hadn't time to move before his hand slammed me hard against the wall. A wave of pain coursed through my back, and the air was knocked from my lungs.

Joe wasn't Dad anymore. He was just Joe. And he was ready to hurt me.

My eyes locked on his, searching for something—anything—that might tie me to him. But there was nothing. Not his eyes, not his mouth, not the way his hair fell in dark coarse strands. There wasn't a single piece of him in me. My blood didn't belong to him. My body didn't belong to him. For the first time in my life, I understood that. And for the first time, I fought back.

My bruised palms connected with his chest with all the strength left in me. I pushed as hard as I could, hard enough to see the surprise flash across his features before he fell backward, landing on the floor with a thud. I was above him, my chest heaving, my body trembling, yet I didn't move. I couldn't anymore. Not for him.

He bared his teeth; his anger was simmering below his skin, like coals, but he said not a word. Slowly, he pushed himself up; his eyes were sharp, seething. Then he turned, his hand shooting out to grab Mel by the arm and yanking her up roughly.

"No!" she shrieked; her voice cracked. "Bree!"

"Shut up," he snarled and his palm met her face with a sickening crack.

She stumbled under the force of the blow, her cheek ballooning in an instant into red welts.

I flung myself at her, but he was quicker, towing her down the stairs along with him. I ran after them, my heart going crazy, but before I even reached them, the door slammed shut. A second later, the sharp click of the lock sounded through the attic like a death knell.

"No!" I screamed, my fists going against the wood. "No! Let me out!"

My voice cracked, my pleading now reduced to guttural sobs, but there was nothing. Just silence. Silence and the faint sound of their footsteps disappearing below, taking Mel with them.

I slid to the floor, my forehead against the door. My nightmare had finally come alive for real, more alive than all those flashes that plagued my dreams. Closing my eyes made it worse.

There, a woman appeared, a woman with golden hair, her soft silhouette stepping out of the shadows into the light. A memory, a dream, something buried deep enough that it felt unreal.

I had a family once; he took me away. And now he had taken Mel too.

I pulled back, palms digging into my scalp as it all crashed down. All the years of pretending, of forgetting. It was not survival; it was surrender. He had taught me to lie, to obey, to believe that nothing more but what he had molded me into existed. And each new town, each supposed escape, not a freedom; just another layer to the chain.

He hadn't just robbed me of my family. He had stolen my future. He had broken me into pieces, molding me into a scared, fragile girl who didn't know her own name or her own worth. But something snapped in me then. I was tired of being lost. I was tired of living half-dead, walking through a life that didn't belong to me.

He'd taken Mel, and I wouldn't let him keep her.

Tears streamed silently down my face, hot and relentless. "Oh, Mel," I whispered into the darkness. "Why us?"

No answer came. Because there was no reason. Some people are just born evil.

I heaved myself up, bruise after bruise screaming in protest. My ribs were sore to the touch with each agonizing breath. I refused to stop. I just couldn't. The attic seemed to be choking me. I had to get out. Immediately, my eyes went toward the window, the very place where he tried sealing me in. I felt the cracked glass and tugged the wooden spring until it gave. The glass released, and with one last heave, I pushed it out.

The cold air nipped my face as I stepped onto the slanted roof, my balance teetering, fingers aching while I held tightly to the edge. And there below was a ladder, so old and half concealed by thorny branches, but it was the only way out.

I let out a shaky breath and started to work my way down, slow step after slow step. Scratches tore at my arms and snagged at my clothes, but I didn't care. When my boots finally hit the ground, I exhaled a breath I hadn't known I was holding.

I turned back to the house; its dark windows seemed to stare back at me like empty eyes. I knew what I was supposed to do. I was supposed to lie down and die today. To give up. But I wouldn't. Not anymore.

"I'll ask him to return my life," I hissed to no one, sounding shrill and uneven, "and take someone else instead." With that, I ran. I didn't look back. The snow crunched beneath my feet as I sprinted into the woods, my breath escaping in short, ragged clouds. I didn't know where I was going, but I knew who I needed to find. The Snowman.

I walked an hour through the woods, though it felt like an age in the silence, the quiet snow crunching beneath each footstep, the light hum of water somewhere nearby breaking into the stillness. The sounds drew me deeper, speaking to me in a whisper as I approached the river's shore.

The water ran crimson red, jarring against the white snow around it. A scene out of a nightmare, felt like someone had painted the river in blood and let it stain the white world around it.

I moved closer, dropping to a crouch on the edge, my huff misting in the icy air. I dipped slowly into the water. For a moment my skin was shocked by the temperature, but still, as the water ran through my fingers, I understood. There was no blood. Cleaned, the water became just water over mud or rocks.

"There's no blood here," I whispered, trying to make the words ring true. I probably wasn't sure if I believed them or wanted to believe them.

There was a smooth rock in the river, much larger than the others, almost inviting. Smoothing my hair back, I took off my shoes and dipped a toe in them. The icy water shot right through it, and I shivered as something crawled up my spine. I let it slide anyway. The pain in my body was loud—the bruises reminded me of everyone I'd survived with.

One step, then another. The water numbed me, but I trudged forward until I reached the rock. In one quick, trembling movement, I leaned against it, first crouching before slowly relaxing to sit on my heels and let the stone warm my feet again. Then I sat still, the river whispering beneath me as if it held secrets that only it could understand.

"You're far away from home," a voice called from behind.

I whipped my head around, startled. Standing on the riverbank was a woman I recognized, the same woman I'd seen the first day we moved here. Her long hair was braided tightly and she held a thick rope in her hands, leading a black horse. Its breath misted in the cold air as it pawed the ground restlessly.

"I needed some fresh air," I said and swung my head back toward the river.

I could hear her approaching; the soft slapping of her horse's hooves in the shallows announced their arrival.

"You good?" she squeaked, short of sleep, it seemed, as she ran her hand gently over the horse's mane as habit had undoubtedly taught her.

"Yeah," I said, quite quietly, exhaling only so that the word might take some of the weight off me. Now I looked up, with quiet eyes watching her.

"You know the woods can be dangerous, right?" she said, spitting something onto the ground.

I nodded weakly and looked closer. Her hands were scarred, with round, rough-skinned marks that told of a lifetime of hard work. She pulled a cigarette from her pocket, lit it, and blew smoke into the air.

"It is impolite to stare, " she caught me.

"I'm sorry," I said quickly, and my gaze shifted away as the cold rose to my cheeks.

"No, you're not," she said, the ghost of a smile playing on her lips. "But it's okay. I'm used to it."

"I didn't mean to," I said again and with more sincerity.

Her eyes snapped to mine, sharp and knowing. "You apologize a lot, kid." She pulled on the reins, releasing the stirrup of her boot as she swung herself onto her horse in one smooth motion. The horse snorted and dismounted as she let it gallop slowly, steadily across the riverbank.

"You shouldn't," she said, looking back at me.

"Thanks," I muttered as she passed, the words tumbling out before I could stop them.

Just as I had turned my head, her voice cut through the air once more, a little louder this time. "The woods get dark after five. You should head out before then."

"I will," I lied, continuing to look out over the river. She didn't press the subject. Her silhouette faded into the distance, horse and rider becoming a part of the forest until they were well out of sight.

I sat and remained where I was, perched on the rock in the middle of the river, staring into the crimson water that was only water, but still felt like something else. Something waiting.

I stood in front of the woods, staring into their dark expanse. Ten minutes seemed to be an eternity. With every blink, it was as if the trees stretched out wider, swallowing the horizon whole. The sun slid lower, its pale light fading as the shadows deepened. The air grew keener, colder. It nipped at my skin and made me shiver.

"This was a stupid idea," I muttered to myself, my voice barely a whisper against the wind.

Slowly, I got down from the rock. My bare feet hit the icy water, sending shivers running like a thousand needles through my body. I closed my eyes and willed my legs to move. Step by step, I made it to the riverbank where my shoes waited in the snow, half-covered in frost. I crouched down, reaching for them—Hands.

Hands came from behind and grabbed me, yanking me back with such force I gasped.

"No," I breathed, my voice catching in my throat.

And then I heard them—the voices. Their voices. Familiar. Mocking. The two boys from the woods two days ago. Josh and Vic. They were here. Waiting. Watching. Like shadows that followed me every time I stepped into this cursed place.

"Let me go!" I shouted, wrenching my body to the side. But it was no use.

Vic, the taller of the two, was spinning me around like a rag doll and pushed me to the ground. I went down hard, skinning my palms against snow and ice. His laughter was cold and mirthless.

"We came to finish what we started," he sneered, looking back at Josh.

I flailed around, reaching for one of my shoes, and I threw it with all my might. It hit Josh with full force right in the chest.

"Bitch!" he snarled, doubling over for a moment.

I didn't wait. I turned and crawled, my hands raking at the frozen ground. My knees plunged into snow, cold searing through, and yet I couldn't, wouldn't, stop.

A yank.

Vic had my ankle and was pulling backward. I hit the bottom with a dull thump, screaming, and kicking wildly in every direction, but only he was the one who laughed.

"Where you going?" he chided, tugging hard to draw me closer and closer to the river.

"Vic, man, let's have some fun," Josh said, his ginger hair catching the last light of the dying sun. He stepped closer, his grin wide, his thumb scratching absently under his nose.

"Thirsty?" he jeered.

Before I could do anything, much less let go, he stomped on my hand. It pinned painfully into the mud and snow, the crunch of bone echoing in my ears, and I screamed.

Then his hand was on the back of my head.

No.

The word never came out.

He shoved me. My face plunged into the river, the water racing over me, slamming me with its coldness, and stealing my breath. I gasped. My mouth parted beneath the surface, and immediately I inhaled mud and water. Red clouds swirled in front of me, I was clawing blind, arms pinned, Josh's knee weighting into my wrist.

Panic roared in my chest. My body fought instinctively, jerking and trembling, but I couldn't break free. My lungs were on fire. I screamed into the water, but no sound came, only bubbles that popped and vanished. This is how I die. The thought flickered in my mind while my limbs started weakening. He jerked me up then, suddenly, just as suddenly as he started. My head broke the surface, and I gasped, choking violently as my body heaved for air, water streaming from my nose and mouth. The cold sliced through me, but I couldn't focus on anything more than breathing.

Josh knelt in front of me, still grinning, as if this were a game.

"This is what you get when you scream like a bitch," he said, his voice keen with cruel humor. He sniffled loudly, his thumb still jerking beneath his nose.

I wanted to fight. I wanted to scream. And my body didn't want to listen; my limbs were heavy and numb as my sight swam.

"Do it," I heard Josh say in a low, eager voice. "We'll blame it on the serial killer. They'll believe it."

The words jolted through me like ice. I felt Vic's hands on me, yanking me backward across the snow. My arms were wrenched above my head, my body too weak to resist.

"Vic, do it!" Josh barked.

Vic straddled my arms, the weight of his body pinning me to the ground, pressing me like prey.

"We just want to warm you up," he laughed, the tone twisted and mocking.

I felt the tug at my coat, peeling away into shreds of fabric as his cold and wrong hands moved with precision to touch areas of my skin that created a very real, rather feral burn in places deep inside. A scream built up in my throat, and though I shook from its intensity, still I could not force my voice past a quaked whisper. My jeans slid, the chill in the winter air outside nibbled with icy morsels at my lower skin.

I squeezed my eyes shut. Darkness. I greeted it. I don't want to watch. I felt myself slipping, falling into a void where the cold couldn't reach me, where their laughter couldn't follow. Just for a moment, I let go. For a moment, I was gone. Today, I had a reason to live. But now, I had another reason to die.

NINE

SNOWMAN

Every step I took crunched the snow, gnawing at the promise I'd made to her: I will find you. It was like a scratched record, just a line running in my head. A promise that, at its core, was a blade digging deep with every minute she wasn't here. Taking her away, disappearing together, and escaping all this just lingered in my brain like a far-off dream of a happy ending. But I wasn't entitled to happy endings. People like me did not get to escape quite so easily.

I had walked in circles for what felt like several hours, her trace every time slipping through my fingers. With every blink of my eye, the woods stretched a bit wider, the sun was almost swallowed by the oncoming night. The cold wind whirled through the trees and cut through my sweatshirt, chilling me to my bones.

Then I heard them.

Laughter. Distant, familiar, two voices carried the breeze like a curse. My body froze; my instinct kicked in, and I ducked behind a wide tree.

Josh and Vic.

The same ghosts haunting me two days ago, here they were again. Following. Waiting. Always waiting.

"We finished what we started," the words seemed to ring within my head in Josh's voice, cold and cutting.

I was only a few meters away from my kill kit. I'd buried four of them around these woods, always ready, always prepared, but for now, I just remained hidden, watching.

"Man, she was good," Josh said, shoving Vic as they stumbled along; their laughter was sharp, grating. Josh was the chief of police's son, Jan Johansson's golden boy, or so everybody acted. Wherever he went, trouble trailed behind him and his daddy wiped it clean: rehab, dead friends, assault charges—all covered, dismissed, forgotten.

Vic had been different, once. A coroner's son, quiet, a kid who never knew better but followed all the rules. And Josh had pulled him down with him deeper and deeper into that hole until the town, too small where everyone knew everybody without knowing a thing at all, was whispering and telling legends only.

Legends like Nøkken, the spirit said to rise from the crimson river, stealing loved ones into the dark. People here believed in those tales. They believed snow brought new beginnings. But I knew better. This town wasn't blessed. It was cursed. And I belonged to it as much as the darkness did.

The papers had taken to calling me Snowman for months now. Their headlines screamed 'fear,' but all they knew was a smidge of the truth. I killed with no intention of making any snowmen, just buried monsters who came cloaked in plain skin. At one point or another in my life, I had vowed that I wouldn't ever be like him, my father, but I hunted people such as him; people should make sure legends remained in the literature and evil rotted six feet under.

I shifted, and my breath steadied, as Josh and Vic, too stoned to take notice, passed by me. A gut feeling told me to head toward where they'd come from. I followed, my footsteps slow, and cautious, the woods quieting around me as I moved further from them.

Then, suddenly I heard the river.

It was a familiar sound, constant, louder as I approached, but another thing drew my attention.

A coat of red color.

It lay crumpled in the snow near the riverbank.

My chest tightened, the panic swirling inside me like a vortex. I was running. My breathing was fast and hard, and my heart hammered so loudly in my ears that I could barely hear the rush of the water. I reached her and fell on my knees, touching her pale, numb face with shaking hands.

"Bree...," I whispered, my voice cracking.

She was so still, her skin cold. I pressed two fingers against her neck and searched for a pulse. It was faint, so faint that I might have sworn that I had imagined it. The jeans were halfway off, the white sweater stained with dirt; the red coat was unzipped, gaping open in a silent scream.

My teeth ground together, my jaw aching with the anger flooding through me. My fists curled, and for a moment, all I could see was red, the kind that filled rivers.

I carefully worked my arms under her fragile body and lifted her into my chest. She didn't stir; her head fell limply against me.

"I've got you," I whispered, though I wasn't sure who I was reassuring, her or myself.

The run back to the cottage felt endless. The world blurred, a rush of branches and snow as my boots pounded the ground. She was weightless in my arms, and that terrified me. Her body didn't fight. It didn't feel like hers anymore.

By the time the cottage came into view, my breath was ragged, my pulse racing. I stumbled onto the porch, fumbling for the key in my pocket, almost dropping it in an attempt to unlock the door.

"Come on, come on," I muttered, growling under my breath as my fingers shook.

Finally, the lock clicked, and I pushed inside, kicking the door shut behind me. I carried her to the bed, setting her down gently. Without hesitation, my hand plunged once more into her neck as I searched for that faint beat of life.

It's still there, barely, but it would do. I slapped the heels of my fists onto her chest, bringing it all to an end. "C'mon, Bree," I gritted out, voice cracking. "Fucking fight."

I pressed my fists into her chest rhythmically, relentlessly, until finally, her body contorted and she gasped in air. The sound was weak and fractured, but there. I exhaled loudly, my hands trembling, as I sat back a moment staring at her. She was alive. Barely, but alive.

I didn't waste another second, yanking my black sweater from the hook by the door and turning back to her. Her bright red coat was soaked and heavy; it clung to her. I tugged it off her carefully, the zipper scraping, letting my hands move through it. Then her sweater, her jeans—cold, wet, stuck against her skin like some dark, damp shroud. I left her in underwear now, her body shuddering hard, her lips purpled. She lay before me so white, so small.

I didn't like the fragile image of her that lay in front of me.

I slipped my sweater over her head; it was on her, yet still clung loosely around her. I gathered her gently together, pulling her up towards the top of the bed, and wrapped her up in the thick blanket up to her neck, trying to get warmth in her body. Her breathing was shallow but steady now. That was good enough.

"Who did this to you?" I whispered, my voice low, and angry, and I didn't even try concealing it. I lowered myself onto the edge of the bed and locked my eyes right on her face, paler than the snow outside. Her lips were purple, that ugly color, a shade I hated to see on her.

I had seen it before, far too many times. Twenty-six times to be precise. I knew that color, that cold, that fragility. On her, though, my stomach churned over. My jaw stiffened, and I found myself looking away, commanding my breathing to steady itself.

She'd crawled beneath my skin, slipped inside like a thorn, and had become so deeply embedded that pulling her out would have meant blood and pain. Without warning, without rhyme or reason. It wasn't supposed to happen. Not to me. Maybe it was fate, maybe some cruel joke, or maybe someone somewhere had finally figured out how to punish me for what I'd done.

And yet, here she was. The answer to questions I didn't even know I was asking. How could someone like me, someone who took lives without hesitation, care about hers? Care so much it made me mad? I'd thought I was hollow, numb to everything, to everyone. And yet, here she was, melting the frost I'd been carrying in my chest for years.

I loathed it. And I required it. I stood, walking slowly toward the window. The woods beyond had grown dark again, stretching the shadows between trees in wide veins of blackness. I tugged on the blinds in a single, fluid motion, cutting off the view. Turning around, I turned on the tiny lamp on the nightstand beside my bed. Delicate and airy, it cast across the room a weak veil.

I looked at her one more time, her breathing in short, shallow gasps, her chest rising and falling softly with each intake of air under the blanket. She was safe for now.

I turned and slipped out of the room, shutting the door softly behind me. I leaned against the doorframe, my hands coming up to bury into my face. My breath came heavy.

It was her.

I'd never felt this, not like this. Not knowing what this was at all, all I knew was that she made me feel alive in a way I never wanted to be.

She made me want to tear off the mask I'd spent years perfecting of the killer, of the monster, of the

Snowman. For her, I wanted to be more, someone normal. A man who could take care of her. A man she deserved.

I had never felt so defeated in my entire life. Hours passed, and yet she didn't wake. Her breaths were shallow, her body unmoving, a pale ghost of herself. I couldn't bear it any longer. I carried her to the hospital.

Inside, the fluorescent lights above me buzzed cold as I spoke with the nurse at the front desk. I lied. I told them I found her on the road, lying there alone. A nameless Jane Doe.

I said I didn't know her, just that I'd seen her around town before. My voice was steady, and practiced, the mask slipping easily back into place, but underneath it, my insides were twisting.

I stood in the waiting room, hands shoved deep into my pockets to keep them from shaking. People came and went, families, children, nurses, all ghosting around me. But I stood my ground, my eyes fixed on the door behind which they'd disappeared with her, waiting for someone to say something, anything.

It wasn't until the doctor finally came out, his expression was grave.

"She was assaulted," he told me, as though those words did not carry the whole world upon their backs.

The room tilted, my heart dropping to my stomach as rage and grief joined in a storm inside me. I bit hard into the inside of my cheek, the metallic salt of blood flooding my mouth as I forced back my reaction. I couldn't scream. I couldn't break. But God, I wanted to, to tear the walls down, to rip apart the whole damn town that had let this happen to her.

It's my fault, the thought repeated, sharp as a blade. If I hadn't left her that night. If I'd found her sooner, just an hour earlier. If I'd been stronger, smarter, more in control. She wouldn't be lying there in that sterile hospital room, alone, broken.

The guilt consumed me. For years, I had worn the mask of a killer who didn't feel, a monster who buried his heart deep enough to forget it was ever there. But standing here now, I was melting, breaking apart for a girl I had no right to care for.

She was just a stranger, a girl who shouldn't have mattered. And yet, in one touch, one look, she had awoken something inside me I didn't think I still had.

Love. Kindness. Warmth.

Things this town had buried long ago, things that were dead inside me, all being dug up anew.

I clenched my hands in my pockets and stared with a frown down at the hallway where they pulled her. Her face danced in my head, fresh bruises, pale lips, the way her body weight had felt so fragile in the circle of my arms when I'd lifted her: all these still alive now in my memory.

I had let her down, and it was something that I was never going to forgive myself for.

I finally faced the glass doors of the hospital and stepped towards it, and outside, through the window, snow fell in thick, heavy flakes. I stepped outside into the cold air which bit my skin, yet I did not feel it.

I will make it right, I whispered to myself, my breathing a cloud in the freezing air.

I will make them pay.

TEN

BREE

I WOKE UP FIVE minutes ago in a sterile white room. The walls were blank and expressed nothing. The steady beeps of the heart monitor rang in my ears like a cruel reminder that I was still alive. Every time I blinked, I was underwater again, drowning, gasping for air that would never come. My chest felt tight, as if a brick sat heavily against my ribs, pressing harder and harder until I thought my bones would shatter.

And just like that, tears slid down my cheeks without permission, when I had no control over my body. I could feel them yet—the hands, their weight—pressing down upon me. I heard laughter, their haunting laughter that echoed around in my ears. Their eyes, watching. Always watching.

I tugged the hard white blanket up to my chin, curling in on myself like I could disappear beneath it. Shame burned inside me, spreading through every limb. I wanted to tear away every piece of myself, to wash it all clean, but I couldn't even sit up. I was trapped, broken porcelain scattered into a thousand pieces no one would ever bother to pick up.

A soft knock broke the silence, but I didn't respond. Unwelcome guests came anyway. The door creaked open, and through the window reflection, I saw two men step into the room. My face was a mess: my cheeks were red and blotchy, and my lips cracked and dry. My hair hung greasy and tangled around my face, curled from the cold air outside. I was like a ghost, a shell of who I used to be.

"Bree," The voice was soft from behind; it came from Detective Thor Karlsson sinking into his chair beside me, but all he could offer now was, "The doctors have asked for us," as he added. He reached again toward my face, his brown eyes delving for my own that refused to meet his gaze.

"This is my new partner, Isak Storm," he continued. "Perhaps you can tell us what happened?"

I turned my head enough to be looking at Isak, and for one brief second, our eyes met.

Blue. His eyes were blue.

My breath caught, and I dropped my stare to the blanket I gripped like a lifeline.

No.

My mind whispered to itself, searching.

"Bree?" Thor said again, his tone soft. "If you need time, we can come later."

I swallowed hard against the lump in my throat, forcing myself to tilt my head slightly. My eyes lingered on Isak now—long enough to study him. Brown hair, tied back neatly into a bun. Strong shoulders. A beard that framed a sharp jaw. He was tall, solid—like all the men in this town.

But his eyes... his voice...

Something about him made me search. I had only seen his eyes—the Snowman's eyes—in flashes, but I carried them with me. Dark. Cold. And yet, I had imagined warmth hidden just beneath.

"No," I finally managed to whisper. My voice was small but the word decisive. "It was Josh and Vic."

Thor's eyes sharpened. "Josh Johansson and Victor Lundqvist?" His voice was careful, even. "Are you sure?"

I nodded, my throat too tight to speak again. The names were out now, spoken into existence. I'd chosen to speak. I couldn't be silent anymore.

They exchanged a glance, a glance that twisted my stomach. They didn't write it down; they didn't need to. It was as if voicing their names sealed something they knew but rather did not acknowledge. Isak leaned in, sitting on the edge of my bed. His blue eyes bored into mine, as if he searched for cracks, for lies.

"Sometimes we get confused," he said softly, his voice deep, almost too calm.

Of all the things, it was his voice that shook me most of all, that deep timbre, so close to his, Snowman's.

It can't be, I thought as my mind went racing, out of control.

Isak's gaze lingered a moment longer, heavy and unreadable, before Thor pulled him back. "Isak, can you give us a moment?" Thor's voice was firm, brooking no argument.

Isak stood slowly, watching me as he left the room. I tracked his movements out of the corner of my eye. Broad shoulders. Heavy footsteps. He glanced back just once before disappearing through the door. I exhaled a shaky breath, my hands clenching the blanket tighter.

I wanted so badly for Snowman to be normal, be someone I could see in the daylight and believe was kind.

Maybe that's why I continued to look, searching for parts of him in the features of strangers. In every man who walked into my life, I searched for the monster who had haunted my mind. Because if I could find him if he could be real, maybe I could fix him.

But that was an illusion, and I had to wake up. I couldn't love a killer, couldn't love a cop, and I had to find a way to love myself first, but that part of me was gone, taken.

"Bree," Thor said softly, drawing me back. He leaned in closer, his voice low and even. "Josh Johansson is the son of the chief of police. Are you sure it was him?"

My eyes dropped, but I nodded again, wordless.

Thor's thumb stroked across my chin, raising it so I had to look up at him. His face was solemn, not cruel.

"I believe you," he said softly. "But they won't."

His words hung in the air, a weight I couldn't carry. I knew what he meant, and that was this wasn't a town for people like me. It was for them, the Johanssons and the Lundqvists, those whose sins were buried under snow and silence. I swallowed hard, the tears threatening to spill again at the echo of Thor's words in my head. "They won't believe you."

But I had spoken. For the first time, I had spoken. And that would have to be enough.

I turned my head to one side, a tear welling silently down my face. "All my life I've been silent, and now, when I do finally speak up, you are telling me to keep my mouth shut."

"No," Thor said, crouching down beside me. His voice was soft, and steady, meant to comfort me, but it didn't reach me. "I want you to tell me everything."

I stared at him through the blur of tears. How can I ever trust anyone now? The question screamed in my head, much louder than his words.

My mouth opened; my lips were trembling, but before words could pour out, the creak of the door opening distracted me.

A man with ginger hair stepped in. Instinctively, my body went numb.

"I heard there was some sort of emergency," the man said, almost too casual to the point of light. He faced Thor, without giving any attention to me, "Could you call the doctor, detective?"

Thor's jaw clenched, his fists curling at his sides. He looked once at me; his face was unreadable. Then he turned and walked out of the room. I watched him go, feeling a pit form in my stomach.

The man approached me, his movements slow. He sat down beside the bed, too close.

"Pretty," he murmured, reaching for a lock of my hair. His fingers curled it around lazily, playing with it as though it were nothing but a toy. "I spoke to the doctor earlier," he said, his voice low, almost kind. "He said nothing happened."

"But it did happen," I choked out, my voice cracking. Tears streamed down my face again, hot and relentless.

"No one will believe you," he whispered, leaning closer. His lips curled wryly and his eyes narrowed to blue slivers. Then he winked like it was some kind of joke I was supposed to laugh at.

I shrank back, further and further against the mattress as though to squeeze into its fibers and never come out again. I was shaking all over.
 Make him leave. Somebody, make him leave.

Thor returned, the doctor following close on his heels holding a clipboard, which he barely looked at despite my presence in the main attraction. He didn't even look at me, he didn't want to.
 "Johansson." He greeted cheerfully, shaking his hand like this was such a casual, friendly. "Pleasure."

I glared at the doctor as he strode closer to my bed. "Miss here fell and hit her head," he said, continuing to flip through the chart. "She may have a concussion. We're still running checks, but that's all it is."

"No!" I shouted my voice raw desperate. "You're

wrong! That's not what happened!"

The doctor had turned his back to me as if I wasn't in the same room.

"I think this is a very troubled young lady who needs care," he said smoothly, ushering Johansson out the door. The man turned once to look back at me; that sick smirk still plastered on his face as he disappeared into the hallway.

Thor stood still for a moment, his face unreadable again. When he finally approached the bed, I tried speaking, trying to make him hear me. "Thor, please—"

"I'm sorry," he said quietly, cutting me off. "But there's nothing we can do."

He turned his back and walked away. My chest ached, and the anger bubbled up from deep in me. My hand reached instinctively for the pillow beneath my head, and I threw it with as much force as I could muster. It hit the back of his head and bounded to the floor. He didn't stop. He didn't turn around. He kept on walking, disappearing out the door like everyone else had.

I felt empty like I had nothing left inside. No one cares,

I thought bitterly. Not even him.

Isak leaned and picked up the pillow. He set it gently on the bed beside me, his fingers brushing the blanket. His eyes were steady as he leaned closer, voice low. "I'll teach them a lesson," he whispered. "I promise."

I swung to him then, my face wet with tears. My voice was shaking; the words came out in broken bits. "I want them dead. All of them."

His palm touched briefly on my arm, an almost reassuring squeeze before standing. He said nothing further, only turned and walked out of the room. I curled onto my side, tugging the blanket up to my chin as if it could protect me from the world.

The tears didn't stop, but when a person becomes too tired, they no longer fight them back. I squeezed my eyes shut and let the sobs shake through me as silently as I could. I was back in the circle again, the one I couldn't seem to get out of.

The endless loop of bad luck, of pain, of voices I couldn't silence.

Life is hell, I thought. And I don't know how to stop it.

Every time I closed my eyes, it was the same. The same hands, the same laughter, the same icy water pulling me under. This time, the steps were soft, light as whispers in the quiet of the room. I could hear them coming, heard them stop. I held my breath, pretending to be asleep, curled up small enough to disappear. The steps remained dragging. Then, finally, they faced and faded away, leaving me to my tears and the weight of everything I could not escape.

ELEVEN

SNOWMAN

I WISHED FOR A clock that could turn back time. I wished for someone to pull me out of the present and take me back to the past. Back to when she wasn't broken, back to a time before her pain began. I wished I could erase every scar printed onto her body and soul, leaving nothing but her—whole and untouched.

Regret is the heaviest burden a man will ever carry, a shadow that lengthens with each passing day until all that's left is taken. And with regrets, sorrow, a trickle turning into a flood till everything's drowned and none is left but darkness.

But I wouldn't live with regret. I couldn't. I didn't have a clock to turn back the time, nor someone to carry me into the past. All I had was what I knew best: an axe, a knife, and a gun.

I couldn't erase what had been done to her. I couldn't fix her fractured heart, her fragile soul. But I could make sure no one ever laid a hand on her again.

I zipped up the black nylon jumpsuit and felt it cling to my body like a second skin. In my hand, I held the faceless plastic mask that had become my identity. It stared back at me, blank and cold. I stood in front of the mirror, but all that stared back was emptiness, just a hollow man with a hollow face.

On the counter beside me lay the local newspaper. The front page showed a picture of an Asian reporter standing outside my last victim's house, a microphone clutched tightly in her hand. The headline screamed in bold, black letters: "Snowman Hunts Again.". They pressed heavily upon my chest, so real. I had once hoped to save this town, to rid it of its corruption and decay. But evil within people cannot be cleansed, no more than a disease can be healed. You can hide it or remove the tumor, trying to drown it, but it will always resurface, wearing a new face. And I was tired. Tired of chasing shadows, tired of wearing this mask, tired of the cold that seeped in through my bones and turned me into what I was. An ice monster.

But I couldn't stop. Not now. Not when she was still hurting. Not when they were still out there. I knew where they hid, where they skulked in, the places they thought made them untouchable. I would find them. I would make them suffer for every bruise, every scar they left on her body and soul.

They thought they could take her away from me, hurt her, and simply walk away. But they were wrong. This wasn't about justice. This wasn't about the town or headlines or the mask.

This was about her. And they would pay for all of it.

The fog hung heavy over the woods, curling around the trees like ghostly fingers. Each step I made, had a reason behind it. And as the crunch in the snow beneath my feet had been muffled under that dense air, the axe swung low in my hand, chafing a thin cut across the snow.

Their laughter, ahead, cut like razor-sharp edges, so cruel and careless. Not loud enough to hide where they were. They lay by the river, in the very same spot where she was, mocking and joking about it, reliving a night they had gotten away with.

Something inside me clicked off. Like a distant switch that flipped and everything became cold, focused.

I moved closer, as quiet as the fog itself. Their voices sharpened, distinct now; Josh's lazy drawl; Vic's nervous titters, following on as he always did.

As soon as I was near enough for them to make me out through the haze, I swung the axe down into the snow, the sound cracked like a shot.

"Good evening, boys," I said. "Ready to die?"

Josh lay on his back, hands behind his head, and didn't even bother opening his eyes. "Yeah, man, whatever," he mumbled, his cocky smirk carved into his face.

But Vic wasn't quite that calm. He moved himself up into a seated position, his eyes wide as they darted between me and Josh. His voice cracked as he slapped his chest.

"It's... it's S-S-Snowman!" he shouted, scrambling to his feet. He tripped over his own boots, went face-first into the snow, but then clawed his way to his feet.

"Fuck," Josh cursed, finally snapping out of his trance. In an instant, he got upright, the laziness gone from his poise. He didn't glance back at Vic as he took off running toward the river.

"Well isn't this going to be amusing," I said out loud as I watched Vic try to stumble after him.

I raised the axe and was off, running with steady, sure steps as adrenaline coursed through me like wildfire. The icy water of the river splashed against my boots; I barely felt the cold. My heart pounded hard in my chest, matching the frantic rhythm of their footsteps crashing through the woods.

The fog thickened, curling around the darker part of the forest where the trees stood higher, their branches clawing for the sky. I followed the sounds of their movements, their panicked breathing, frantic steps.

Vic didn't get very far. He fell behind a tree, pressing himself against the ground like some sort of animal that was afraid. His tall body stuck out awkwardly, his feet poking out from the shadow of the tree. He thought he was hidden.

He wasn't. I circled silently, moving behind the same tree he cowered against. The fog wrapped itself around me, masking my presence until I was a single breath away. I hunched low and leaned close enough to him to hear his ragged, shallow breathing.

"Oh shiny, swingy axe," I softly sang, the words slipping from my mouth like a lullaby.

I swung the axe in the air, the blade whistling on and on before it bit into the bark of the tree just inches from his head.

"Went chopping through the woods," I went on, my voice low.

Vic screamed, his body trembling as he pressed himself harder against the tree.

"Down came the chips..." I pulled the axe free, letting it slice through the air again. This time, I buried it in the root of the tree just beside his foot. "...as the tiny dick bitch in front of me stood."

I laughed then, sharp and cutting, as his wide eyes, teary with unshed tears darted to the blade. It was a whole body stutter before he slumped forward, unconscious.

"Pff, coward," I grumbled.

I reached down, hoisting his limp body onto my back with a grunt. Compared to the satisfaction flooding me, his weight was close to nothing. The axe hung loosely in my other hand as I started to walk. The woods darkened the farther north I went, and the river's sound faded behind me. I had to move ahead, where my kill kit was buried.

I heard behind me the soft crunch of footsteps and dropped him roughly to the ground, turning toward the rock where Josh was hiding. A panicked uneven breathing was now giving him away. I inched forward, my movement slow, surrounded by the fog.

He saw me before I was close enough, turned, and ran, his feet pounding the snow.

I chased after him, the cold air burning my lungs. He was faster than I had expected, his panic giving him speed. But adrenaline coursed through me, sharpening my focus, I leaped, tackling him to the ground.

"What's up?" I said as I pinned him beneath me. His wide, terrified eyes met mine, and I couldn't resist. "You like my body on top of yours, you little slut?"

His face went crimson, his lips trembling, and then I felt something warm and wet spreading beneath him.

"Seriously?" I muttered, rolling my eyes. Josh had pissed himself, and the wet stain on my suit was growing cold. "You couldn't hold it for five minutes?"

His only response was a desperate, guttural sound as I punched his face. The satisfying crack of impact silenced him, and his body went limp beneath me.

Scooping him up, I slung his unconscious body over my shoulder and carried him back to where Vic still lay stretched in the snow. My irritation grew as the cold wet spot from Josh's piss soaked through my suit, raising a shiver.

I dropped him beside Vic, both of them lifeless like a pile in the snow. I snatched up his shirt, yanking him out of it and quickly tearing it into strips. I used the fabric to bind their legs together, pulling it tight, making sure they couldn't escape. Grabbing the loose end, I trudged forward through the snow, dragging their bodies behind me.

The sound of their weight sliding over the ground, scraping against branches and rocks, was like a pleasing melody to my ears.

Five minutes. That's what separated us from the spot where I hid the kill kit.

As groggy voices began to return, their screams mingled with the crunch of snow. They were clawing at branches, trying to break themselves, but it was pointless. Every scratch, every bruise—they would feel it all.

"My dad's the chief of police!" Josh yelled, desperation cracking his voice. "You'll rot in prison for this!"

I stopped abruptly, the shirt pulling tight in my hand. I turned more slowly, letting their bound legs fall to the ground.

Josh, motivated by the pause, tried again. "That's right," he spat, his voice rising. "You better untie us now!"

I crouched down, and with slow motions, I leaned forward and untied his legs. He stood up, then, brushing the snow away from his pants.

"Who's scared now, huh?" he sneered, his grin wide.

I said nothing. I merely kicked the snow aside with my boot, revealing a box buried beneath. His smile faded as I pulled it out and opened it.

"You," I growled.

His confidence shattered, and he struggled to his feet to run, but I was faster, slamming him back to the ground. Vic fainted again, his body going limp.

I pulled out an injection of epinephrine from the box. Adrenaline was the perfect fuel for pain. I rammed the needle into Josh's arm, his eyes jerking as his body twitched when the medicine hit.

"You will feel it all," I calmly said as I tied his hands behind him and strapped a rope tightly around his waist.

Throwing the rope over a thick branch, I pulled, hoisting his body just high enough that his toes barely brushed the ground. He struggled, twisting and turning, but the adrenaline coursing through his veins made his fear more visible to my eyes.

I turned to Vic, repeating the process, injecting him with the remaining dose. Immediately, his eyes snapped open, wild with terror, and I tied him up, leaving him on the ground for now.

"W-what are you going to do?" Vic stuttered, his voice shaking.

"I'm going to make you pay," I said, my tone icy, with no emotion. The white plastic mask reflected the faint light on my face, I was like a ghost, searching through my tools.

I pulled out a small hunting knife from the toolbox, its blade sharp and shiny. I just tuned Josh out as he came near, begging and promising me money and connections.

"Stop crying like a bitch," I told him, slicing his shirt down the middle and pulling it off.

"Let's start with an R," I muttered, laying the blade against his chest. He screamed as I cut into his skin, the letter welling with blood down his torso.

"A...," I went on, the knife digging deeper, "P... I... S... T."

His screams echoed through the trees. His chest heaved as I stepped back to admire my work. "Now," I said, my voice low, "let's take care of the rest."

I unbuttoned his trousers and couldn't help a smile as I saw his shriveled, pathetic attempt at masculinity.

"I have a better idea," I whispered, my voice little more than a murmur. I left him hanging in confusion and turned to Vic.

I leaned out, snatching the rope tied to his middle, my fingers clamping down on it and tugging him upright. His feet stutter-stepped as he struggled to find his balance while his eyes went large, frantically wide.

"You're going to take your fist," I said, "and shove it in his ass." I laid my palm on his shoulder, steadying him, feeling the fine trembling of his body.

"N-No," he stuttered, his voice breaking as he shrank back. Disgusted, his face screwed up, a deep furrow forming between his brows, and he shook his head violently, taking a few backward steps.

"I might let you go," I said with a very slow, taunting grin, "might."

He froze, his body rigid. The bark of the tree met his back, he was trapped, and I closed the gap between us. Without hesitation, I grabbed his wrist, yanking his hand toward me, and began unrolling his sleeve, exposing his bare skin up to the elbow. His pulse thudded beneath my fingers.

"No, please," he cried, his voice breaking, desperate. But I didn't respond to his pleas—just as they had ignored hers.

I yanked him forward, dragging him toward Josh, the tension in the air thick with fear. Both of them screamed for help, their voices raw with panic, but the sound was swallowed by the dense trees around us, vanishing into the woods.

I pulled down his trousers, sliding them down his hips, his body stiff with resistance. His ass cheeks clenched together, his breathing rapid and shallow.

"You wouldn't," he whimpered, but there was no hesitation in my movements.

I couldn't bring myself to care anymore—not when they had never cared about her.

"Spit on it!" I barked.

Vic froze, his body stiff, a fear running down his spine, but I wasn't done. I leaned in closer, my gaze never leaving him, my words just a challenge. "It has to slide in."

He shook his head again, his face contorted in disbelief, refusing to give way. I drew my knife from its sheath, pressing its cold steel against the skin of his neck. The sharp edge bit into him just enough to send a shudder through his body.

"Do it," I ordered.

His willpower shattered like glass as he slowly, with his trembling hands, parted the cheeks of Josh's ass in ragged breaths.

"No, man, no!" Josh yelled but Vic didn't hesitate. His fingers stirred, trembling, desperate to obey.

I leaned in, a cold smirk curling on my lips. "Treat him like a slut," I said, my tone flat, "the way you did that girl before; give him the same treatment."

His face contorted in distaste as he moved, his actions driven by something he couldn't suppress. Josh's screams echoed through the night, his voice cracking with a mix of pain and fear. Then, together, they cried—two broken sounds that filled the air with desperation.

"How does it feel?" I asked coldly. "Do you feel like you are nothing?" I pressed the blade to his neck, digging the sharp metal into his skin just enough to remind him of my control. "Do you regret it now?"

Their bodies were shaking, caught in a rhythm of violence neither one wanted to be a part of. I watched them, the raw emotion in their eyes telling a story of helplessness.

But even as Vic struggled, Josh's body betrayed him, reacting in ways he could not hide. My anger flared like a fire in my chest. I stepped closer to him, my presence suffocating, every inch of me radiating rage.

"You think you are in control?" I raised my voice. "Pathetic."

Anger surged within me, more intense than ever before. I used to take my time, letting them suffer slowly, but with this, all I wanted was for them to pay—so I could rush back into her arms. I needed to be with her, at that very moment. To comfort her. To show her that not all men are the same.

My hand was firm, gripping the knife tightly as it stabbed into his flesh, slicing through his cock as coldly as if it were just a branch standing over him. The scream that tore from his throat echoed through the silence of the night, piercing and harsh, sending ripples through the forest. Far away, crows and owls, startled from their sleep, flew into the sky, their wings beating the air in a frantic escape from the chaos happening below them.

His severed cock fell to the ground, penetrating deep into the snow as blood ran down his inner thighs. Now, watching him trying to breathe, screaming, closing his eyes, I could tell he had paid and would not do it again, ever again.

I stepped back toward Vic, shoving his shaking body away as he sobbed, tears streaming down his face. My grip on him was heavy, and with one hard pull, I yanked him aside, pulling him before Josh. And when he finally saw the humiliation laid out before him, a feral scream ripped from his throat. His body tensed, and as I pulled tight on the rope he crumpled to the ground. Fear and disgust hung in the air, heavy with him, the noxious stain of blood that had seeped into the ground in front of him tearing at his eyes, which now looked only at the severed cock in the white snow.

I picked up the cock that was on the ground, shoving it deep into his mouth, even though his lips were tightly closed, pushing away the dead flesh on them.

He gagged as it filled his mouth, but I didn't care, I flung him against the bent bark, wrapping his arms with the rope and tying knots as the weight of my fury tightened. The rage ran wild inside me, pure and merciless, and the memories of what they'd done to her surged anew, setting fire to my blood. Every part of my body screamed for revenge, to feel that one helpless moment that she had felt.

I wanted them to disappear, to take them out of existence until their actions were a whisper, lost in the winds of time. My hands clenched, shaking with the hunger for justice, for the blood of those who had caused so much pain to her.

I stripped him of his clothes, the cold night air biting against his skin, adding to his torture. His eyes were wide, full of fear, but I couldn't bring myself to care.

I turned and walked away, the thud of my boots echoing through the stillness of the woods. I was at the edge of the clearing when I saw the axe. I gripped the handle tightly, knowing that when I returned, the moment would come when they would finally learn the price they had to pay.

TWELVE

BREE

16 YEARS OLD

I NEVER WENT TO school. I never had a friend. My world was small, just my family and Mel. That summer, though, something shifted. For the first time in what felt like forever, we convinced our parents to let us go to the beach alone. They were always so overprotective, they always wanted us close, always within arm's reach, as though letting us go too far might shatter something fragile. We thought it was love, a strange kind that they didn't show but couldn't let go of.

The still morning was suddenly bursting into sound. It was barely six, the kind of early where you felt the world was stuck in a dream. An aged Greek, his raspy voice suddenly shattered the quiet outside, yelling out beneath our window.

"Fresh cherries! Sweet, fresh, buy!" And his voice boomed louder and louder, breaking through the morning fogginess.

"We don't want your damn cherries! Go away!" Mel shouted, leaning out the window. She turned to me, grinning, a laugh bubbling from her chest as she collapsed onto the bed.

"Malaka!" the man barked, shuffling off with a glare, his muttered curses fading as he went.

"You really pissed him off," I said, biting my own laugh back.

Mel looked at me, her face softening into that knowing gaze she always wore, the look that made her seem so much older than fourteen. She was always the wise one, seeing through the world's little tricks when I clung too closely to the stories told to me, trusting too much by half.

She wordlessly crawled to her bed and pulled something from underneath the mattress. The glossy magazine she had taken when Mom wasn't looking. She flipped it open to a page with a model draped across a page in his underwear.

"This," Mel said, poking her finger at the picture, "this is why we're going to the beach alone today." She gave me a wicked grin. "And don't give me that saint look."

I tried to keep a straight face, but a giggle managed to sneak out. "You think anyone will even notice us?"

Mel didn't answer right away, instead tugging my hand to pull me to my feet and spinning us toward the mirror on the old wardrobe. The reflection showed two girls caught in a moment, dark blonde hair falling wild around her face, my lighter locks brushing my shoulders. She rested her chin on my shoulder, her eyes following mine.

"Are you kidding?" she whispered, "Look at you. You're fucking beautiful."

Her words hit me, and I turned to her, wrapping her in a tight hug. "I fucking love you, you know that, don't you?" I murmured against her hair.

"And I love you, malaka," she said, giggling, the word spilling from her mouth. "Even though I have no idea what it means."

She pulled back and spun us to face the mirror again, her hands clamping down on my shoulders. "This is our year. No more locked doors. No more rules. Just us, and maybe some of those gorgeous men out there."

Her squeal of excitement echoed through the room, her hands clapping together as she bounced on her toes. For the first time, I let myself believe her. Maybe this really could be our year.

The beach was supposed to feel like freedom, but it didn't. Not with our parents at the bar above, watching us from their shaded perch in case we disappeared if they happened to look away.

"Minors need supervision," Dad told us before we left. Their rules clung to us, every step we made.

Mel didn't seem to mind. Lying on her towel, her arms outstretched, seeking the sun, her skin already a deep pink. But she didn't move, she lay there, and her body needed to feel it, to leave a mark on it. All I could do was sit and wait, let the rhythms of the sea sway me, like a melody I couldn't help but hum.

I stood and wandered toward the shore, my feet falling onto the hot sand, and eyes searching smooth cool rocks at the edge of waves. Restless, the sea was crashing into rocks, sending sprays of salt water upwards, through the air. I let mist stay on my skin as it settled from it, closing my eyes to the roaring sound of the ocean.

When I opened them, I wasn't alone.

A woman was standing there, leaning on rocks with the shimmering sea acting as a backdrop, her blonde hair pulled back into some sort of ponytail. She wore sunglasses propped high on her head. Her eyes caught mine, an odd feeling of being stuck in her cool blue-eyed stare. She seemed strange to me, familiar and at once unattainable, like a momentarily forgotten dream.

She took a step closer, again not very sure if she should approach. Her gaze did not waver, nor did it shift to another place. My chest tightened a little because I did not know what to do, whether to leave or stay when she suddenly spoke. "Zara?"

Her voice had cracked and was barely more than a whisper. Then louder, with rising desperation, "Zara, is that you?"

I froze.

The name hit me like an unexpected cold wave. I turned slightly, looking behind me, certain she was talking to someone else. But when I looked back, her eyes hadn't left me.

She took another step closer, then another, her pace quickening. Something, hope, lit up her face. Before I could say a word, her arms wrapped around me in a tight embrace.

"Zara!" she sobbed. "Oh, Zara, mommy found you!"

I stiffened, my breath catching in my throat. "I'm not Zara," I managed to say, my voice shaking. "You've got the wrong person."

But she didn't let go. Tears streamed down her face as she clung to me, her grip tightening. "Mommy found you," she repeated, words tumbling out like a plea as if she could make them true if she only said them enough.

I tried to pull back, panic rising in my chest. The desperation in her voice made me want to comfort her, but I couldn't. From the corner of my eye, I saw Dad. He was coming down the stairs from the bar, his strides long, fast, his face dark with anger.

In an instant, he was beside me. He pulled my arm, whirled me behind him, and stepped between the woman and me. "Leave her alone!" he shouted, his voice edged, a cutting sound.

The woman took a step back but refused to leave. Her face twisted in anger. Lashing out, she struck the side of his face, leaving a red trail of her palm behind. "You won't take Zara away from me!" she shouted. "Not again!"

I saw Mel running towards us, her bare feet kicking sand. She stopped beside me, her eyes going back and forth between Dad and the woman. "What the hell is happening?" she whispered, her voice low but urgent.

"I don't know," I whispered, the loudness of my heartbeat muddling my words. I turned back to the woman, who by now had streaks running down her face, her chest heaving as she stared at me like the answer to a question that only she knew. "I'm not Zara!" I yelled louder than I intended. "My name is Bree!"

Mel snorted, breaking the tension with a half-laugh. "You're a magnet for lunatics," she murmured in a teasing voice, holding her hand tightly in mine, pulling me away.

Mom was waiting for us at the bar, sitting under the shade of her wide-brimmed hat. She didn't even look up as we approached. Instead, she sipped her drink, as though nothing in the world could disturb her peace.

"What happened?" she asked coolly, her sunglasses reflecting the late morning sun.

"Some woman attacked Bree," Mel said, her voice light, free of the weight of it all.

Mom lowered her sunglasses enough to see me. "Are you okay?" she asked, softer.

"Yeah," I said, sinking into a chair beside her. My voice felt small and shaky. "She thought I was someone named Zara."

"Zara?" Mom repeated, her lips curling into a faint smile. Then she laughed—a quiet, dismissive laugh. "Well, that's a new one."

I forced a laugh, too, but it felt fragile like it might crack under its own weight. "Yeah. It is."

Mom smiled, then set her drink down and stood. "Let's go home," she said, adjusting her hat with a careless flick of her hand. But as she turned away, I could have sworn I heard her murmur, soft as the breeze. "Zara..."

I looked at Mel, trying to read her face for some sign of what she was thinking, but she didn't give anything away. It was just one of those moments that was too weighty, too weird to talk about.

The walk home was overbearingly quiet. Neither of us said a word. The only sounds were the dull slap of our sandals against the ground and the distant hum of waves breaking upon the shore. Every step was like stretching time and by the time we reached the apartment door, my chest was tight, still, I couldn't say a thing.

Mom turned the moment we stepped inside. Her eyes were sharp, her posture tense, like she already knew something had gone wrong.

"There are people out there," she started, her voice wasn't rising above low. "People who will never mean well, people who want to hurt you."

She took another step closer, her hand rising to rest against my cheek then Mel's, the touch was soft though the words weighed as rocks upon both of us.

"Now you understand why your dad and I are trying so hard to protect you," she said, turned, calling us upstairs without waiting for the response.

We were halfway up the stairs when the front door burst open, the force of it slamming against the wall. The sound made us all jump, and we turned to see Dad standing in the doorway. His face was scratched, and his chest heaved as though he'd been running. There was something wild in his eyes, something that made my stomach drop.

"We're leaving," he said, his voice raw. "Pack your things. We're leaving. Now."

The room was silent. Mom didn't ask why, didn't argue. She didn't even flinch. Her lips pressed into a tight line, and she gave a single, curt nod.

And that was all. Another trip cut short, another frantic, frenzied scramble to get packed up and go with no answers. It was always that way—his way, or no way. No explanations, no warnings. Just the command to go. I hated it, that feeling of powerlessness. What could I do?

We never had choices. We did what we were told, swept along in the storm of his decisions.

PRESENT DAY

A few minutes earlier, I had told the doctor my name, the same doctor who had failed to protect me from the police chief not so long ago. His silence was louder than my questions, his eyes heavy with the answers he had never given. All I wanted to ask was why, but the words seemed to evaporate in the sterile air from my mouth. No explanation, nothing.

A nurse came in clutching an old white brick telephone of the type that seemed to belong to ages past. She was really hesitant, her eyes darting between me and the white brick in her hand.

"Miss," she said, almost whispering. "I tried running your name through the system, and nothing came up. No file." Her voice hitched. "Detective Karlsson is on the line. I had to call him. I'm so sorry."

She held the phone out toward me, her hand extended. I stared at it, shaking my head. I didn't want to talk to him.

"Please, miss," she pressed. "It's important."

I took the phone, my hand stiff. I pressed it to my ear and snapped, "What?" It was sharp, bratty, but I didn't care.

"Bree," Thor said, his voice as even as his features. He didn't flinch at my obvious hostility. "We ran your name through the database and found nothing. Is Bree short for something?"

"No," I said curtly, "that is my name."

There was a pause on the other end, and then his voice softened. "You're not lying, are you?"

Something inside me snapped. The anger I'd been bottling up boiled over, spilling out in a sharp burst. "First I'm a delusional, troubled young woman, and now I'm a liar too?" I shouted, my fingers clenching around the phone. "Aren't you the detective? You tell me. Why am I not in your database?"

"Bree," he said, his voice firm without trembling, trying to break into my anger.

I didn't let him finish. It was just too much, and in a surge of frustration, I let my anger boil over. I pushed the phone back at the nurse, turning and burrowing into myself. She didn't hassle me further but took the phone and headed out; the soft ticking of her shoes trailed down the hallway.

I pushed the pillow aside, angry, not at him, but at myself for trusting him, for letting myself believe even for a moment that he could help me. Turning to the other side of the bed, I stared at the wall while my mind was a vortex of frustration and exhaustion.

A soft knock sounded in the room, breaking the silence. I didn't answer, I refused to turn. That was when I saw him, his figure reflected in the window ahead of me. A black hoodie covered his body, paired with blue jeans outlining his legs.

"Isak?" I asked, sitting up slowly before I turned to him.

He came into the room, holding a white rose in his hand. He approached me and reached out to hand it to me. "This is for you," he said softly. "White, just like snow."

Snow.

I took the rose, a smile spreading across my face despite myself. "It's beautiful," I said, my voice barely above a whisper. "I've never gotten flowers before."

Not from anyone. Ever.

For a moment, the walls I'd built around me cracked. The simple gesture—his presence—stirred a flicker of hope. Maybe, just maybe, someone could save me after all.

"Just a small gift," he said, sitting down beside me.

"Thanks," I muttered, the smile still lingering. "White's my favorite."

I lied.

It wasn't. Red was.

Red had always been my favorite. The color of strawberries, of fire, of life itself. Maybe I loved it because it was something I couldn't have. My allergy to strawberries had only made their rich, forbidden red more tempting. Over time, the color had attached itself to me, a symbol of everything I wanted but couldn't have.

But white, white was safe.

"I figured," Isak said, his voice soft, the tips of his fingers brushing my cheek.

I closed my eyes at the touch, leaning into it for the briefest moment before pulling away. My breath caught as I pushed his hand back, shaking my head.

"I'm not ready," I said, my voice trembling.

He nodded, his eyes understanding, but sad. He didn't say anything, just let the moment hang in the air between us.

I had dreamed of this, of someone coming to save me. Of a prince on a white horse, riding in to take me away from everything that hurt. But life wasn't a fairy tale, and closure didn't come from someone else. It came from within. I had to fix myself. Heal myself. It wasn't fair to force my broken heart to try and love when all it needed was time to mend.

I knew that, deep down always had. But sometimes the pain was overwhelming, and all I wanted was an easy way out. I wanted someone else to take it away. To save me. To make it all better. But it didn't quite work that way. And I wasn't ready to let anyone in, not yet.

THIRTEEN

SNOWMAN

Since childhood, life has so cunningly trained me to be cold, to bury my emotions deep, no matter what storm blew my way. Every breath I took carried the weight of knowledge that someday I would face the world alone. That time would shape me into what I am, not what I was meant to be.

   I grew up in a house where survival was something earned: if you wanted to eat, you hunted; if you wanted to drink, you worked; if you wanted to matter, you fought for it. Loneliness wasn't just a feeling but a condition of air and ground beneath my feet. And in that isolation, I have built walls so high that no one would ever be able to climb. I pushed people away before they could get too close. Now, when I've finally found someone who can melt my frozen heart, I don't dare take off the mask I've worn for seven years. It was much easier to hide, to be a nobody instead of a somebody. I just became a ghost, someone no one sees but everyone fears. Because it was easy, for me.

I walked to the edge of the woods, the axe heavy in my hand. My grip tightened around the handle as anger roared in my chest. The thought of ending this, of walking into that hospital and telling her the truth, burned in my mind. I wanted to say, "I'm here now. I failed you, but no one will hurt you again." But then again, she probably thought all men were the same, that I was just a stalker who was willing to hurt her, while I was willing to hurt the world for her.

I could see them. Josh was hung unconscious, his arms stretched above him, attached to a tree, he just dangled inches from the ground in a frozen rigor. His face was slack and pale.

Vic was lashed against the trunk, a dead flesh of cock stuffed in his mouth. Their skin had taken on a sickly hue, mottled with purple from the cold. When Vic's eyes met mine, there was a flicker of hope—pathetic and misplaced—that I had changed my mind. But he didn't understand.

I wasn't here to negotiate. I was here to finish what I started.

"Cold?" I asked as I stepped closer and watched him shiver. His body was trembling violently, but he just shook his head, refusing to answer.

I crouched before him, my hand slipping into his mouth. The gag of cold, dead cock was slick as I yanked it free, tossing it onto the ground. His breathing fogged in the icy air.

"Why did you do it?" I asked calmly, yet sharply, like a blade at the ready.

I wanted an excuse, a reason, any scrap of justification that would let me, finally, end this thing. But he gave me no reason.

"She was pretty," he rasped, coughing wetly. "She was running away. We wanted to show her no one runs from us."

My jaw locked, and my hold on the axe tightened so much my knuckles burned white.

"Is that so?" I whispered, deadly edges slipping into my words.

"Yeah," he went on, not noticing the oncoming storm behind my eyes. "She didn't put up much of a fight." A sly grin quirked at the corner of his mouth. "Even let us switch sides."

The words hit like a hammer, each one driving nails into my chest. My heart pounded so hard it felt like it might tear free. Before he could spit out another word, my hand shot forward, fast as lightning, and seized his tongue. His eyes widened in shock, but it was too late.

I forced his tongue onto the cold iron of the axe blade. The muffled screams filled the air, steam rose from his breath. In a second, his tongue was sliced, warm and bloody, into my hand. I dropped it in the snow as if it was trash.

"You should have chosen your words more carefully," I said, trying to keep my voice calm against the rage that flooded through me. I stepped backward, kicking the severed tongue towards him.

"You stole her life, her freedom, her choice. And all you can say is that she did not fight much?"

"God," I snarled, lifting the axe high. The blade came down hard, cleaving through his wrist. His scream tore through the forest as his severed hand fell into the snow. I didn't pause. The axe swung again, severing his other hand in a spray of red. His body, fueled by adrenaline, trembled while his wide, disbelieving eyes stared at the roots of the tree.

I moved away, ignoring his desperate cries.

The untouched snow gleamed under the pale light as I knelt and began to roll it into balls. Slowly, I packed the snow, the wet crunch filling the silence. I rolled the snowballs larger, stacking them one on top of the other until the snowman stood tall, up to my knees.

I dunked my thumb within the blood pooling at my feet and painted crude eyes and a jagged mouth on its face. Finished, I stepped towards the tree, took his severed hands, and pressed them into the sides of the middle ball like crude bloody arms. Stepping back, I observed the perfection of my work.

"See?" I said, turning to him with a satisfied grin. "Perfect."

He attempted to mutter something, his mutilated mouth fumbling over the sounds that never formed a word. I cupped a hand to my ear, mocking him.

"What's that? Can't hear you..." I chuckled, lowering my hand. "You don't have a tongue, do you?"

He sobbed, the bloodied tears streaming down his face. His cries were pitiful, a wretched gurgling mess.

"Aw, poor thing," I said, laughing. "What's the matter? Cat got your tongue?"

I motioned to the bloodstained snow and burst out in a cold, cruel laugh.

"Don't cry about it. You're the king of a silent party now!"

His eyes rolled back, and finally, his shock and pain caught him, but I leaned over into them, grinning.

"Oh shut up," I mocked. "Oh wait, you can!" I laughed as I turned back to glance at the snowman. "At least you are good at keeping secrets."

My laughter echoed through the woods, cold and hollow, as he hung there, silent, broken, defeated.

Josh stirred, a low groan escaping his lips as his head lolled. His bleary eyes slowly opened, and as they focused, he froze, staring at the snowman, the hands, his mutilated friend bound against the tree.

"Look," I said, smirking, "it's your girlfriend.".

Josh's confusion turned to anger, his body tensing as he shouted, "I'll kill you!" His voice was strong, raw with fury, but as he took in the scene of blood, the snow, the lifeless limbs, he cracked. He fell silent, his wide eyes darting between me and the snowman.

"Well," I said, tilting my head, "you can try."

He did not say another word. His silence said it all.

I hunched down, tugging loose the knot that bound him to the tree. The rope went slack, and his body collapsed to the frozen ground with a muffled thud. He'd barely shifted before I was atop him, straddling his chest, my weight pinning him down.

"Why did you do it?" I growled, my gloved hands clamped on his collar as he struggled beneath me.

A sneer contorted his face, his voice spewing words with hatred. "I wanted to taste the bitch," he spat. "And I don't regret a thing."

My jaw clenched, my anger bubbling just below the boiling point. But he wasn't done.

"I fucked her three times," he said, his laughter cruel. "And she didn't even fight back."

She didn't fight back.

The words echoed in my mind, haunting me.

She didn't. She couldn't.

My vision blurred for a moment, tears threatening to fall, but I bit them back. I couldn't let her melt me, not yet. I needed to stay cold, just a little longer.

My hands rose to his face, thumbs pressed into the soft flesh below his eyes. He fought it, his laughter faltering, but that only fed into my determination. I dug harder, my fingers sinking into his skin. His blood leaked from the corners of his eyes and seeped over onto my gloves, but I didn't care. I wanted everything gone, all taken away from him, even his sight, his strength, his memory of her.

His screams rang through the silence of the woods. Tears mingled with his blood as I kept on and on, unmerciful, till both eyes came loose. Two soft, slippery globules lying on my palm warmed.

"There," I said, my voice cold. "Now you've got a better point of view."

Josh crawled on the ground, writhing and screaming, blind and broken.

I dropped his eyes into the snow at my feet, the red staining the white. Ignoring his cries, I knelt and started rolling fresh snow. The crunch of the icy flakes under my hands was so satisfying, almost soothing.

One ball. Two. Three.

I stacked them, forming another snowman beside the first.

Dipping my thumb in the bloodied snow and painting on crude buttons and a jagged grin across the face of it. Then I crouched again, picked up the eyeballs, and pressed them deep into the snowman's head, where they stared blankly. I stepped back to overview my work.

"Perfect," I whispered, a crooked smile tugging at my lips.

Josh's broken sobs echoed through the air now, as he crawled forward, hands outstretched and feeling his way upwards through the snow.

Staggering forward, I picked up two sticks that were lying nearby and then stuck them into the snowman, completing it.

"There you go," I said, stepping over him. "Now you've got company."

If you hear voices, they'll call you mad. Treat the voices, and they'll call you sick. Take them to your grave, and they'll call you a man who's endured too much. I never heard voices—never feared them—but I had an image. It floated in my mind until I made it real. That image took me, dragged me through endless loops, breaking me in ways no one could fix. No one truly knows what hides in your head, what monsters you wrestle with, or the weight of a story you never said. People pretend they understand, but they don't.

The world sees the cold monster I've become, the mask I wear, and deep down, I am afraid of it too. Not that I will be found and punished, that is easy to accept. What really terrifies me is that one moment when the mask slips and Bree sees the real me behind the mask. That she'll leave, treat me like the monster under her bed, and one day I'll disappear from her life. I'll fade to nothing more than a whisper she carries to her grave.

I pulled the phone from Josh's pocket. He'd had it all along, tucked away like some kind of secret he thought I wouldn't find. I wasn't worried that anyone would come looking for him; his father, Chief Jan, always cleaned up his messes. But he never cared where Josh was or what trouble he got into.

Before I could bury them, I had to melt the frozen ground.

I made a circle of fire, the flames popping and spitting as they heated the ground. Then I dug the hole deep enough for them both. Now they were underground together under the pile of earth and snow, above them snowmen with their parts marking the grave, and beneath that earth, they took their last breaths.

I scrolled through Josh's phone until I found the number I needed. Jan, the chief of police. My finger hovered for a moment, then I dialed, the line connecting with a sharp click.

"Josh, what is it?" Jan's gruff voice was barking on the other end.

I spoke, my voice low and cold, "I have eyes that cannot see, hands that cannot touch or plea. A frozen soul, a fleeting grace. In warmth, I disappear without a trace. What am I?"

There was silence, heavy. Then I heard his breathing—sharp, ragged, and close.

"Snowman," he hissed, simmering with rage. "Where is my son?"

I laughed quietly, letting it hang in the air like frost. "I stand above his grave. Silent, still, the frost his slave. His hands instead of branches, his eyes served as coal. But soon he'll melt. and lose his soul."

"WHERE IS MY SON?!" Jan roared; it crackled through the receiver like static.

"Tick tock, tick tock," I whispered, my voice plunging to a high, mocking tone. Then I disconnected the call and let silence swallow his anger.

I tucked the phone into my pocket, turning my back on the snow grave and moving toward the cottage.

Jan would tear through the forest looking for his boy, searching everywhere. I could see the search teams, the hounds, and the radios crackling with orders. They would rake over every inch of that forest. I could leave nothing to chance.

I hurried to the cabin. The walls reeked of the crimes we had committed here, and I was not going to let their sins leave a trail that led back to me.

I staged a fire, stacking wood and dousing it with accelerant until the air was thick with a sharp, acrid smell. Then I lit a match. The flames rose, consuming everything in their path: evidence, memories, all of it. I had left enough false trails to lead them in circles, far from where I would be.

He had failed me when I needed it most, leaving me to fend for myself in a world without justice. Now it was my turn to fail the system—to strip it of its power, piece by piece.

I watched the fire burn, feeling no regret—no guilt. Just a cold pleasure.

In the distance, a snowman stood, his smile frozen in time, marking the grave of a new beginning.

FOURTEEN

BREE

17 YEARS OLD

Last month, I turned seventeen. Just one more year, I thought, and I could finally leave home. The only thing that got me through it was the thought of escaping and building something better. I dreamed of coming back for Mel, of giving us both the life we'd always talked about, a life that often felt impossibly far away.

Days dragged like molasses, every second heavier than the last. Time appeared to freeze, keeping me imprisoned in a home where hope was never in reach.

Homemade pasta steamed the kitchen as I stepped inside, where the rich warm, comforting aroma mingled with the crisp autumnal cool air that slid through the window and opened a crack. Mother stood by the counter, nimbly working with the dough, gentle white flour was dusted over her fingers.

Her hands moved with a gentle sway, almost hypnotic as if she were at peace. She looked up and caught me watching her, her lips curving into a small smile.

"Bree?" she asked softly. "What's wrong?"

I hesitated, my feet shifting on the worn tiles. "Uhm, nothing much," I mumbled out, my voice hardly a whisper.

She turned to me, smiling, her hands wiping across the apron. "What is it?" she pressed again, this time facing me.

I swallowed hard, my fingers twisting nervously. "I dreamed about her, the woman I met last year in Greece," I said, my voice catching in my throat slightly.

Her face hardened and the warmth in her eyes cooled to something much icier. "That crazy lady?" she asked, with a bitter tone. She stepped closer and ran her hands over her apron again, though it had been clean, and landed with palms on my shoulders. "Bree, we've talked about that."

"But it felt so real," I said, the words tumbling out in a rush. "I was only four in the dream, and she was younger too, and—"

"Bree," she cut in, the sigh brushing me off. "We often dream of the life we want, not of the one we live." The tone of her voice softened some, though her eyes didn't. "I know how I haven't been the mother you wanted, and maybe you're just looking for something in that woman that I couldn't give you."

Love.

Love was what I had been seeking the whole time. In one second I saw more love in that woman's eyes than I had ever seen in my mother's eyes. I kept that to myself and swallowed it like a bitter pill, knowing that I had always desperately convinced myself that one day this would get better and I would feel something. Anything.

"But," I started, wanting to ask more, but her patience was already gone.

"No buts, Bree," she snapped, raising her voice. "I don't want to talk about crazy anymore, okay? Just drop it. Please." Her hands fell away from my shoulders as she stepped away, the touch replaced by a cold emptiness in their wake. "Just go to your room, you're upsetting me."

"I'm sorry," I whispered as I stepped toward her, wanting, needing to bridge the gap between us. I reached out, desperate for a hug, but she moved, pushing me away like I was a stranger, someone unwanted.

My vision blurred with tears as I turned and walked out of the kitchen; the sting of her rejection cut deeper than her words ever could. The hall seemed endless as I trudged toward my bedroom, my head hung low, my shoulders slumped in defeat. The quietness of the house swallowed me whole. And with each attempt I made, every time I would even try and share the least fragment of myself, I got put to silence, pushed aside, and forgotten.

I sank on the bed, the weight of the day resting on my chest. I closed my eyes and let the tears fall freely. Sleep was my only escape, a place where I could at least live the life that real life hadn't given me. My dreams, were where I could live without the suffocation of the real world. I could finally breathe.

Soon I found myself in Greece, in my dreams, falling into the arms of a woman, a mother I didn't know I had. Her arms were so warm and loving. The love I had always wanted but never had. For a time, I wasn't alone. Someone could hold me, love me, and be loved by me. It was perfect.

Suddenly, something jarred and stopped, a hard thud awoke me. My eyes snapped open to darkness. Night had fallen. What had seemed like mere seconds of sleep had turned into hours of sleep. I blinked dazedly, a dream of Greece gone, replaced by the harsh, cold reality of my bedroom.

I stood up quietly, my bare feet tapping lightly on the floor as I tiptoed toward the hallway. My heart pounded in my chest, and a strange unease washed over me. As I approached the kitchen, soft sounds reached my ears—low moans, muffled sounds. My throat tightened as I drew closer, each breath shallower than the last.

Then I saw them.

Mel lay sprawled across the kitchen island, her body bare, her legs spread. Dad stood behind her, his hands tugging hard on her hair as he moved against her. His face twisted in pleasure, an evil grin I'd never seen before. Their bodies moved together, their gasps and moans filling the room. Mel bit down on her palm, trying to stifle the sounds, but it wasn't enough. The sight was searing, unbearable.

I gasped, the breath escaping me before I even knew it was coming. Mel's head snapped toward mine, her eyes wide and horrified. She shoved Joe, scrambling off of the counter as panic set into her face, now.

"Bree!" she called, desperate. She ran toward me, outstretched hands and all, but I was faster. I turned and left, slamming my bedroom door behind me and locking it with trembling hands.

Inside, my heart was racing, hard, and it felt like it would tear out of my chest. I slumped against the door, my knees buckling as the image replayed in my mind. I couldn't believe what I'd seen. I didn't want to believe it.

"Bree, please!" Mel's voice came from the other side, frantic and pleading. She banged on the door. "Please, I can explain! Just let me in! Please!"

Her wails were muffled by my own silence. I pinched my arm to a sting, to wake from the nightmarelike scene, but I was not sleeping.

"Please, let me in," she begged, her voice cracking. "Bree, please."

"Go away!" I shouted, finding my voice at last. My body shaking, I pushed myself upright, but my back remained pressed against the door.

"I'll tell you everything," she sobbed. "Just let me in!"

Then I heard it, the sound of his footsteps approaching. A fresh wave of nausea rolled over me.

I hadn't thought, had only unlocked the door, yanked her inside, and slammed it shut again, locking it fast. She half-stumbled into the room, her face streaming with tears.

"What the hell, Mel?" I yelled, my voice shaking in anger and disbelief. "Are you outta your mind? What the fuck's wrong with you?"

She flinched, her hands shaking as she tried to steady herself. "It happened in Greece," she started, her voice weak, but I couldn't bear to hear it.

"No," I said, hands covering my ears. I flung myself onto the bed, curling into a ball in desperation to shut her out. "Stop. I don't want to hear it."

"He was nicer than usual," she said, dismissing me. "And I..."

"You what, Mel?" I snapped, my voice colder than ice as I whirled my back to her.

My stomach churned with the bile rising high into my throat. "That's sick. You're sick. I can barely." I faltered then, slapping a hand to my mouth, hard.

"I know," she whispered.

She took a step closer to me, her hand glancing over my shoulder. "He touched me and I... I know this is wrong, but I liked it." Her words cut through me like a razor.

My body went stiff as the waves of repulsion washed over me, hot and uncontrollable. "I think I'm going to be sick," I said, trying to get to my feet in one motion; I almost fell.

My stomach was churning and I doubled over, clinging to my knees as I struggled not to let the nausea win. Mel broke down, sobs erupting through the room. And I couldn't comfort her. I couldn't look at her.

"He's not our dad," Mel whispered, her words shaking as if they could break her themselves.

I froze. Her words hung in the air like smoke, choking me. "He's not. What?" I whispered, while my breath hitched in my throat. "Was that woman right? Was I her daughter?"

Mel sank onto the edge of the bed, her face buried in her hands. "I don't know," she said, her voice breaking. "I really don't."

"Mel, this is sick," I told her, the words spilling from my mouth like cold razor blades. "What if?"

"I love him," she cut in, her voice barely audible but laced with raw emotion. Tears streamed down her face as she sobbed, "We wanted to escape together. He took me places, and when we're together, it feels so right."

Her words hit me like a gut punch. My stomach was churning violently, and I doubled over, grabbing at my abdomen. "I'm going to puke," I muttered, my knees hitting the floor as nausea rolled through me.

But I didn't.

"I swear, Bree, I don't want to hurt you," she cried. "But please, not a word to Laura, she'll freak out…"

"You think?" I yelled, cutting her off. My voice cracked, and I stared at her in disbelief. "You're fucking her husband," I whispered venomously, the disgust lacing every syllable. "I can't even believe I'm saying this."

Mel flinched but pressed on, her voice growing wilder. "All I know is we're here because of her. She pointed her finger and chose us." Her tears fell freely now, her hands wringing together as she spoke. "Joe just wanted her to be happy."

"This is sick," I said, my voice trembling as I stood. "All of it. This is all so fucking sick."

I turned, heading for the door, the walls closing in around me. I needed air. Space. Something to pull me out of this nightmare. But as I reached for the doorknob, Mel grabbed my hand, her grip desperate.

"Bree, please," she begged, her voice cracking. "Don't—don't go."

I yanked my hand free, my chest heaving as I stared at her. We stood there, crying, broken, standing at the edge of something we could never take back. We somehow ended up on the top of the stairs, both our emotions tangled in a storm of regret and despair.

And then, everything spiraled. A sudden pull, a shove. Which of us moved first, I will never know. It was as if time slowed, and the next thing I knew was weightlessness.

Everything around was a blur; the world flashed from dark to light as we tumbled down the stairs, rolling. It was a loud crash, deafening, but then all of a sudden there wasn't anything. No noise, no pain, void. We floated there, carried off somewhere to a point out of time. Just the two of us.

PRESENT DAY

Isak was still here. He'd fallen asleep in the chair by the window, his head tilted at an awkward angle. I didn't mind. Somehow, knowing someone was there with me made the silence feel less heavy, the night less suffocating. His soft, steady breaths were a reminder that I wasn't completely alone.

But then I heard the soft sound of footsteps. My heart raced as I slowly turned my head to the left. Thor appeared from the shadows, quiet, almost too quiet. He was holding something, a small box.

"I won't stay long," he said in a low, almost hesitating voice. "I just wanted to see you."

"Okay. You've seen me," I said, defensively crossing my arms, my tone sharper than I had intended.

He looked different. His hair was shorter now, the dark strands framing his face in a way that softened his features. It suited him, made him look older, maybe even wiser. But I refused to acknowledge it. I wouldn't give him the satisfaction of knowing I noticed.

"Yeah," he said, smiling faintly. "I did."

He cleared his throat and finally wore a serious expression. "I'm sorry," he said. "If I hurt you, in any way, that was never my intention."

"Well, you did," I said, slicing through the apology like a knife.

He hesitated. My words were hanging between us, yet he didn't argue; instead, he held out the box and placed it gently in my lap.

"Anyway," he said now with a softer voice, "this is for you."

"A gift?" I asked, narrowing my eyes and turning to the box.

"A phone," he said. "I put my number on speed dial. All you have to do is press one. That's all."

Curiosity finally got the better of me, and I opened it to find a simple phone. I got a phone for the first time in my life. A slight grin tugged at my lips despite myself.

"Thank you," I said softly.

"I won't bother you anymore," he said and stepped back. "Isak will care for you better than I ever could."

A lump formed in my throat, and I swallowed hard, the ache almost unbearable. So long, I'd wanted Thor to be my Snowman, the one who could take my heart. But maybe all along, I'd been looking for someone to save me from the Snowman.

"Bye, Bree," he said, his voice hanging in the air as he turned to leave.

I watched him go, the shadows swallowing him whole as he disappeared into the hall. The phone felt heavy in my hand. My thumb hovered over the button marked "1," the urge to call him back was overwhelming. I wanted to tell him I was sorry too, to ask him if his eyes weren't brown at all but icy blue. But the world doesn't work like that, and I'm not that lucky.

I set the box on the table next to my bed, a small table with a vase full of Isak's white roses. Light danced across the soft petals, carrying the sweetest, lightest scent in its breath. I huddled under the blanket again, picked up the phone, and held it tightly to me as if it could somehow fill the hole gnawing at my soul. I closed my eyes for a moment and wished—wished he would come back. That he would tell me I was wrong. That there was a world where he could be both: the man I needed and the one I feared.

Isak woke up, a faint smile spreading across his face as he leaned closer, his palm brushing my hand. "How do you feel, birdie?" he asked softly.

Birdie. There was a trap.

A game he was good at, he played me like a string. First, he showed me the sky and made me believe I had wings, only to clip them whenever I started to fly.

Even with the cage door open, he had the power to drag me back down. I stared at him, his icy blue eyes piercing, his hair tied in a loose bun at the back of his head. He was perfect—too perfect. His smile, his presence, his whole being weighed upon me. I could feel the hunger in his gaze, the want radiating from him like heat.

But all I wanted was a moment of peace. Just a little bit of freedom to stretch my wings. To fly, even briefly. But he wouldn't let me. He called to me, pulling me into his arms.

My lips parted as he leaned in, his mouth finding mine. His lips pressed against me, his tongue forcing its way into my mouth. He didn't ask; he took. A tango of forbidden love he commanded, and I didn't fight. I let him steal my first kiss, and another piece of me surrendered to another man who would only take more.

When he finally pulled back, I smiled faintly, masking the pain inside. Then I heard it: "Hello?" The voice was faint, distant. My heart froze as I realized my thumb had been pressing the number one on the phone the entire time.

My body was screaming for help, my heart wanted love, and my mind was screaming for freedom; I couldn't have it, not one piece.

I brought the phone to my ear, a tear slipping down my cheek. "Sorry," I whispered. "It was an accident."

"I see," the voice replied, and it wasn't coming from the phone.

Thor stood in the doorway, his figure framed in shadows. His eyes locked onto me, flicking briefly to Isak, then back again. The disappointment was plain on his face, cutting through me like a blade.

"Thor." I began, but his upraised hand cut me off.

Isak chuckled, leaning back as if all this meant nothing. "Man, we—"

"No need to explain," Thor cut him off, his voice cold, detached. "You're both adults. You can do whatever the hell you want."

His fist was clenched at his side, but he didn't raise it. He merely turned and walked away, the heaviness of his footsteps growing distant as he disappeared down the hall.

"Maybe," I stammered, trying to push gently on Isak's chest. "Maybe we're moving too fast?"

He snorted and pushed my hand away.

"Since you've been here, Bree, I've been watching you," he said in a low tone that seemed to make my heart skip beats, the timbre of his voice almost possessive. "I needed to have you."

My heart sank. "Have me?"

He nodded, his smirk spreading as he leaned in closer, his body weighing down on mine.

"I knew it from the very beginning, birdie," he whispered, his hand moving to my throat, his fingers curling around it with a gentle yet firm grasp. "I knew you would be mine."

Mine.

The word echoed in my head.

How?

I couldn't. Not again. I couldn't let this happen again.

Fine.

I am fine.

But I wasn't fine. Not even close.

FIFTEEN

SNOWMAN

12 YEARS OLD

I SAT ON A green bench in the park, my eyes fixed on the playground. It was late 1994, and I had just turned twelve. Mom had gone to pick up medicine for my younger brother, Erik, leaving me to wait out front. The city had changed so much since the last time we were here; more people, more noise, and more strangers I didn't want to meet. I watched other kids play, their laughter and shrieks ringing through the crisp autumn air as they ran and pulled on each other, lost in their games. None of them came near me. If any of them had, I would've said no, but, it would have been nice to be asked.

I saw Mom come out through the glass doors of the pharmacy, brown paper bag in hand. She was wearing her blue coat and matching hat, her other hand tightly clutched to Erik's as she led him toward the car. She waved at me, calling for me to join them. I stood ready to go, but then a little girl appeared beside me.

"Hey," she said, her voice bright. "Wanna play?"

I turned to her. She couldn't have been more than six, her blonde pigtails tied up with red ribbons matching her dress. Her wide blue eyes stared up at me, searching my face for an answer. For a moment, I hesitated. I wanted to stay. I wanted to play. But I couldn't. If I didn't go straight to the car, we would all pay the price later.

I shook my head and turned to run, leaving her standing by the green bench staring at me hopefully as if expecting me to turn backward.

By the time I reached the car, Mom was waiting with a knowing smile, her arms across her chest. "If you keep running away from girls like that, you'll never have a girlfriend," she teased, chuckling.

"I don't want a girlfriend," I hastened to say, plunging into the back seat.

Erik was already there, leaning against the window, his face pale and drawn. His head leaned limply against the glass, where his breath fogged it. I reached over and touched his hand; it was warm, too warm. My stomach twisted as I turned to Mom.

"Is he going to be okay?"

"Yes," she said. "It's just frostbite," the words sounded thin, like a tarp too small to make anyone warm.

Frostbite, that was what she called it, when we got sick afterward from one of Dad's "lessons." Last night, he had left us in the woods once more, wanting to "toughen us up." The cold had seeped into our bones while the woods, with all their whispers and shadows, crept into our minds. Erik had felt it worst of all.

The drive back to the farm took half an hour. The silence in the car was thick, with only the soft hum of the engine and Erik's shallow breathing breaking the stillness. Finally, we pulled up, and Mom turned to us, her voice hushed. "If your father asks where you were, just say you went to visit Aunt Ilda."

We nodded, knowing full well that we didn't have to be told twice. We knew what Dad was capable of, how quickly his anger could turn violent. We'd learned to lie, to play the game. It was the only way to keep Mom safe.

As Mom got out to unlock the garage, Erik turned to me, his hand reaching for mine. His grasp was weak but urgent, and his wide, feverish eyes searched mine, and he whispered, "It's not frostbite."

"What do you mean?" I whispered back.

"I saw something," he said, his voice shaking. "Something they didn't want me to see."

"What did you see?" I asked, a tinge of fear creeping into my chest.

"They take them," he said, all the while his hand tightening mine. "Dad and Joe—they take them to the river and..."

He didn't finish, but then again he didn't need to. His words seemed to hang in the air, the unsaid saying it all. It grew colder in the car, darker, as though some of the shadows of the woods had followed us home.

But just as Mom came back into the car, Erik suddenly clammed up, bringing a finger to his lips. He turned back toward the window to stare out, as though nothing had been said.

"If you want to play with that little girl, we can ask Dad to bring her home," Mom said, looking at me through the rearview mirror light, almost teasing.

Erik shook his head, fast, his face unreadable. I did not understand why. All I knew was that she was so beautiful, that little girl. I wanted her near me, to play with me, to build snowmen in the yard. And so I nodded enthusiastically, a grin spreading across my face. This strange idea filled me with an even weirder feeling of happiness, like getting a forbidden toy that I had always wished for but never dared to ask for.

For the first time in a long time, something good may happen, I thought.

PRESENT DAY

I stood for two hours in the shade of the forest and saw the cottage burn. The fire roared and hissed, swallowing wood, memories, and evidence until nothing remained but ash and smoke curling into the cold night air. The silence afterward was almost holy.

Hiding behind the trees, I watched Jan Johansson arrive; his headlights cut through the smoke. He'd tracked his son's phone, thinking he was closing in on answers. But what Jan did not know was that his son's grave lay far from here, deep, buried beneath frozen earth. His lungs would fill with nothing but dirt and frost by the time he found him.

I promised myself a long time ago that no one would stop me. Not from doing what I had to do. My father's sins shaped and molded me into what I am, and in that darkness, I found a purpose. The thirst for blood had settled in me long ago, but I kept it focused: only on those who truly deserved harm.

Deep down, I knew this was wrong; everything I did was wrong. But it would have been worse if I'd let myself take anyone, killing without reason. Then I wouldn't just be a villain. I'd be a monster. But villains can be good, right? If someone cared to hear their side of the story.

I stepped into the hospital, my footsteps sounding inaudibly on cold tiles. In the corner of the lobby stood a man clutching a bouquet of red roses. He set them softly down on a bench and leaned against the coffee machine, fiddling with some change.

I moved quietly, slipping close enough to pluck a single rose from the bouquet. I thought of taking the whole thing but then noticed the teddy bear tucked beside it with a handmade note: You did it, Mommy. My conscience got in the way, and I didn't have the heart to take all of it. All I needed was one rose, one for Bree.

She deserved a thousand, but for now, this single one would have to speak for all the days ahead when she'd be free of those monsters who stole her choices, her safety, her innocence.

Even if I couldn't see her, even if she didn't want me there, I needed to leave her this one small gift.

I stood in the hall, holding onto the rose for dear life, and just waited for that perfect moment. It wasn't until she finally shuffled out of her room, wrapped up in those hospital pajamas, making her slow way to the bathroom, that I had my chance. As the door clicked shut behind her, I slipped inside and gently laid the rose on her bed.

"Birdie," I whispered into the stillness. "From now on, you'll be safe with me."

Every step away from her room was like a knife twisting inside my chest, digging a void that only she could fill. Every step reminded me of the stories that would never be told, the future that was never meant to be.

By the time I got to the hall, my phone vibrated in my pocket, drawing me out of the pain of a silent goodbye. Erik's name flashed across the screen.

Call me as soon as you get this.

His urgency chilled me through more than the winter air did outside. I slipped out of the hospital as fast as I could, making sure nobody was watching. The cold nibbled at my face, the only warmth was my breath against the frozen night. Outside, under the pale streetlights, I hit number two on my speed dial and put the phone to my ear. Erik's voice answered almost at once.

"Hey," I said into the phone, my voice low, my hand shoved deep into my pocket, trying to keep the cold from seeping further into my bones. "What is it?"

"I found her," Erik said, his voice steady, almost grave. "I found the girl."

"Speak," I snapped, the urgency in my tone sharper than I intended.

"Lower your damn tone," he barked back, "or the only thing you'll hear is the slap I'll give you when I see you."

I couldn't help but chuckle despite myself. "Yeah, sorry. It's been... a day."

"I heard," he replied. "The chief even called me in."

I exhaled, my breath visible in the freezing air. "What did you find?"

"Both girls Joe had in that house? They've been missing since 2001," he said. "And they weren't the only ones."

"Why am I not surprised?" I muttered. "Is the case still open?"

"Yes," Erik said. "But they're tying it to another cold case."

I pulled the phone slightly away from my ear, staring blankly ahead, frustration brewing inside me. "Yeah?" I finally said, my voice taut.

"Remember the little blonde girl? The one you wanted to play with at the park in '94?" His voice carried a note of hesitation like he wasn't sure he should say the words. "She's been missing since then. They think it's connected."

His words hit me like a punch to the chest. I sank to the cold ground, my head in my hands, my chest tightening with an ache I couldn't name. My voice broke when I spoke. "I want to see what you found."

"Julia and the little one just went to sleep," Erik said, his tone softening. "Come over. We can go over it in my office."

I managed a small, tired smile. "Sure," I said. "How are they?"

"Do you really want to know?" he asked with a chuckle in his voice.

"Not really," I replied, chuckling faintly in return.

He paused. "How's Bree?" Then, after a beat, "And does Mom know?"

"She doesn't know," I said. "And Bree... she'll be okay."

"Okay," he murmured. "See you soon."

"Yeah," I said quietly. "Soon."

I hung up, still sitting in front of the hospital, staring at the empty stretch of sidewalk ahead of me. For a moment, fleeting thoughts of normalcy rushed through my mind—what life could've been if things were different? But the illusion shattered as soon as I closed my eyes.

All I could see was my reflection in a cracked mirror, staring back at me through the hollow eyes of a white plastic mask. The sins of my father were so heavy on me, but I bore them willingly. Not for myself, but so Erik wouldn't have to.

We grew up together, but we came from different worlds. Even though I was the youngest, I always felt the need to protect him. He was the fragile one, the one who cracked under the pain Dad tried to place on us. Our father had big plans, the Family, as he called it, but there was never anything familial about it. Joe, the oldest from his first marriage, was the favorite. The golden child. Erik was stuck in the middle, and I was an afterthought, the youngest.

He refused to let us have sisters. He said daughters would make him weak, and that women brought softness and vulnerability to the family. I never understood why then. But now, as I see Erik fiercely protective of Julia, and I want nothing more than to do the same to Bree, I understand. He never wanted us to go against him, to worry about anyone else. Control was his only goal, and for a time he succeeded.

Joe... Joe was Dad's shadow, his mirror image, but without any of his stability. When I think of Joe now, it's like I'm looking at a reflection of everything I could have been if I'd followed in their footsteps. And as I sit here, in the cold, staring out at the empty streets, I understand why Mom did what she did when I turned sixteen.

She didn't want us to be his pawns. She didn't want us to become any more broken than we already were.

PART TWO

SIXTEEN

BREE

DECEMBER, 2016

> "Hold him gently in your hands.
> He has been cracked enough as it is,
> and his heart is more
> shattered than he lets on."
> — Unknown

THEY SAY EVERY PAIN is temporary, but I never understood why mine felt like it stretched forever. Maybe it was because my pain didn't have an ending. Maybe I was meant to carry it with me.

They say the pain will mute you, will steal your voice, yet here I was, drowning in it and somehow finding a voice that begged to scream. A voice that wanted to tell the world how hard it was to be me.

Bits and pieces of the past started to surface, fragments I had locked away: the accident, the mental hospital, the doctor—memories sharp enough to cut through the fog. They were almost to the moment when Joe took me from kindergarten, pretending to be my uncle. They were almost to the night they snatched Mel from her bed while I sat in the car, clutching a doll and humming a lullaby. They were almost to the plan they made to erase me when I started remembering too much.

Now, they'd called someone to pick me up again. They locked the doors, their voices calm, insisting I was dangerous, that I had a history of mental issues, and that I might try to escape.

I was trapped. Again.

They returned my clothes—clean, folded neatly, the same ones I had on when they brought me in. The memory of who brought me here was hazy, but the smell was still there; cedarwood, smoke, and musk. The scent clung to my skin like a stain as I slid into the freshly washed fabric. The itchiness of the clothes wasn't from dirt; it was from knowing they had scrubbed them clean of evidence. The evidence they thought I would forget. But I hadn't.

I wanted to burn the clothes, and maybe myself along with them.

Sitting on the edge of the bed, I held the phone Thor had given me. It was small, black, and simple—made for calls and nothing else. I stared at it, knowing they'd search for me before I left. I needed to hide it. Tying my hair back into a ponytail, I carefully wrapped the phone into the strands, twisting it into a bun. Standing in front of the mirror, I checked from every angle. It was invisible. But it was there.

I thought about leaving the phone behind, but the thought of calling him one last time was too strong. Even if it would be the last time I ever heard his voice.

Footsteps echoed down the hallway. I grabbed my red coat and stood, waiting. The door creaked open, and there they were—Mel and Mom, standing in the doorway. I ran to them, the need for a hug overwhelming every other thought in my mind.

Mel's arms wrapped around me tightly, and the tears came, unstoppable. I couldn't hold them back, even if I tried. For a moment, the pain dulled, replaced by the simple warmth of her hug.

We walked to the car together, the cold touching my skin through the thin coat. Joe was waiting inside, in the driver's seat, his silhouette framed by the light. As we climbed into the car, he spoke without turning around.

"We're moving tomorrow morning."

The words hung in the air, but this time, I couldn't sink into silence. I couldn't be the quiet Bree he knew.

So I asked, "Why?"

He glanced at the railway window, his reflection distorted by the frost. "You know why," he said simply.

I met his eyes through the mirror.

"Yeah," I said softly, a bitter edge on my tongue. "Unfortunately, no accidents will hide the truth now."

The car fell into silence. That same, muted, heartbreaking silence that always followed when the truth lurked too close. No one said a word. Maybe they were afraid that if they did, I'd finally tear down the curtain they'd so carefully hung over our lives.

The engine roared to life, and we drove off. The house loomed in the distance, each turn of the wheel taking us closer to it for the last time.

Not much happened between morning and afternoon. As soon as we arrived, all we got were instructions to pack. I found myself in the bedroom, surrounded by the faint smell of old wood and stale air. A purse sat on the bed, and inside it was my notebook.

I sat down, pulling the notebook out. The last entry was from the day we arrived here. It felt like yesterday—but it wasn't. Almost a month had passed. Time had slipped by so fast, yet every second felt like a nail driven into me, an excruciating pain that refused to let up.

I turned the page and began to write:

Date: December 6th, 2016.
Mood: Fine.
Thankful: For life.

As I finished, a tear fell, smudging the ink. I pressed my palm to my lips, stifling a scream that clawed its way up my throat. My fingers gripped the pen tighter, and with a trembling hand, I scratched over "FINE" and "LIFE" so hard the paper tore. In the jagged space next to it, I wrote:

Date: December 6th.
Mood: Sad.
Thankful: For truth.

Something in me had died that day by the river. Maybe it was the quiet version of myself—the one who didn't fight, the one who hid behind silence. Now, what was left was someone louder, someone desperate to stop pretending.

I sat there, realizing for the first time that it was okay not to be fine. It was okay to stop wearing the mask. But it didn't make it easier. I was so tired. Tired of pretending, tired of feeling alive when every breath felt like it shouldn't belong to me.

The door creaked open softly. Mel stepped in, holding a steaming cup of tea.

"Hey," she said, her voice gentle as she closed the door behind her. She placed the cup in front of me. "This might help."

"Thank you," I said quietly, taking the tea in my hands. The warmth seeped into my palms, grounding me, if only for a moment.

"They told us what happened," she said softly, sitting beside me. Her hand rested on my shoulder, and I saw the tears welling in her eyes. "The first time... it's the hardest," she whispered. "But over time, it gets easier. You learn to accept that it's something you... need."

Her words sliced through me. A tear slipped down my cheek.

"Need?" I shouted, my voice trembling. "Is that what you think happened?"

Mel hesitated, her brows furrowing. "Well... yeah. You slept with them, didn't you?" Her voice wavered, as though unsure of her own words.

"No, Mel," I said, my voice cracking. "I didn't."

"It's okay," she started, but I cut her off.

"No," I said, standing abruptly. My movements sent the tea shaking, and I placed it on the small table by the bed, turning to face her. My breath quickened as anger bubbled to the surface.

"It's not okay," I said, my voice rising. "They followed me." I closed my eyes, the images flashing behind my lids—muddy red water, hands around my neck. "They almost drowned me," I said, my voice breaking. I clutched my throat, mimicking the grip they had on me. "They choked me," I cried, "and then they threw me on the ground like I was nothing."

My breaths came in short, sharp gasps now. I could feel the heat of anger and shame rise in my chest, burning like fire.

"Do you think that's okay?" I shouted, my voice shaking.

Mel shook her head, tears streaming freely down her face.

"They forced themselves on me," I said, each word sharp and raw. "They took the only thing that was truly mine. Then they left me there to die." My voice cracked under the words. "Do you think that's okay?"

Mel shook her head again, harder this time. Her trembling hand rose to wipe at her tears. She tried to speak, but no words came.

I sank back onto the bed, my body trembling. Mel sat beside me, her hand hovering near mine as though she wanted to comfort me but didn't know how. I stared at the notebook, the words "Mood: Fine" still visible beneath the scratches.

"I'm not fine," I whispered, more to myself than to her. And for the first time, I allowed the words to sit with me, to be real.

"And no one believed me," I cried, my voice cracking under my tears. "Because they think it's okay." The tears came harder now, streaming down my cheeks.

"I believe you," Mel said, her voice trembling, her body almost shaking. "But... sometimes it's easier to cover it up, to wrap it up. It hurts less that way."

"No, it doesn't!" I shot back, my fingers clawing at my skin, as though I could scrape away the memories etched into it. "No matter how many times I've rubbed my skin with soap, their touch doesn't wash away. It **never** washes away."

"I know," Mel broke down, her sobs spilling out in waves. "It's easier to tell myself he loves me. If I let him do what he wants, I'm safer. It's safer if I don't fight back."

Her head fell onto my chest, her tears soaking through my shirt. She was breaking in my arms, breaking apart in a way that uncovered the truth we both had buried for too long.

"It was so much easier," she choked out, "when I couldn't speak. When I couldn't move. It was easier when I was numb."

"Oh, Mel," I whispered, pulling her closer, my arms wrapping around her as tightly as they could. "There's still hope. Maybe—"

"No," she cut me off, her voice shaking. "That night, when I saw you laying in blood... I died, Bree. I died with you."

Her hand found my cheek, her palm warm, trembling. "You'll go out there," she said, her voice quieter now, but firm. "You'll tell them our story. And you'll save us both."

Her words were a dagger in my chest. "No," I said. "You deserve to go with me."

"You have to go to the police station," she whispered, leaning closer. "Tell them everything. Tell them how we were both held here against our will."

A lump formed in my throat, and I swallowed hard, my voice faltering. "They won't believe me, Mel. They didn't when..." I trailed off, my eyes shutting tight. The memories clawed at me—the pulsating sound of their laughter, their breath against my skin. It was all still there, haunting me.

My hand instinctively went to my hair, pulling out the rubber band. The phone hidden within fell into my palm, its weight suddenly feeling like the heaviest thing I'd ever held.

"I can call a friend," I whispered, clutching the phone tightly. "He can help."

My finger hovered over the number one. Pressing it felt like jumping off a cliff, but I held it down until the line rang.

After three beeps, he answered. "Bree?"

"Yes," I whispered. "I have to tell you something." My throat tightened, and I paused, hearing only silence on the other end. "Joe," I said finally. "My dad... he took Mel and me when we were kids. I think he's planning something."

"Where are you?" he asked, his breathing quickening.

"Home," I said, my voice shaking. "We're in my room."

"I'll be there in ten minutes. Twenty, tops," he said. "Will you two be okay until then?"

"Yes," I whispered, clutching the phone. "Thank you."

"Bree," he said softly, his voice steady, "please, just stay safe. Okay?"

"Okay," I replied. The line clicked, and the silence returned.

I lowered the phone, pulling Mel even closer to me.

"We'll be okay," I promised, though my voice quivered. "I promise."

Her tears fell harder, her bloodshot eyes meeting mine. "I can't take it if he touches me again," she whispered. "I pretended I was okay, but I'm not, Bree."

She rolled up her sleeves, revealing a patchwork of cuts and bruises. "He takes my blood," she said, her voice dropping into a broken whisper. "He drinks it... after." Her hands flew to her face, covering it as she sobbed. "I can't do it anymore. I can't."

I pulled her into my arms, holding her tighter than ever, our bodies sinking together onto the cold floor. My heart shattered as she shook in my hands, her pain pouring out in waves.

Suddenly, a loud knock at the door startled us. Our heads snapped up as Laura pushed the door open slowly.

"Dinner is ready."

SEVENTEEN

BREE

We stepped out of the bedroom, and there they were, two little girls sitting by the table, their feet barely touching the floor. They looked like ghosts from our past, dressed just as we had been at their age. The smaller one, maybe five, had blonde curls that framed her face, and a black bow tied neatly on top of her head. The older one, about eight, sat with her back straight, her pale skin almost the same as the snow outside.

Joe sat between them, his chair creaking as he leaned forward, his eyes locking onto ours. He smiled, his lips stretching too wide.

Laura stood nearby, her red dress tight around her body, red lipstick smeared slightly at the corner of her lips. Her ponytail swayed as she shifted her weight, her arms crossed loosely. To an outsider, this might have looked like a picture-perfect family, but something was deeply, horribly wrong.

"Bree, how is your dinner?" Joe asked the older girl before turning his gaze toward me.

"It's very delicious, Daddy," she said sweetly.

He kissed the forehead of the younger girl and asked her, "And yours, Mel?"

She nodded, looking up at him. "Perfect, Daddy."

Mel's grip on my hand tightened as she started shaking. Joe's eyes bore into us, making the world feel warped and surreal. Then he stood up, taking both girls by the hand and guiding them upstairs toward the bedroom. As we watched them disappear, we moved closer to Laura.

"Mom, what is going on?" I asked, my voice trembling.

She tilted her head. "Who are you?"

"Mom, it's me, Bree!" I said, stepping closer and pointing toward Mel. "And that's Mel!"

Then she laughed, "My daughters are five and eight. You're too old to be my daughter."

Faint footsteps sounded behind us, and as I turned, Joe was already there, standing just a few feet away. He held a knife in his hand, the blade catching the light, making my stomach drop.

"I'll give you a choice," he said, his voice calm. "One of you will get out alive," he continued, his dark eyes flicking between us. "And one of you will be dinner."

Laura began clapping her hands, her face lighting up. "Dinner time!" she sang out.

"What the fuck?" I stammered, stepping back with Mel.

Joe ignored me and turned his focus to Mel.

"Imagine," he said softly, "no more touching, no more late-night baths, no more pleasing anyone." His voice was hypnotic, his tone almost convincing. "All it takes is one little decision," he added, his eyes darker than before.

Mel took a step forward, hesitant. She turned to me, her face soaked with tears.

"I'm so sorry, Bree," she whispered, her voice cracking as she reached for the knife in his outstretched hand.

"No, Mel!" I screamed, the sound ripping from my chest. "We can't do this!"

Tears streamed down her face as she gripped the knife tightly, "I'm so sorry," she repeated.

I stumbled backward, nearly tripping with every shaky step I took. But she kept moving toward me, her eyes distant but focused, a knife gripped so tightly in her hand that her knuckles turned white.

My chest tightened, and I could barely breathe. Those twenty minutes Thor promised felt like forever. It felt like there was no way out of this nightmare.

"Mel, please," I begged, pressing my hands together like I was praying. My voice cracked, trembling just like my legs. "This isn't you. You don't have to do this!"

"Kill her already," Laura's sharp voice cut through the air. She leaned against the doorway like she had all the time in the world, her face curled into a smirk. "I've waited years for this."

"You're sick!" I screamed at her, anger mixing with fear, my voice shaking. "You're both sick!"

Laura shrugged, unbothered.

"We tried to do this the night you two fell down the stairs," she said, so casually, like we held no meaning to her. "But you had to lose your memory. You see, fear makes it better. All that adrenaline... pumps the blood. Makes the taste richer."

"Go to hell!" I shouted, slamming my hands against the locked door. My fists stung, but I didn't stop. "Mel, please! Don't listen to her. Please!"

Mel's hands were trembling now, the knife shaking as she clutched it tighter. Her lips quivered, but her eyes wouldn't meet mine. "I'm sorry, Bree," she said, breaking. "I just... I can't do this anymore."

I couldn't let this happen. I refused to let this happen.

I had to run. Turning on my heel, I sprinted out of the living room and toward the bedroom. My feet slammed against the floor, the wooden boards creaking with each step. Behind me, I heard Mel chasing, her breaths sharp and uneven. My heart felt like it might escape, the pounding in my chest so loud it drowned everything else out.

I reached the bedroom and threw myself inside, slamming the door shut behind me. My hands fumbled with the lock, twisting it until I heard the soft click. My knees hit the floor beside the bed, and I reached for the phone on the nightstand. My fingers were shaking so badly I could barely press the buttons, but I pressed number one. Again and again.

Finally, his voice came through. "Bree, I'm almost there. Just hold on!"

"It might be too late," I whispered, tears choking my words. "Thor, I don't know if—"

"No," he cut me off. "I'll be there. Just hide, okay? Hide!"

Before I could answer, the door burst open. The lock shattered, and Laura stormed in, dragging Mel by her hair. My stomach twisted. The knife had fallen from Mel's hand and hit the floor with a dull clatter. Her face was red, streaked with tears, and she didn't even try to fight back.

I screamed, so loudly, the sound ripping out of me before I could stop it. It wasn't just fear, it was anger, grief, and desperation all at once.

"Bree!" Thor's voice crackled through the phone in my hand, but I couldn't respond. I dropped it onto the floor as Laura stepped closer.

"Your choice, Bree." She shoved Mel to her knees, gripping her hair tighter. "You or her."

I took a step closer to Mel, my eyes searching hers, and she looked so lost, so sad. She never truly lived, had never even known the world, and maybe, deep down, neither had I. But still, I wanted her to have that chance. I wanted her to know everything, to have everything. Even if it hurt me to admit that my promises had been nothing but lies.

I stepped again, my voice rising. "Come and get me!"

Mel's cry shattered me, "Bree, no!" she yelled, her voice breaking. She shoved Laura back, turning to me with tears in her eyes. "Run! The window... slide it to the side. Go!"

"No!" I shouted back, the words cutting out of me. "You're coming with me!"

She shook her head, her jaw tight, her hands trembling as she held Laura off. "This time... it's my turn to protect you."

And then it happened. Laura twisted in her grip, the blade flashing. And it happened too fast, too brutal, and the knife sliced across Mel's neck. And in the room, the only sound was the gurgling noise of Mel drowning in her own blood.

She was gone. Mel was gone.

"Enough!" Laura screamed.

"Mel!" I staggered forward, my body screaming to go to her, but my legs refused to move. Her blood was everywhere, staining the floor, her hands, my heart. She had given herself for me. For me.

I had no choice. I forced my legs to move, spinning toward the window. My hands fumbled, the cold air rushing in as I slid it open. I climbed through, my chest heaving, my vision blurred by tears.

"No!" Laura tried to catch my hand, "Nooo!"

I didn't stop. My feet hit the frozen ground, and I ran. The sharp wind sliced my face, and the snow crunched beneath my boots, but all I could hear was my heartbeat, hammering like it wanted to tear itself free from my chest.

Behind me, footsteps. Fast. Closing in.

I pushed harder, my legs burning, my lungs raw from the icy air. My body begged me to stop, but I couldn't. Not now. Not after what Mel had done. Every step forward felt like it carried her with me, like stopping would mean leaving her behind. I wouldn't do that. I couldn't.

The footsteps were right behind me now. I felt a hand grab the back of my shirt, jerking me back. My body snapped backward, slamming into a firm chest.

I didn't think—I just fought. My arm swung out on instinct, my hand connecting with a face. The blow made us both stumble, my feet catching on the snow. I tripped, pulling him down with me, and we hit the ground hard, the icy cold biting into my skin.

Then his hands were on my face. Firm. His voice cut through my panic, "Bree."

My eyes shot open. For a moment, all I saw was his face, his eyes, but one was icy blue, the other chestnut brown. I froze, everything else was just falling away.

"Thor?" I whispered, my voice cracking. "You..." My throat tightened, the words tangling together. "How?"

My hand lifted before I could stop it, brushing against his temple. My breath caught as I stared into his mismatched eyes. "Your eyes... they're blue," I murmured, my voice trembling, barely more than a breath.

"No," he said nervously, lifting himself off me. His voice was thin, uncertain. "They're not," he added, looking away. "They're brown."

I stood up, steadying myself, my gaze fixed on him. He tilted his face, trying to avoid my eyes.

"No," I said, pressing my palm against his cheek. I turned his face toward me, not letting him escape. "Don't call me crazy, Thor. I know what I saw."

He just stared at me, silent. His lips didn't move, not even to protest.

"You're him, aren't you?" I whispered, my voice trembling.

"I don't know what the hell you're talking about," he muttered, pushing my hand off his face. But the way he said it... It didn't sound convincing.

"You're Snowman," I said. "But how? How is that even possible?" Tears welled up in my eyes, spilling over before I could stop them.

"Fuck, Bree," he said, exhaling sharply, his hand dragging through his hair. "Maybe you just want me to be."

"Look at me," I begged, my voice shaking. He tilted his head slightly but didn't meet my eyes. "Look at me!" I shouted, the desperation clawing at my chest.

"No," he whispered, so quiet it was almost like he didn't say it at all. He turned his back to me, his shoulders stifled.

"You stalked me," I said, stepping closer. My voice was tight, trembling with anger. "Then you came into my home, pretending to be a cop. You gave me that phone, but why? Why?" My voice cracked. "So you could track me? Is that it?"

"No," he said again, still not turning around. His tone was flat, his back refusing to give me anything.

"I trusted you," I said, choking on the words. Tears blurred my vision. "I still do," I added, my voice dropping to a whisper.

His head moved slowly to the side. "What do you want from me?" he said with a low growl. "I can't give you much."

My chest tightened, the pain twisting deeper.

"A hug."

My hand hovered above his back before I pressed my palm lightly against his coat. My fingers trembled as they curled into it.

"A hug?" He finally turned his head, his eyes narrowing as he scanned me. "That's what you want?"

"Please," I said, meeting his eyes, tears still sliding down my cheeks.

His jaw tightened, his lips pressed into a firm line. Then, without a word, his hand reached for my arm. He pulled me to him, our chests colliding. His arms wrapped around me, pulling me in as though I belonged there. His head rested against mine, his breath warm against my hair.

And I broke. My sobs came in waves, uncontrollable. I buried my face in his chest, my tears soaking into his coat. I cried like I hadn't cried in years, each sound ripping out of me as if it could tear the pain away. And with each sob, his arms tightened, holding me closer, grounding me.

It was everything I didn't know I needed, just a hug that made the world disappear. One that let me fall apart completely without fear. I'd never had this before. My first kiss was stolen, my innocence taken. I had never been given something so simple. But now, this hug was his, ours. And I could've stayed there forever.

He might be a monster. He might be made of ice. But right now, he felt more real than anything else.

The tears kept falling, and with them, pieces of my heart. Everything I had lost, today, yesterday, Mel, it all came rushing in, crushing me.

Slowly, he eased his grip, pulling back just enough to see my face. His fingers brushed my cheeks, wiping away the tears as his eyes met mine.

And then I saw them.

They weren't brown anymore.

They were ice blue.

His eyes. Blue.

I froze, my breath catching in my throat. My stomach twisted, and I felt my knees weaken beneath me. How had I not noticed? How had I missed this?

He pushed me back slightly, just enough to see my face. His hands brushed my cheeks, wiping away the tears, his touch steady despite the storm in his eyes. I met his eyes, those eyes. They were ice now, sharp and cold. He must have taken out his contacts. I hadn't even noticed. I felt stupid for missing it. The icy blue of them crushed with the ocean blue of mine, like it was meant to be.

My heart pounded in my chest, too fast, too loud. I felt it in my throat, my stomach flipping in knots. My arms trembled as I held onto him, his stare was almost too much. My lips parted, and I realized how close we were, close enough that I could feel the soft warmth of his breath against my mouth.

"You're my worst nightmare, Bree," he said.

His eyes didn't waver, as if searching for something in mine, even as he seemed to lose himself in them. "You're haunting me."

His lips brushed against mine as he leaned in, his whisper so warm. "But I wish I could be your dream."

I didn't wait. I pressed forward, my lips finding his. His mouth moved against mine, his tongue thrusting inside, making my knees weak. It wasn't just a kiss, it was everything, pulling me under his skin. I wrapped my arms around his neck, my fingers twisting into his hair, holding him as tightly as I could. We kissed until we were both out of breath and even then, neither of us wanted to stop.

When I finally pulled away, gasping for air, I let my forehead rest against his shoulder.

"What now?" I whispered, afraid of the answer.

He tilted his head, his breath brushing my ear. "Now," he said, his voice deeper, growling, "now you're mine."

His.
The word settled over me, heavier and more real than it ever had before.
I was his.
Only his.

EIGHTEEN

SNOWMAN

She sat in my car, quiet, but I could feel her anger, her pain. She knew now.

Every mask I had worn in front of her, every lie I'd let her believe, she saw through it all. She knew exactly who I was. And somehow, I felt relief. Like the weight pressing on my chest for years had suddenly lifted. For the first time, I wasn't pretending.

But what she didn't know, what I couldn't let her know, was that I was driving her out of town. Not to protect her, not really. I had to hide her, lock her away for now. She was vulnerable, and vulnerable people... they break too easily. I couldn't risk her telling anyone. Not yet.

The road ahead was just a stretch of dark woods and endless asphalt. The headlights carved out pieces of the night, but everything else blurred into shadow. The rumble of tires, the silence in the car, it all seemed far away, as if we weren't there. Just echoes of ourselves.

I looked over at her, just for a second. She was staring out the window, her face pale and streaked with tears. Her shoulders trembled with quiet sobs.

Tonight, I won. But she? She lost everything.

"Bree," I hesitated.

I reached out, my hand finding her thigh. I gave it a small, reassuring squeeze. Her body stiffened, but she didn't pull away. My hand nearly wrapped around her whole thigh. She got so thin. She felt like she could break.

"I lost Mel," she whispered, her voice barely holding together. Her eyes stayed fixed on the window. "Laura... she... she slit her throat."

Her words hung in the air.

"What?" I turned to her, the car wobbling slightly on the road.

"And Joe," she continued, her voice cracking. "They had two little girls..." She swallowed hard, her breath hitching. "They said they... they will eat her."

I blinked, my brain struggling to make sense of the words. "Eat her?" I repeated, my voice harder now. My hands gripped the wheel, knuckles whitening. "What the hell are you talking about?"

Her hands trembled, resting on her lap, and she let out another broken sob. I pulled my hand back from her thigh and grabbed my phone, dialing Eric with one hand while keeping the car steady with the other.

When he picked up, I didn't wait. "I have Bree," I said, my voice flat, controlled. "But her sister's still in the house."

"The younger one?" Eric asked. "Do you need back-up?"

"Yeah," I said, looking at Bree. "But I need some time alone with him first."

"Want me to call Mother?"

I felt my jaw tighten at the mention of her. My grip on the wheel hardened, the leather creaking under my fingers. "Tell her to meet me at the farm."

I hung up, shoving the phone back into my pocket. Gripping the wheel with both hands, I yanked it hard, spinning the car around. The tires screeched against the frozen road, the smell of burning rubber filling the air. Bree gasped, holding the door handle as the car swerved.

"Are you out of your damn mind?" she shouted, looking at me.

"We have to go back," I said, my tone steady, but my foot pressed harder on the gas. The car moved forward, the needle on the speedometer climbing. I looked at her, my eyes locking with hers. "Do you trust me?"

She hesitated, her lips parting like she wanted to argue. But then she nodded, her red eyes glistening. "Why do I feel like I shouldn't?"

I pressed my hand to her thigh again, this time holding her gaze. "Because you shouldn't," I said honestly.

After a moment, I added, "But tonight, you can."

Her lips trembled. "Why do you..." She hesitated, clearing her throat. "Why do you kill people?"

Her question caught me off guard. For a second, I didn't say anything. I kept my eyes on the road, the yellow lines blurring as I drove faster.

"When I was twenty-five," I said finally, my voice quieter now, "I was the youngest detective on the force. My first case..." I stopped, exhaling sharply through my nose. "It was a man who killed his wife. They had a twelve-year-old boy at home."

"The guy was best friends with Jan Johansson," I continued, looking at Bree. "The guy walked. Case closed."

"But how?" she asked, confused. "How does that happen?"

"Self-defense," I said bitterly. "There wasn't enough evidence to convict. He walked. And when I went to the chief, angry as hell, you know what he told me?" I paused, my jaw clenched. "He said I could walk away, pretend nothing happened, or they'd make sure it was me who would take the fall."

"The point is, Bree, someone had to do something. Snowman... he's just a mask. Most of the time, I don't even remember what he does."

She hesitated. "Why did you kill that woman?"

"She took a boy," I said, cutting her off. "Brought him here, abused him for years. And her friend Donna? She knew. She covered it up like it was nothing."

Bree swallowed, the movement making her throat bob. Her voice cracked when she spoke. "And why me?"

"Curiosity." I locked my eyes with her just for a second, then looked away. "I never planned to kill you, Bree. I just..." I let out a breath, trying to piece the thoughts together. "I just wanted to know you."

"Know me?" She let out a bitter laugh. "You don't 'get to know' someone by scaring the hell out of them."

"It was a mistake," I admitted with a slight shrug. "An honest rookie mistake. It won't happen again."

She rolled her eyes and shook her head. "Because now you know me."

"I don't." I turned toward her, tilting my head. "I still have no idea who you are."

She looked away. "Maybe that's for the best."

I didn't respond.

The silence between us stretched, filled only by the faint rumble of the tires on the road. Up ahead, the farm came into view, and the sharp stink of pigs and horses stung the air. It hit me like a slap, dragging me back to memories I tried so hard to bury. Memories that never stayed buried.

The car slowed, bumping gently to a stop near the gate. I turned to Bree, catching her eyes in the night. "We'll get our chance," I said quietly, reaching out to tilt her face toward me.

She held my gaze for a moment before her eyes fell.

"Why did you stop calling me Birdie?" she asked, her eyes lingering on my mouth.

My jaw tightened as I let go of her face, my hands clenching into fists.

"Birdie?" My voice softened as I cupped her face again, my fingers trembling against her skin. "When I heard him say it, I felt like I was losing you."

I lied.

I didn't remember ever calling her that. The word had slipped out once, maybe twice, when I was driving with Isak. He took it like it meant nothing. Like it was just a word. But it wasn't. Not to her. Not to me now.

Her eyes filled with tears, one breaking free and sliding down her cheek. "He stole my first kiss," she whispered. "And I let him... because I thought he was Snowman."

Her words hit me hard, sharp. I leaned in, pressing my forehead to hers, trying to hold her together.

Trying to hold myself together. "And I hate myself for it."

"I always wanted it to be you," she whispered, the words like a quiet confession. "I know this is wrong. All of it. But... I still want it."

Her breath mingled with mine, and I felt her hesitation, her vulnerability. My lips brushed her forehead gently, lingering. "Does it help if I say I've wanted it too? Since the first day I saw you?"

A small, trembling smile formed on her lips as she wrapped her arms around me, holding me close. "Just don't let go."

"I won't," I promised, pulling her tighter against me. She rested her chin on my shoulder, and we stayed like that, locked in a moment that felt almost real enough to last.

Then, a sharp knock shattered everything. The thin glass of the car's window rattled, the sound cutting through like a blade. She screamed, so loud, sending shivers down my spine.

I turned, my heart pounding. Lena was standing there, her hands pressed flat against the glass, her face close, peering in.

I reached for the door and pushed it open. She took a step back, serious. The cold air rushed into the car, and I forced myself to meet her eyes.

"Hello, Mother."

"You brought her here?" Her eyes darted to mine, questioning me.

"Yeah," I said quietly, meeting her gaze for a moment before turning back to the car. I leaned inside. "Bree, come on out."

The car door opened softly, and Bree stepped out, her shoulders hunched. She moved toward me, her fingers brushed against mine, tentative, before slipping into my hand. She clung to me, staying slightly behind, her body so fragile and small in comparison to mine.

"You," Lena said, her tone shifting as her eyes fixed on Bree.

Bree stepped further behind me, her grip on me tightening.

"Does she know?" Lena asked, looking at me.

I nodded, sliding my hand to Bree's back and pulling her closer. "She knows."

Lena's mouth pressed into a thin line, and then finally, she tilted her head toward the house and said, "Come inside."

We followed her down the path, the pig pens were alive with snorting, shuffling, and the occasional squeal. The smell hit like a wave, harsh and overwhelming.

Bree raised her sleeve and covered her face with her hands, muffling a soft gag. I reached for her hand again, gripping it as we continued walking.

The snow crunched with each step, the sound rhythmic, almost distracting. Up ahead, the house came into view. It sat low, its wooden walls stained dark from years of storms.

It looked smaller than I remembered, more worn, as if time had taken more from it than the paint itself.

Lena pushed the door open and let it swing wide. Inside, a soft breath of warmth, along with the faint smell of old wood and metal.

The space was cramped, with closed walls and worn furniture. A staircase in the middle led to the bedrooms, while the kitchen and living room took up one space. It was cluttered, not messy, but the whole place suggested that no one had cared for it for a long time.

The radio on the counter crackled, a buzz of static broadcasting the news. My gaze fell on a framed photograph on the far wall, the black-and-white image faded, the faces slightly blurred with age. Bree looked at it without saying a word. She paused before the picture, staring at it with wide eyes. Her breath misted the glass as she leaned closer, squinting as if she recognized someone.

I moved and stood behind her, my hands brushing her shoulders. She was stiff under my touch but didn't pull away. "I have to go," I said softly, leaning down. "You'll be safe with Lena."

She didn't speak, just nodded, her arms folding around herself. She sat down in the chair beneath the photo, her head tilted down.

I stepped back, turning toward Lena. I pulled my phone from my pocket and handed it to her. "Call me," I said simply.

She took it without a word, and the expression on her face was still unreadable.

I turned back toward the door, my boots scuffing against the floor. I didn't look at Bree. I couldn't. Her silence stayed with me as I walked away.

My hand gripped the doorknob, the radio went from humming to sound, and a sharp voice came out, reporting; "In the woods near Isla, police discovered a burned cottage containing the remains of a young woman in her twenties. Authorities have identified her as Ingrid Berg, missing since 2001. Detective Isak Skalsgard confirmed the case is being reopened, with new evidence suggesting a serial killer known as 'Snowman,' believed to be a man in his fifties or sixties, may have accomplices."

I tilted my head toward them, frowning. "Fifty?" I said, the word coming out sharper than I meant. "And who the hell is Ingrid?"

Lena raised her eyebrows and let out a low laugh. "Oh, boy. You're in trouble," she said, shaking her head. "Maybe call Erik and get to work, Thor."

I sighed, trying to ignore the sinking feeling in my chest.

"Yeah," I muttered.

I stepped out the door, hesitating. Bree was still there, watching me.

I hated I was leaving her behind, but I couldn't make this about her right now. I couldn't even look at her as I shut the door behind me.

The yard was the same disaster it always was, scraps scattered across the ground like no one had bothered to clean up in years. I shoved my hands in my pockets, moving through the mess as I headed for the car.

As soon as I sat inside, I grabbed my work phone off the passenger seat, flipping it over to see Erik's name on the missed call. I pressed to call him back.

"Chief called us all in," Erik said the second he picked up. "See you at the station."

The line went dead before I could even grunt a reply.

The police station was surprisingly large for a small town. Three stories high, it seemed almost out of place. The first floor held the reception area and cells, the second floor held the chief's office and a row of desks for detectives and officers, and the third floor was quieter, mostly for officers dealing with paperwork. And outside, in a separate building nearby, were the lab and the coroner's office.

I went inside and climbed the stairs to the second floor, feeling eyes on me with every step I took. The building had that smell of stale coffee, stale air, and the faintest trace of bleach. When I reached the room, everyone's attention was not on me, but on the transparent board with evidence and clues about the Snowman serial killer. The chief stood in front with Donna, the coroner. And their faces said it all, their eyes rimmed with red, an exhaustion that was deeper than a bad dream.

On the clear board behind them were the photos; of Josh, Vic, Sigrid, and Ingrid, strings of notes and crime scene photos surrounded their faces.

I kept moving forward, weaving through desks until I reached Isak and Erik. They nodded as I joined them, and when the chief noticed me, he gave a quick nod to the officer at the door. Without a word, the man left, the door clicking shut behind him.

"Now that we're all here," the chief began, "let's get started."

He turned to the board, picking up a marker, but the way he held it told me his mind was elsewhere. I leaned toward Erik, lowering my voice. "What's going on?"

He shrugged, his eyes glued to the board. "You'll see."

The chief wrote something on the board, then stopped. When he turned, in red was a sketch of the snowman, like a mocking signature.

"What do we know about this guy?" he asked.

Isak raised his hand, but the chief just sighed, pinching the bridge of his nose. "Isak, for God's sake, this isn't school. Just talk."

"Right." Isak cleared his throat and stepped forward. "He hunts at night, and every victim has a record. The first one we found was dumped by the road. She killed two teenagers in a car accident back in 2003."

"We thought it was a truck driver at first," a woman stepped in. Her hair was pulled back neatly, and she looked like she hadn't slept in days. I didn't recognize her. She was new. "He was moving south to north, so it made sense at the time. But none of these victims are random. He picks them."

"He cuts his victims into small pieces," someone in front added, "leaving trails and pieces of them for us to find."

"He is cold and calculated," the woman said, "and he will do it again."

The chief's voice broke in, colder now. "He's been taunting us for years. Playing some hero, deciding who deserves to live or die. But we still don't have a damn clue who this bastard is."

"He's local," the woman cut in, arms crossed tightly. "No one else would know the area this well."

Donna stepped forward. "There's a pattern," she said. "The way he cuts his victims... it's not random. He's skilled. Trained. It's surgical. Every single one of them was drained of blood, clean, controlled. And torture?" She paused, looking around the room. "That's personal."

For a moment, no one spoke.

The silence that followed was stifling. Everyone stared at the board, at the drawing of a snowman, as if it might suddenly tell us something we hadn't seen before. The chief's shoulders slumped as he stared at it, exhaustion written all over his face.

"Do you think he's searching for something?" I broke the silence. "Or is he just interrogating them for what they've done?"

"Yes," the woman replied without hesitation. "I think he's acting like a judge, pushing for confessions. And once he gets them? He kills them."

She stood up again and turned towards the room, I felt like she was looking for him in the room.

"There are four types of serial killers," she said, counting them off on her fingers. "Visionary. Mission-oriented. Hedonistic. Power/control-driven. But this one?" She paused, letting the words sink in. "He doesn't fit into any of those. He's all of them mixed into one."

She walked to the board, picked up a marker, and began to write. Each word came slow: **Experienced. Antisocial. Dissociative.**

She turned back to face us, pointing to the words as she spoke.

"He's experienced. He's antisocial. And he likely has a split personality." Her eyes moved across the room like she was daring someone to argue. "He might think he's a doctor," she added.

Wrong.

"Or," she went on, "he could believe he's on a military mission."

So wrong.

"Maybe," she mused, her voice softer now, "he's an abused girl trying to avenge her past."

So fucking wrong.

"Or maybe," she said, changing her tone, "he doesn't fully understand what he's doing. He has a good face, a part that feels guilty, allows him to justify it, and a bad face that picks on people he thinks are bad, deserving of punishment."

Bingo.

Erik leaned back in his chair with a smirk, glancing at me before turning to her. "If that's the case," he asked, "how do you explain the snowmen?"

She tilted her head, thinking. "Maybe even a third face, a child," she said calmly. "Building snowmen is his way of creating something he lost in childhood. Or maybe something he never had."

"So, what you're saying is," I said, leaning forward, "this guy is lonely, sad, desperate, and old? Isn't that half the population of Iceland?"

A ripple of laughter broke through the room.

"This isn't a joke," she snapped, her voice cutting through the noise. "I was sent here to profile this man because none of you have been able to close this case. Ten years, and it's still open."

Ten years?

"What about his latest victim?" I asked after a pause, trying to get the conversation back on track. "Does she fit the profile?"

She paused, her jaw tightening, her eyes narrowing slightly. When she finally answered, her voice was flat. "No. She doesn't."

"We think someone saw the cabin burning and decided to throw the body into the flames," Donna said, her voice low, almost resigned. "She was already dead, at least a year before the fire." She paused, shaking her head. "And the bastard left nothing. Not a trace."

Again silence, then a few murmurs rippled through the team, fragmented whispers that didn't dare take form. Then the chief broke through it, his voice cutting.

"That bastard took my son," he said, his tone cold and steady, though his fist tightened on the desk. "And I'm going to make him pay."

No one said a word. We didn't have to. Everyone knew what was left unsaid. Everyone knew that if Josh's case file weren't covered by his father, it'd be as thick as the Bible.

"You're dismissed," the chief barked, waving us off without looking up.

We left quietly, the tension following us into the hallway. Erik and I walked together to my desk. He dropped into the chair across from me, flashing that crooked smile he always wore when he was about to cause trouble.

"Where are your contacts?" he asked, leaning back as if he had all the time in the world. His smile widened. "Does she know?"

"Just bits and pieces," I said, opening my desk drawer. I pulled out a small box and opened it. Shoving the contacts in, I blinked a few times, feeling the familiar sting.

"I went to see Joe," Erik said suddenly, his tone shifting like he was letting me in on a joke. "He's at his house." He paused, the grin returning. "Well, technically your house. He doesn't know that part."

"Does he know it was you?" I asked, trying to sound casual as I shut the drawer.

Erik leaned forward, resting his elbows on my desk. "I wore your mask. Don't worry," he said, glancing away for a moment as if weighing his next words. "I got there just in time for the younger one, though. She's in the hospital."

I scanned him, waiting for more, but he hesitated, his eyes dropping to the floor.

"I need to tell you something," he said finally, his voice softer than before.

"What?" I asked, leaning forward slightly, my pulse quickening.

Before he could answer, Isak's voice broke through, startling both of us.

"I just came back from the hospital," he said, approaching my desk. His face was tight, his jaw clenched. "I asked about Bree, but they said she'd already left. Do you two know anything about that?"

I let out a dry chuckle, turning to face him. "Why would we know? She's your girlfriend."

"Do you have her address?" Isak asked, ignoring the jab. His voice cracked.

I looked at Erik, who raised an eyebrow. "We do," Erik said slowly, "but we can't give it to you. You're too close to this. It's personal."

Isak's shoulders dropped slightly, but his voice didn't waver. "Then call her. Please. I need to talk to her."

"Why?" I asked, my tone sharpening.

Isak leaned in, whispering. "I think she believes I'm the Snowman. I need to clear that up before the new profiler drags her in and paints me as the prime suspect."

The room seemed to get smaller. Erik shifted in his chair, the grin on his face curved at the corner of his mouth.

"Oh," I said. My gaze didn't leave Isak's face. "Should we be suspecting you?"

"No, man, I swear," he said, his voice jittery, barely keeping it together. Erik stepped in closer, resting a heavy hand on his shoulder. The grip tightened just enough to make a point.

I ignored them and pulled out my phone, pressing my number. The call connected after a couple of rings.

"This is Detective Thor Karlsson," I said, keeping it formal. "May I speak with Bree?"

"What's this about, you shmuck?" Lena snapped, clearly unimpressed. "But yeah, hold on. She's here."

There was a muffled rustle, and then Bree's voice came through, soft. "Hi."

"Hey, Bree," I said. "How are you?"

She paused, and for a second, I thought the call had dropped. Then, quietly, "Bad. I'm... waiting for you."

I closed my eyes, took a breath, and focused. "I need to ask you something. Be honest, okay?"

"Okay," she whispered.

"Detective Isak wants to see you," I said. "Do you want me to give him your address? It's completely up to you."

"No." Her voice cracked, but the word came out firm. "Please, Thor. I don't want to see him again."

"Got it," I said. "Thanks for letting me know. Goodbye, miss..."

Miss you.

The thought hovered in my head as I hung up, but I didn't let it stick. There wasn't time for that now.

I turned to Isak, who had been standing nearby, arms crossed like he owned the room. "She said her family's out of town tonight. You can stop by tomorrow morning."

"Right," he said, a smirk creeping across his face. "Perfect."

"I'll send you her address half an hour before," I added, keeping my tone clipped.

"Thank you." He gave a slight nod, then turned and walked off, his footsteps fading into the background.

I looked at Erik, who had been watching everything without a word. "We have to go," I told him.

He stood and grabbed his coat from the back of the chair. No words, just a quick nod. We had a plan.

NINETEEN

BREE

I sat in the corner of the dark living room, my knees pulled to my chest. The air felt so heavy, thick with the smell of mold, smoke, and lingering animal fur, maybe. Lena's soft humming sang faintly as she moved through the house, lighting candles one by one. Their light cast long shadows across the room, making it even smaller, and more stifling.

I looked around, my eyes catching on the framed photos on the walls. Images of her and Thor's family stared back at me, their faces stood frozen in time. I couldn't connect it, any of it, no matter how hard I tried. Never in a million years would I have guessed the woman who greeted Joe and Laura, on the day we arrived, was Thor's mother.

Was this his house all along? If it was, he only told me half of the story, or maybe even less.

I looked toward the kitchen. There were papers everywhere, sticky notes taped on surfaces, each with scribbled words as reminders. They didn't feel random, and Lena didn't seem like the kind of woman who forgot things often. I knew there was something else behind it. The whole house was like a puzzle as if every creak of the floorboards and every whisper of air contained some piece with a deeper meaning.

I shivered and wrapped my arms around myself tighter.

The place felt alive in a way that made my skin crawl. I lowered my head, pressing my face into my arms, letting the tears come quietly. My chest burned with the weight of it all.

Soft footsteps came closer.

"Why tears?" Lena said calmly, almost detached.

I looked up, meeting her eyes, sharp and cold. She saw right through me.

"If you miss him," she said, lighting a pipe and slipping it between her lips, "he won't be back soon." She lowered herself into a wooden chair, crossing her legs. Smoke curled around her face as she leaned back, and exhaled.

"I..." My throat tightened, and I swallowed hard. "I lost my sister today."

Her hand paused close to her face, the pipe resting just shy of her lips. She didn't react the way I expected, no pity or shock. Instead, she scanned my face like she was turning my words over in her mind, expecting something else from me.

"When you're in pain," she said after a long moment, "it's better to keep your mind busy. Ask me anything. I'll answer. Maybe it'll take your mind off her."

I nodded, but my thoughts felt like a scattered glass all over me. There were so many questions I wanted to ask, but none of them formed. My eyes moved back to the kitchen, to the yellow sticky notes dotting the walls and counters.

"Why all the notes?" I asked finally, looking back at her.

Lena didn't answer right away. Instead, she stood, taking the candle from the table with her.

"Come with me," she said, the pipe still between her teeth.

I followed her to the stairs near the entrance. She led the way, slowly moving, one hand holding the wooden railing. Each step groaned under her, the sound so sharp in the stillness around us. The air got colder as we reached the last step, and my heart panicked just a little.

At the bottom of the stairs, she stopped in front of a door and pushed it open. The room inside felt so dark, with low light. I could still see the sticky notes, they were everywhere. The walls were covered with them, a sea of yellow squares scrawled with handwriting that ranged from neat to hurried.

Lena moved to a lamp in the corner, using the candle to light it. The warm glow lit the room, and she turned back to me.

"How much do you know about Thor?" she asked.

I hesitated. "I know about Snowman," I said finally, my voice barely steady. "If that's what you mean."

Her lips twitched like she might smile, but the expression never fully slipped to her lips. "No," she said.

She plucked a sticky note from the wall and handed it to me. The paper was flimsy between my fingers.

"I knew Thor was different from an early age," she said. "He used to have nightmares, and when he woke up, things would just disappear. Sometimes it was just small objects that he moved without remembering. Sometimes it was more than that."

"Sleepwalking?" I asked, staring at the note in my hand. The words on it were so far away as if they weren't meant for me to see.

Mommy: No.
Erik: No.
Dad: Yes.
Joe: Yes.

Lena reached over, gently tugging the paper from my fingers. She folded it back into itself, then set it down where it had been.

"No," she said quietly, shaking her head. "He wasn't sleepwalking."

"Why is Joe's name on there?" My knees felt weak as I lowered myself onto the first step of the staircase, the wood creaking under me.

She hesitated, her lips pressed tight before the words slipped out. "When Thor turned seven, the blackouts got worse. And his behavior... shifted. One night, I asked him who he was." Her voice broke, and her eyes were distant as if she was reliving it. "And he told me, 'Mommy, I'm [1] Snjókarl.'"

The name hit me. "Snjókarl?" I repeated, testing the word.

Snowman.

Lena nodded, her gaze lowering to her hands. "I had him write a list of everything in the house. Everything! So that when he became Snjókarl, he'd know where to put things back. I knew something was wrong, but his father..." She clenched her jaw, her tone hardening. "He didn't believe in doctors. He believed in The Family."

I felt my stomach twist. "Are you saying Thor doesn't know?" My voice cracked. "That he's... Snowman?"

1.

Lena looked at me sharply, her expression solemn. "Oh, Thor knows. He had always known. But Snjókarl doesn't. He believes he's here to fix the world."

Her words sent a chill through me. "But why is Joe on the list, Lena?" My voice dropped, trembling.

She let out a shaky breath, like the words were clawing their way out. "Joe is Thor's stepbrother," she said softly. "My husband's first child."

She rose from the chair, moving to a drawer where she pulled out another piece of paper. This one was older, worn at the edges, with two names crossed out—Joe and Dad.

She turned to face me, her face still cold, without any emotion. "Thor was abused," she said in a low voice. "His father... he did things to him. And Joe? Joe helped."

A tear slipped down my cheek, unbidden, and everything he had been through pressed on my chest until I couldn't breathe. All I wanted was to wrap my arms around him, to tell him he wasn't broken, that maybe, we could figure this out together.

"Snjókarl protected Thor," Lena continued, her voice trembling now. "But as he grew, as life kept throwing darkness at him, Snjókarl changed too. He became... darker."

I swallowed hard, forcing out the question. "What is The Family, Lena?"

She drew in a deep breath, staring at the floor. "My husband started it in 1986," she said. "Back then, it was just seven of us. But people kept joining. The worst kinds of people. They would come, and then... they would disappear. The whole town suspected us. But no one said anything. Then the famine hit, and people were starving. Yet somehow, my husband always had meat."

She fell silent for a moment. "That's when I figured it out. We weren't eating animals, we were eating them. The missing members."

I felt bile rise in my throat. Her words were so plain, so cold, almost unreal.

"A few of us survived on plants, berries... scraps," she went on. "But most left. I stayed. I gave birth to Erik. Then Thor. And in the end, it was just the four of us. And Joe."

I stared at her, my stomach churning. "You're saying Joe was part of the cult? All of you?"

Her eyes flicked to me, and for a second, I thought I saw regret there, but she was still cold. "When my husband died, Joe left," she said. "But I think he took you and your sister because he wanted to start over. To finish what my husband started."

"I'm going to puke," I said, my hands pressing against my lips. My stomach churned, my chest tight. "I feel sick."

"We never thought Joe would come back," she said, standing slowly, like the words themselves were pulling her up.

"Why did you tell me all this?" I shouted, my voice cracking as I stood. "Why?"

She raised her arms, her scars etched deep against her skin. "These," she said quietly, "Snjókarl did this."

"He won't hurt me," I said, my body sinking, almost folding in on itself. "He wouldn't."

"You're his type," her voice cut through me, the same words she told me when we first met. Her gaze was heavy, unwavering. "Broken. Beautiful. Easy to manipulate."

"No," I said, shaking my head. "He..."

"He would," she snapped, her eyebrows shooting up, her tone rising sharp. "And he will. You have to run. This time, you can't hesitate. Run fast. Change your name, your address, your hair—everything."

"No," my voice was breaking, tears falling. I felt them drip off my chin. "I'll wait. I have to."

"You stupid, stupid girl," she spat, her face twisting in frustration. "You can't save him. No one can."

"Even if I can't," I choked on my own words "I'll keep trying."

She stared at me for a moment, her shoulders tense, before she let out a long, harsh breath. "Fine," she said, turning away. "Your funeral, not mine."

I slumped onto the steps as she walked upstairs, her footsteps fading behind me. I didn't look after her. I couldn't. My eyes just scanned sticky notes plastered all over the walls. They called to me, I needed to know.

I stood up, drawn to them, and started counting. One by one, tracing their edges, feeling the paper under my fingertips. I needed something to hold onto, even if the truth was hard to hear. I counted one hundred and one pieces just on one side of the wall.

My chest felt tight. My heart was sinking. I searched for something—anything—that could explain him. I was desperate to find the boy he used to be, the one his father had hurt. I wanted to see a clue, a crack, a piece of him that I could fix.

He had two faces. One soft, warm, and full of care. The other, cold and distant, cruel. I told myself that if both of those faces cared for me if I could keep both, I'd be safe.

But deep down, I wasn't so sure anymore.

An hour had passed. I was curled up on the bench by the wall downstairs, hugging my knees to my chest. Lena had gone out and still hadn't come back. Around me was nothing but silence, broken only by the faint creaks of the walls behind. My eyes stung from crying, my throat raw, and exhaustion pulled at me. But I couldn't rest. Not yet.

I heard the door open. My heart jumped, but I didn't move. I stayed curled up, too drained to care, even as heavy footsteps thudded against the floor. Only when they grew closer did I open my eyes and sit up.

He was there, standing at the top of the stairs. His white shirt was stained with blood, stains, and spots dark against the white. His hair was slicked back, damp, and messy, and his eyes weren't the same. They were darker like something inside him had died. He held a white plastic mask in his hand, the edges of it stained with blood.

For a moment, he didn't move. He just looked at me, his chest rising and falling, short breaths. Then he took a step forward, and another, until he was in front of me. Without a word, he pulled me into his arms. My head rested against his chest, and despite the blood, the smell, everything, I clung to him like he was the only thing left in my world.

My stomach twisted in knots. How could I fall for someone like this? Someone born to destroy, to kill? Someone who could so easily hurt me?

I pulled back just enough to see his face, my hand pressing lightly against his chest. I needed to see his eyes, to find something in them, anything. My breath hitched as I looked up at him. His icy blue eyes met mine, and for a second, I thought I saw something soft beneath the surface. But the metallic smell of blood hovered at the tip of my nose, sharp and suffocating. My gaze flicked to the mask in his hand. It wasn't him, but it was. The face he showed me never changed, but the masks always did.

"Lena said," he started, "you know."

My throat clenched as tears rolled down my cheeks. "How could I know..." I couldn't complete the thought.

"Who should you choose?" he said, sliding his hands to grab my face. His touch was kind, and his fingers brushed the tears off my cheeks.

"No," I said softly, my voice cracking. "Who you are?"

His eyes softened, just enough to make me want to believe him.

"Bree," he paused, "I will be whoever you need me to be." "But no matter who I am, I will always choose you."

I leaned in again. "I'm so tired," I said. "I don't think I can fight anymore."

His arms tightened around me, holding me up, and I was slowly falling apart. "Then let me fight for you." He leaned back just enough to look into my eyes. "Just don't give up, Bree. Not on yourself."

"I'm not giving up, I just..." I whispered, my eyes closing as I tried to steady myself. "I know I've been through a lot. Mel's had it worse. You've had it worse." My eyes opened slowly, locking onto his. "I can't even compare the pain or the hurt... but I'm so damn tired." The tears came again, slipping down my cheeks. "I should be grateful I survived. I know that. But I'm not. I feel like... like I already lost the fight."

His eyebrows pulled together as he looked at me, his grip tightening just enough to ground me.

"Stop," he said. "Stop ripping yourself apart because another person's grief appears different. Everyone has their own troubles. It doesn't make yours any less."

"Fuck, Bree." He ran a hand through his hair, his frustration bubbling over. "You matter. If not to anyone else... you matter to me. Don't you get that?"

I shook my head, my voice trembling as I whispered, "I'm not enough. I'm not whole. I don't know if someone as broken as me can do anything but make it worse. I'm scared... scared that I'll hurt you, or ruin whatever this is."

"I don't need saving," he said as he pulled me closer. His arms were tight around me, and I could feel the strength behind his words. "You can't save me, Bree. Even if you tried. And you won't ruin anything. Trust me, you couldn't."

The tears came harder now, and I tried so hard to see his face through the blur. My voice cracked as I asked, "Can you fix me?"

"You don't need to be fixed," he said, his hand brushing against my cheek, wiping away the tears as fast as they came. "You just need to be loved."

Loved.

How could I even think about love when I felt so empty? What was left of me to love? Could he even love someone like me? Could anyone?

I loved before. Now, I am wounded. I don't know how to protect myself. I don't even know if I want to.

I was lost. Completely lost.

TWENTY

Snowman

I ONCE HEARD SOMEONE say that some people die at twenty-five, we just wait until they're seventy-five to bury them. Looking at her now, her shattered pieces scattered like glass—I could see it. She was dying, and she was only nineteen.

I knew that feeling too well. I'd died a long time ago, back when I learned how to abandon my feelings and start over. I knew what it was like to wake up each day not remembering who I was yesterday, let alone what I'd done to make today any better. The truth was something I'd buried deep, waiting for someone else to dig it out of me.

But her? She was so fragile, so painfully breakable. I caught myself wishing—just for a moment—that her pain was on the outside. If only there were wounds on her skin instead of the ones carved into her heart. At least then I could patch her up with a bandage and tell her she'd be okay. But a wounded heart isn't that simple. It takes time, and I... I needed her now.

A single tear slipped down her cheek, and I brushed it away with my thumb. Her skin was cold against my hand.

"Erik can take you to the hospital," I said softly. "To see Mel. She made it."

"She did?" Her voice trembled, disbelief clouding her face. But then, just barely, a smile tugged at the corner of her lips, fragile.

"Do you want to see her?" I asked, my hand gently cradling her face. "We reached her parents. They're taking her home on Friday."

Her gaze dropped to the floor, her smile fading as quickly as it had come. "Maybe I shouldn't," she murmured. "Maybe... maybe it'll just hurt her more."

I leaned closer and pressed a kiss to her forehead. "How about you decide later?" I said, my voice low. "I need to finish something first, but I'll be back soon. Okay?"

She nodded, her eyes still fixed on the floor. "Okay," she whispered. "Okay."

"I know I'm not the person you wanted or needed," I whispered against her lips, my voice breaking. "But I'll try my best to make you feel better. Fuck, Bree, I'll try."

She leaned back against my chest, her eyes fluttering shut as if the weight of the world was finally pulling her down. I let her rest there for a moment, breathing in the quiet between us before I gently pushed her away. My gaze drifted to the wall, to the sticky notes plastered in uneven rows. One caught my eye, a memory I wished I could burn, and it sent a shiver down my spine. Swallowing hard, I pressed my lips to her forehead one last time, and then I turned and left.

I had to leave. I just had to.

The door creaked as I approached, its worn wood carved with grooves and scratches, traces of a childhood I had spent trying to forget. The faint scent lingered with the cold air seeped through the cracks, and Lena and Erik were waiting outside.

Lena rocked in an old chair, her pipe glowing faintly as she exhaled, the smoke curling like a ghost against the midnight sky. Erik leaned against the fence, staring into the barn, his face as blank as the snow around us.

"What's the plan?" Lena asked, her eyes narrowing as she looked me over. "We've gotta be smart about this."

"No one is coming for him," Erik said without looking at her. His gaze shifted to me, his head tilting slightly. "You know that, right?"

I met his eyes and nodded.

"So?" I said. "Shall we?"

Without waiting for an answer, I started to walk toward the barn.

The snow blanketed the property in a suffocating white silence, broken only by the crunch of our boots as we trudged through the dirty path leading to the barn. The only tracks were ours from moments earlier when we dragged Joe here. Now, we were leaving a second set, marking our way.

Inside, the air was foul. The stench of pus hit me first, nauseating, forcing my stomach to flip. I winced but kept walking. None of us spoke, we didn't need to. This wasn't the time for words, more for answers.

The barn had the weak light from the open window casting long, uneven shadows across the frozen floor. Joe sat slumped in a chair at the center, his shirt half-open, his skin pale and slick with sweat despite the cold. Blood dripped from his face, staining the wooden boards beneath him, but he still managed to grin. A twisted, mocking stretch of his lips sent rage boiling in my chest. His half-lidded eyes fixed on me as I approached, unblinking, defiant.

In the corner, Laura was crumpled and still, her wrists tied in knots and her face slack. She hadn't woken yet—hadn't seen what was coming. I swallowed the lump in my throat and clenched my fists. I wasn't hesitant. Not anymore.

As I stepped closer, Joe let out a jagged laugh. It was mean, cruel, and utterly devoid of guilt for anything he'd done. Lena moved silently behind me, shutting the barn door with a heavy thud. She moved to the old heater beside the stalls, a piece of trash from when this barn held cows and horses, and turned it on. Joe's laughing drowned out the slight click and hum of the heater.

I laughed with him, folding my arms as I stared down at his broken face. For a moment, the sound of our laughter tangled with the cold. Then he stopped, his voice cutting sharply. "What's so funny?"

I tilted my head, mirroring him. "What's so funny?" I repeated, mocking him.

His body moved against the ropes, muscles straining as he spat out, "I'll kill you!"

"I'll kill you!" I repeated, crouching low. My hand hovered over his knees, a knife glinting in my grip.

"Fuck you!" he snarled, trying to jerk away, but he was tied too tightly.

"Fuck you!" I said, my voice calm as I plunged the blade into his knee.

The scream ripped out of him like a wild beast, primal and shaking through the barn. I twisted the knife, seeing the sorrow spread through his body, the way his head swung back, veins bursting at his neck. Behind us, Laura screamed through the chaos, begging to stop.

"Now," I said, pulling the knife back an inch before leaning closer to his face, "tell me." I tilted my head back and forth, watching the beads of sweat streak through the pores on his skin. "Why did you come back?"

"Why would I tell you a damn thing?" he shouted, saliva flying from his mouth as he glared up at me.

"Why not?" I chuckled, standing and strolling toward the heater Lena had turned on.

Its coils glowed faintly now, the heat pouring outward in shimmering waves across the chilly barn air. Joe's face was covered with sweat, and his body trembled. I let the heat develop while I crossed the room to where my father's branding irons stood on the wall. My fingertips brushed over one of them, the chilly iron imprinted with the words **"Property of T.K."**

I pulled it down, firmly gripping the handle, then dragged it back near the heater and rested the branding iron against it to allow the metal to absorb the heat. The scent of rust and growing warmth soaked into the barn. Then I bent down again, my knife striking his knee once again.

"Why are you here?" I asked with a low voice, almost bored, as I pushed the blade in deeper. His scream came immediately, jagged and high-pitched.

Blood poured from the wound in thick, dark streams, pooling beneath his leg. He was shaking now, his body failing him as consciousness began to slip away.

Before he could say anything, a desperate voice cut through towards us.

"We were called!" Laura screamed. "Please, stop!"

I froze, my head snapping toward her. Her face was pale, streaked with tears, her tied hands trembling as she tried to sit up.

"By who?" I demanded, my eyes still fixed on Joe, who was slumping forward, his head lolling. His breaths came shallow and uneven, his eyes rolling slowly back as his body sagged against the chair.

I leaned to the side, my eyes narrowing on Laura. Her sobs echoed faintly in the barn, breaking by hiccups and gasps. She was a mess but was awake, and most importantly she had answers.

"I don't know," she said. "There was a riddle, and an article from 2006 showing us with Mel and Bree. Whoever sent it threatened to publish our address if we didn't come back."

"Why did you kidnap the girls?" I asked and slowly moved closer to her.

Her gaze dropped, her voice barely above a whisper. "Their parents were the ones who left the cult. Joe wanted them to pay." Her breath hitched as tears streamed down her face. "But he changed after." She broke into sobs. "He gave them blue pills... brought other cult members into their rooms."

I froze, her words slicing through me. "What the fuck, Laura?" My voice cracked. "And you just watched?"

Her quivering fingertips reached up to her shoulder, exposing a familiar jagged scar. My breath seized my throat, I recognized the mark. It was my father's mark.

"You..."

The memory surged forward, her face, younger, softer, in the sunlight at the park. She was the one who wanted to play with me when I was twelve.

"How?" The question escaped before I could stop it. Behind me, Joe's gurgling breaths grew louder, stirring faintly to consciousness.

Laura's body shuddered as she spoke. "Ivar branded me. He kidnapped me the day after I saw you at the park in '94." Her voice cracked, barely holding together. "From then on, he fed me with human meat and tortured me. And when he got bored, he handed me to Joe." She collapsed into sobs. "After that, I had no choice. I depended on Joe. The only food I could eat... was what he gave me."

My fists clenched, nails biting into my palms. "You," I growled, barely able to contain the fury coursing through me. "You, who knew firsthand what it was like... why the fuck did you let him hurt them? Huh?" My voice exploded in a roar. "You disgust me."

"Because I wanted them to pay, all of them!" she shouted, her voice breaking. "Every. Single. One of them. No matter who they were!"

I turned to Erik, his eyes meeting mine. Without a word, he grabbed Laura by the arm, hoisting her off the ground. She thrashed and screamed, but he dragged her to the door and left, closing the door behind him.

Lena stepped forward, her lips curling into a smile. She picked up the red, hot iron brand and pressed it into Joe's cheek with a sickening sizzle. His scream ripped, and all I could smell was burning flesh in the air.

I grabbed a pair of frayed cables hanging near the window, my mind racing. Sparks flew when I brought them near the heater, crackling. Joe's body shook fiercely as I put them on his neck, his eyes flying wide.

"This," I said, leaning in close, "is what I call shock therapy. Minus the therapy."

Lena laughed. "Be quick, son," she said as she strode to the door. "The pigs are hungry." She slammed it shut behind her, leaving us in the darkened barn.

Joe's eyes darted frantically. "Pigs?" His voice cracked with panic. "How? You wouldn't—"

I crouched down, grabbing him by the collar. "Answer me first," I hissed, my voice cold. "Do you know who sent the letter?"

"I don't!" he stammered, his face pale, his words tumbling over each other. "But I... I can tell you what was in it!"

"Then speak, idiot!"

"I know where you dwell, where you wander and stray,
At the end of the road, far, frosty homes lay.
Two diamonds you claimed, their gleam met your eye,
But their truth bears a weight — do you know why?
Before snow's first knock, the prodigal must roam,
Back to where it all started, to finally call home."

He recited each sentence, his voice cutting through my thoughts like a knife. With every word, something deep inside me woke up, something I had tried to suppress for so long. Could it be? Could I have been the one to send the letter? Had I lost the control I fought so hard to keep?

The thought clawed at the edges of my mind, but I pushed it down, telling myself I was fine. I had to be. In a twisted way, I felt grateful. If I hadn't done this, I wouldn't have met Bree. I wouldn't have known about her. And now, it felt like everything was finally coming to an end I never dared to imagine.

"Do you know who it was?" I asked as I reached over and turned off the heater.

"I don't know!" he said, panic written into every line of his face. "But you have to let me go—you have to!"

I laughed, low and bitter. "And why the fuck would I do that?"

"Because..." He grinned, the corners of his mouth curling. "I met someone, a long time ago, who talked just like that." His tone dropped. "Someone who, just like you, couldn't help but spill the truth... Dad."

Every word landed like a punch to my face, but he wasn't done.

"I know you know. But so do I. So what's the point?" I said, my breath hitched as he began to sing, his voice was haunting me.

"Åh, sjung till tallar, låt din röst fly. Där snön faller m jukt i vinterns sky."[1]

"Stop."

My hands flew to my temples, pressing hard, but my thoughts were just like a rising tide.

---

1. Oh, sing to the pines, let your voice fly. Where the snow falls softly in the winter sky.

"Skogen talar sitt urgamla språk. En saga om livet i köldens vråk,"[2] he continued, his tone rising and falling like a taunting lullaby. "Korpen skriker där skuggorna går. Vargar ylar djupt där vinden rår. Men här i stillhet, där hjärtat slår. Hittas friden i skogens spår."[3]

"STOP!" I shouted, my vision blurring. My hand found the axe propped against the hay bales before I even realized I'd moved.

In a blind rage, I swung it with everything I had. The blade connected with a sickening crunch, biting deep below his shoulder. His arm fell in one clean piece, hitting the floor with a loud thud.

His face twisted in pain, his eyes wide with disbelief. Blood gushed from the jagged cut, pooling and spreading like a scarlet flood. His body flicked life draining from him as he fell unconscious.

"Dra åt helvete,"[4] I muttered.

---

2. "The forest speaks its ancient language. A tale of life in the cold,"

3. "The raven screams where the shadows go. Wolves howl deep where the wind blows. But here in stillness, where the heart beats. Peace is found in the tracks of the forest."

4. "Fuck off,"

Turning, I saw Lena standing in the doorway, her face cold like nothing happened at all.

"Laura's gone," she said, her words a sigh of frustration. "Erik's searching for her in the forest."

"FUCK!" I spat.

Lena's lips curved into a faint smile, "You know," she said, "pigs go crazy at the smell of blood."

TWENTY ONE

SNOWMAN

I HAD TO DRAG myself the rest of the way down the stairs and when I did, the thick smell of blood hit me before I was even on the ground. It hung in the air there, pungent and sickening, twisting my stomach. All I wanted was to collapse beside her, draw her into my arms, and squeeze her tightly. She'd been through so much, more than anyone ever should have to face. Her body was fragile, trembling whenever it was against mine.

I knew I couldn't fix her. That thought alone broke me to pieces. But damned if I wasn't going to try. No matter what it took. Even as my own mind seemed to be splitting under the strain of it all, she was the one thing that kept me grounded. I somehow knew, if I made it out of this alive, it would be for her.

The floor below was eerily quiet, each creak of the floorboards echoing as I looked around. Panic began to claw at me when I noticed that she was no longer there. My heart raced faster, my breaths coming out as short gasps as I scanned the empty room around. Then I saw it, out of the corner of my eye, lying on the floor of the room, where the door was ajar.

I ran to her, adrenaline was pumping me up. When I saw her, I felt relief, but it was short-lived, fleeting. She sat with her body slumped slightly forward, her arm over her knee. From a distance, it appeared she had perhaps been sleeping. But as I got closer, I noticed it.

The little red line streaking her arm, drops of blood, dripping slowly down. On the other hand, she held a jagged piece of broken glass, an edge sharp enough to reflect light. My stomach twisted at the thought.

She can't be.

"Fuck, Bree," I grumbled under my breath, dropping to my knees next to her. In a daze, I ripped a strip from my shirt and pressed it against her arm, attempting to stop the bleeding. She felt cold—too cold. Her pale face lay slack, and her breaths were faint.

"Bree," I whispered, stroking her hair back from her face.

I smacked her cheek lightly, having to wake her. "Come on, Bree. Wake up."

Her lids flickered, and for a split second, I saw her eyes. A knot in my chest loosened with relief. Without thinking, I picked her up, cradled her in my arms, and carried her upstairs, my heart thrumming against her cold body.

The cabin was quiet, and the air charged. I shut the door behind us, so no one would be able to come in. I placed her on the old, brown couch and raced back to the kitchen. My hands clumsily drenched the rest of my shirt in cold water, but I didn't let myself pause.

When I returned, I knelt next to her, dabbing her hands and face with the wet fabric. The cold seemed to work, her breathing grew somewhat deeper, and her eyes half-opened.

But seeing her, so fragile and pale, tightened my chest. I couldn't understand why she'd done that, why she'd hurt herself. Mel was safe now. Joe and Laura were gone. We were meant to be beyond this.

But then, deep down, I knew. I'd seen it before. People who had suffered so much pain for so long began to long for it. They thought it was all they had coming. Bree wasn't any different. She had gone through hell, and she had begun to think that was where she belonged.

My throat constricted as I washed the clotted blood from her hands. "You don't deserve this," I said, more to myself than to her. "Not this. Not any of it."

I stared at her, her face still pale, her lips slightly shaking. If pain was all she was worthy of, then I'd rather be the one to carry the burden. I'd rather be the reason she's hurting than allow her to do this to herself again. Because I couldn't take it if she hurt herself. Not again.

I leaned in, resting my forehead against hers. "Why, Bree?" I whispered the words, my voice cracking. "Why are you doing this?" Warm against my hands, her blood soaked through the bandage. "Please... tell me."

Her lips parted, her voice thin, I barely heard it. "I don't know," she whispered. "Just let me go. Please... just let me go."

Her words were like a punch and left me breathless. I swallowed and blinked away tears I did not want to fall. I couldn't let her go. I wouldn't. But I didn't know how to call her back, either.

All I could do was hold her and pray it was enough.

She turned away her back to the couch, shoulders slumped. Her hands hugged the cushions, and she wouldn't meet my eyes. When she finally spoke, her voice was barely there, just a whisper floating in the still air.

"I fell asleep," she said. "And when I closed my eyes, I saw Joe and the others. They were wearing masks... wolves, bears, wild animals. They scared me. I ran, but no matter where I hid, they found me."

"They won't find you again, Bree," I said softly. I took her hand, brushing my lips against it. "Never again."

Her breath hitched, and then the words came tumbling out. "When I was younger, Mel and I... we used to cut ourselves. We liked the feeling. I thought—" her voice broke, a sob hitching in her throat, "I thought if I did it, it'd bring us closer."

I stayed quiet, letting her get it all out.

"Now, sometimes I do it because... I'm punishing myself. For not running away sooner. For not being braver. And this habit..." She shook her head, tears spilling freely. "I'm so fucked up. Aren't I?"

I moved closer, my hand cupping hers. "We both are," I said. "But I don't want you to hurt yourself again, Bree. Promise me."

She curled into herself, knees pulled up to her chest, her voice muffled. "I don't know if I can," she whispered. "It's hard. I'm... it's hard."

"There's a way," I said, my voice low, steady. "But you have to trust me."

She finally looked at me, her eyes red, her lips shaking. "What if I can't forgive myself? What if I see you in that same light, Thor?"

"What if I told you I have needs, too?" I said, my tone barely above hers. I slid my arms around her, lifting her gently up in my hands. "Let me help you."

She didn't resist, her weight light in my arms. We stood there, holding onto each other as if we were the only things standing our ground in a world slowly breaking down. Her eyes searched mine, and I felt her shaking—felt the fear.

"I trust you," she stopped. "I know I shouldn't, but... I do."

"It's fatal attraction," I joked, the corners of my mouth twitching upward.

"It's madness," she whispered, leaning her head against my chest, her voice softening. "Maybe I'm crazy. Or maybe I'm just crazy about you."

"Maybe." I let out a low laugh. "Or maybe you're just a scared little girl."

She pulled back slightly, raising an eyebrow. "Thank God for your personalities," she said with a wry smile, mocking me in a sarcastic tone.

I chuckled, shaking my head. "You've got a way with words, Bree. You really do."

She didn't reply, just rested her head against me again as I carried her downstairs. This time, I didn't take her to the bedroom. I pushed open the door to a dark room, the hinges groaning. The scent of wood and metal felt faint in the air, and cold nubbed my skin. Chains hung from the walls, around the light of candles catching in the cold iron, and in the center stood a heavy oak table.

I set her down gently, her bare feet brushing the cold wood below. She looked around, her brows knitting together.

"Are you going to kill me now?"

"No," I said, lighting the last candle. "I'm going to show you something."

The tools on the walls gleamed in the low light; blades, hammers, hooks, not a romantic setting, but it wasn't supposed to be.

She stayed silent, her eyes darting from me to the room and back again.

"Get undressed."

"Excuse me?" she said, a nervous laugh escaping her lips.

"You heard me. Come on." I raised an eyebrow, holding her gaze. "You said you trust me, didn't you?"

"Yes, but..." She hesitated.

"I don't like waiting," I said evenly, letting my stare rest on her.

Her breath hitched, but she complied. Slowly, almost hesitantly, she lifted her arms and tugged at the top of her shirt. She wasn't sure, but there was a quiet determination in the way she pulled the fabric off her body. Her blonde curls spilled forward as her shirt slipped past her head and fluttered to the floor, leaving her in just her bra. Her pale skin bore nothing but goosebumps.

She looked at me, took a shaky breath, then stepped up to the table. Her fingers fumbled with the button of her jeans—one leg, then the other—and the pants slid down her hips, past her knees, before falling to the floor in a messy pile.

I stood with my arms crossed, watching her in silence, lit candle still in my hand. My eyes roamed, drinking in every curve, every detail. She moved beneath my stare but did not back away.

"Do you know how beautiful you are?"

Her lips smiled, and her body lowered into a squat.

"Lie down!"

She obeyed, stretching out along the cool wood of the table. Her hair fanned around her head, and her breathing steadied.

"Close your eyes."

I moved around her, circling the table slowly, like a predator, my eyes searching for the perfect spot. When I found it, I paused, letting one drop of wax land on her skin. She flinched, a sharp gasp escaping her mouth, but her eyes remained closed. The tension in her muscles eased as quickly as it had built, her lips pressed together between her teeth.

She wanted more.

I continued, one drop at a time, the wax tracing a path from the curve of her neck down to her stomach. Her skin flushed where the heat kissed it, the faintest sheen of sweat catching the light. Each drop seemed to pull her deeper into addiction, and I was here for all of it.

"Do you trust me now?" I raised my brow.

She bit her lip again, her head nodding slightly.

I slid my hand to the edge of her hips, fingers brushing under the fabric of her thong. I pulled at the fabric, sliding it down her legs, past her ankles, until I had them completely off her. The room was still, except for the soft sound of her breathing. Her chest rose and fell in rhythm with her racing heart.

"Spread your legs, Bree," I said, and she hesitated a little, but after a few seconds, she moved her legs from edge to edge of the table.

I moved my hand to her ankle, and my fingers slid gently from her foot to her inner thighs, until I was so close that my hand hovered above her. I spread her lower lips, pulled them gently upwards, and dripped the wax gently on top. She moaned softly, her hands gripped the edges of the table, holding on tightly from one side to the other.

"Do you want me to continue?"

She opened her eyes, locking onto mine.

"Not sure," she said softly, biting her lips.

The answer had already been decided, I asked just to prepare her what was coming next.

I let another drop fall, this time dangerously close to her clit. The wax landed with a soft hiss, the burn sending shivers down her skin.

"Maybe," she chuckled, her eyes closing again, surrendering once more.

I blew out the candle, wax still held its warmth. Slowly, I lowered it down, holding it upright as I positioned it near her clit again. I moved the candle side to side, the gentle pressure making her moan. Her nails scraped against the wood, leaving faint crescents on the wooden edge.

After a moment, I moved the candle and set it at the edge of the table. As the candle dropped, I grasped her legs, pulling her down to me until her hips met mine.

She spread her leg, her hands holding onto the edges of the table, trying to ground herself. She was insatiable, and her eyes consumed me, mirroring my hunger for every part of her.

I pushed her back from the edge, far enough but close enough. I walked slowly to the wall where a smaller axe with a painted edge hung. Taking it in my hands, my fingers traced the edge—dull in some places, but sharp enough. Moving to the middle of the left side of the table, I leaned over her, pressed a kiss to the curve of her stomach, and drove the axe into the edge of the table, right between her legs. She screamed so loudly in panic as the point of the axe board barely lightly brushed the tip of her clitoris.

"You're crazy!"

I moved closer to her, kissing her neck, "Crazy about you, Bree." My lips gently traced the path to her ear, whispering in a soft hum, "Ride that axe like you would ride me."

With a flick of her tongue, she wetted her lips, her eyes fixed on mine. She then retreated to the bottom of the table where the axe was. As she lifted her hips, I moved towards her, and by the time I reached her, she was thrusting the wooden handle inside her. A soft moan escaped from her lips as she adjusted herself around it. When she had taken about half of it in, I gently placed my thumb on her clitoris letting her sway and twirl around the wooden piece. Her weak legs trembled, yet she continued to move against the wood as if it were a dance that would never come again, biting down on her lip, eyes rolling back in pleasure.

As the trembling in her thighs intensified, I moved onto the table straddling over her body. My hands held onto her hips as I joined in this dance of twisted need for more, pushing her faster at times, then slower, and finally more forceful onto the edge of the axe.

I extended a hand to her, pulling her up and into my arms, her frail body collapsing against me. Her strength was spent, but the ghost of a smile graced her lips.

"Did that feel good?" I queried, "Do you want more?"

She responded with a simple nod and a coy bite of her lip. My need for her was growing bigger now. I wanted to claim every inch of her as mine. Only mine.

Unfastening my trousers, I shed them until I stood bare in front of her. I spun her around, her back brushing against my chest. Lifting one leg gently, I parted her ass cheeks, pulling her towards me with a dominant tug.

I am well aware of how big my cock is, I did not doubt that she couldn't take every inch of it. Reaching up, I unhooked a chain hanging overhead and presented it to her.

"Hold on tight," I chuckled lightly as she clung onto it tightly when I guided myself closer and plunged into the depths of her inside flesh.

"Fuck," she gasped out as she held onto the chain with all the strength she had in her.

Ignoring her gasps, my head tilted back in pleasure while my hands secured themselves on each side of her hips; pushing myself deeper and deeper inside her. Each powerful thrust was matched by an equally forceful jerk from both our bodies; our moans mingling in perfect synchrony as she took every inch of me, like the good girl she was.

The chain jangled against her breasts as I continued to thrust further into her. The feeling of her tightening around me was an indication that any moment now would have been filled with cries bearing my name. But before that could happen, my palm silenced her as I continued to thrust deeper into her. Lowering her leg, I leaned forward, straightening my back against hers while spreading her legs further apart.

Her tremors were a clear sign that she had reached her limit and it wouldn't be long before I followed suit. Removing my hand from her mouth, I allowed her screams to fill the room just as a final thrust brought me over the edge and I groaned with her.

Pulling away from her, I turned her around to face me again. Our lips met in a kiss, my tongue exploring every crevice of her mouth; searching for traces of myself.

She took my body, melted my heart, and became mine. And I vowed that she would remain so until forever. There was no one before her, there will be no one after; she is now and forever will be the only one for me.

TWENTY TWO

Snowman

Morning light streamed through the curtains, pulling me out of sleep. I blinked, my eyes blurred at first, then saw her on my chest. Birdie. She was quiet, her head tucked against me like she'd found the safest place in the world. Her breath was steady, soft against my shirt. For the first time, she wasn't crying or looking over her shoulder like she was about to run. She looked... calm.

I stayed still, not wanting to break the moment. If I could wake up like this every day, maybe life wouldn't feel so heavy.

The buzzing of my phone on the nightstand snapped me out of it. I reached over carefully, fumbling to grab it without waking her. Erik's name lit up the screen.

I slipped out of bed, moving as quietly as I could, and gently closed the door behind me before answering.

"Where the hell are you?" Erik didn't even say hello. "Are you ready?"

"Ready for what?" I muttered, still groggy. Then it hit me. "Shit. No, I forgot."

"You've got to be kidding me," he groaned. "This is our shot to get them off our backs, and you're—"

"I can't come to the office today," I cut him off, smiling to myself. "I've got to take Bree to the mansion. She doesn't belong here in this dump."

"You're unbelievable," he said, though I could hear him laugh under his breath. "I miss the old you, you know. The one who had everything under control."

"That guy needed a break," I said simply.

"What's the plan, then?" he asked.

Erik never said it outright, but I could tell he was worried. About me. About everything.

"You'll see."

"Fine. Just... don't overdo it, all right?" He laughed again. "Have fun."

"Always." I hung up.

I shoved the phone into my pocket and headed upstairs to the old filing cabinet. The plan was simple, or at least it felt simple when Erik and I planned it out last night.

We wanted to write a letter from a witness, someone who'd supposedly seen Isak creeping around the victims. The Snowman. It was airtight, every detail thought through. And it had to be because this wasn't just about blame, it was about Bree.

Ever since I saw him with her, I wanted to tear him apart. Not just him, Joe, Laura, the whole fucking mess they dragged her into. Erik had kept me from going on a rampage, though. He said revenge without control wasn't revenge—it was suicide. So, we went with the plan instead.

Once Isak was out of the picture, I'd take Bree to the mansion. That place was safe, bought with the money Erik and I found after our father died. Buried under the floorboards in the stable, it was enough to keep us set for life.

Lena wanted nothing to do with it. She hated the money, hated the memories tied to it, but Erik and I weren't so sentimental. We used it to build something better, or at least something different. We buried the past along with our father, taking new names to make sure no one connected us.

The cult, the Family, it all died with him.

But the past doesn't let go so easily. I could still feel the weight of it, the scars my father left behind. The beatings. The madness in his eyes, when he talked about "the plan" like it was some divine prophecy. Most of the cult left when it fell apart, running as far away as they could. Some left the country, but only some stayed behind.

We all swore an oath: the Family was dead, and no one would ever speak of it again. If the day came, we'd help each other, no questions asked. But some things don't stay buried, no matter how deep you dig the hole.

Joe always tried to be like him, imitating him. But he was never clever enough to pull it off. And honestly, I was relieved. Someone like Joe with that kind of edge would've been dangerous. Easier to deal with him. Easily silenced, easily forgotten.

I pushed those thoughts away. What mattered now was beginning over. Bree deserved peace. Hell, so did I.

I pulled on my gloves and unfolded a clean sheet of paper. My hand hesitated, but soon I began to write, word after word, leaving nothing that could point back to me.

"On the last Friday of November, I was walking my dog when I saw something in the snow. Footprints, a man's, size 45. I'm sure because my boots are four sizes smaller. The tracks were fresh, made by someone in thick-soled boots.

Later, I saw him at the station, during questioning. When I realized he was the one asking the questions, I walked out. I didn't trust him.

Then I saw him again, watching the house of the new family in town. He wasn't hiding it, either, just staring at the girls inside. I followed him. He went into the woods, and I saw him building a snowman. Don't ask me why I didn't stay long enough to find out.

But one thing sticks in my head: he carries a white silk scarf in his pocket. Every time I see him, he's sniffing it like it's something dear to him. He has long hair and blue eyes. You know who he is. He's the new detective, and I think you've suspected him for a while now."

I signed nothing. No name, no trace. At the top, I wrote For the Chief of Police.

As I pushed the letter into a plastic bag, Lena walked in.

Perfect timing.

I handed out the bag to her, and she took it with a doubtful smile.

"Take this to the station," I said. "Use the blue door by the morgue on the left side. No cameras there. Drop it in the mailbox, but don't leave any fingerprints. Take the letter out of the bag first. Keep the bag. Got it?"

"Crystal," she said but paused at the door. "Any sign of Laura?"

"No," I said. "I don't think she made it through the night."

"Yeah," Lena said softly. "You've changed, you know. Since Bree. If she makes you better, maybe... maybe let this go. Live your life."

"I'm trying," I said.

A lump rose in my throat, surprising me. How long had it been since I hugged her? Years? Maybe longer. Before I could second-guess myself, I stepped forward and opened my arms. Lena froze for a second, then let me pull her into a quick, awkward hug.

"See?" I said, letting her go with a faint smile. "We can do normal."

She laughed nervously. "You're creeping me out."

"Fair enough," I said, raising my hands.

She laughed, shaking her head as she opened the door. The cold wind swept inside, biting at my face.

"Lena," I said before she stepped out. "Thank you. For everything. You've done more for me than you had to."

She looked back, her eyes softening. "You're welcome," she said.

Then she was gone.

The house was quiet again. I stared at the closed door, her words in my mind. Lena wasn't a good mother, she never had been. But she'd been the only one who ever tried. And in her way, she was enough.

It was just past noon when we got into the car. I told Bree earlier it was a surprise where I was taking her. She didn't know where I lived, but today, I wanted her to see it. To show her that what was mine could be hers too.

She sank into the seat, leaning back as if trying to get comfortable, her gaze fixed straight ahead. A quiet smile tugged at her lips, one of those soft ones that seemed to sneak up without her noticing.

"It's weird," she said after a moment, brushing her fingers lightly over her mouth. "Smiling this much. My face feels sore."

I laughed, turning the key. The engine rolled to life, and the car eased away from the farmhouse.

"It looks good on you," I said, looking at her.

She shot me a quick look, her smile twitching wider. My right hand stayed on the wheel, but my left drifted without thought, resting lightly on her thigh. The sun poured through the windshield, washing everything in a golden haze. She tilted her head, the light catching her hair in a way that made it gleam.

She leaned her head onto my shoulder, and I reached for the radio with my free hand, hoping for something calm to fill the silence. Instead, the sharp voice of a reporter stated from it.

"Joining us now is profiler Frida Dahl, who successfully apprehended the Snowman Killer this morning. Frida, can you tell us more about the case?"

Frida's voice came next. "A tip early this morning provided crucial evidence, confirming our suspicions about the suspect. With that, we were able to bring him into custody without resistance."

I reached over and twisted the volume down, but not fast enough to stop Bree from catching it. She shifted, lifting her head from my shoulder to look at me.

"What's going on?" she asked, her brow furrowing. "Who's in custody?"

Her voice was steady, but I knew her well enough to hear the undercurrent of worry. I kept my eyes on the road, my grip tightening on the wheel. I wasn't ready to tell her. Not about Isak. Not yet.

"Nothing we need to think about right now," I said, keeping my tone light.

She studied me for a moment, her eyes narrowing. "And where the hell are we going, then?"

"Home," I said simply.

Her shoulders rose in a small huff, but she let it go. Her face softened as she turned back to the window, the tension sliding away. I reached over, brushing her hair back from her neck. My fingers lingered for a moment, and she turned back to me with a smile.

She kissed the back of my hand. "Okay," she said. "You don't have to tell me."

The sunlight caught her hair again as she turned away, making her look almost unreal for a moment. Every second with her felt electric, like my blood was too hot like I was burning up from the inside out. Last night flickered in the back of my mind, her laugh, her touch, the way she'd looked at me like I was the only thing in the world.

The road stretched out endlessly. Twenty minutes of driving felt like hours, but I spotted my house in the distance. It should have brought relief, but it only stoked the fire. I couldn't wait.

I turned the wheel hard, veering onto a side road without thinking twice. The car turned as gravel crunched beneath the tires, and I slammed the brakes, the sudden stop throwing us forward slightly. The road here was quiet, secluded, and forgotten by most, it was perfect.

"What are you doing?" Bree's voice broke the silence.

I didn't answer.

Words felt useless when all I could think about was her. I reached for her face, cupping her cheeks, and brought her lips to mine. The kiss was deep, searching, the taste of her like something I needed to survive. She froze for a second, startled, before melting into me, her arms wrapping around my neck.

"You're crazy," she whispered when we finally broke apart.

"Maybe," I murmured, leaning back and pushing my seat as far as it would go. My heart was pounding, and I grabbed her hand, guiding it to rest against the hardness between my legs.

Her eyes widened slightly, and she raised an eyebrow, her lips twitching in a smirk. "What now?"

"You know what, now."

Her lower lip was caught between her teeth as she slid towards me, the soft brush of her knees against mine sending sparks up my spine. Her gaze never wavered from mine as she positioned herself above me.

My hands traced the curve of her hips, fingers lightly skimming over the fabric of her black pants. I couldn't resist sliding my hands beneath the waistband, my fingertips meeting the warmth of her skin on mine. Her breath hitched in response. I pulled the fabric, ripping through it.

The sound causes her to gasp in surprise. "Seriously?"

"Seriously," I confirmed, pulling her closer and steadying my hands on her hips once more. Our lips met again in a slower kiss this time, every inch between us was a warm sign, making reality itself seem distant in comparison to us.

A giggle escaped from her as she drew closer still while I undid my pants and stood briefly to slide them down; my cock stood still in the air beneath her.

As I settled back down into the seat once more and took hold of myself, I thrust myself along her inner flesh, her moans filled the space around us until finally, she let herself fully onto me, her head falling back in pleasure.

"That's right, Bree, take it all," I encouraged as she moved against me.

My hands locked her hips and guided her movements; the pace quickened to a point where I was losing control. But it wasn't just about me, I wanted her to feel the same intensity that she brought me.

I shifted our position so that Bree was leaning against the steering wheel, my hand slipping under her shirt to gently knead at her breasts while my other hand traced circles over her clitoris. Her palm hit the window beside her as she teetered on the edge, but I withdrew my touch just in time, driving into her with such force that the honking of the horn echoed our shared pace.

"That's right, Bree, let everyone know you're mine," I chuckled as steam began to fog up the windows. The cold outside was no match for the heat inside. We didn't make love, it was raw and primal sex. She was an addiction I would go to hell for, a temptation I craved completely.

Resuming my attention on her clitoris once more, I sent waves coursing through her until she began to shake from their intensity. She pressed back against me again and moved as her desperate cries filled the car.

"Fuck, fuck," she moaned out breathlessly.

Now it was my turn to take control. Lifting myself to meet each thrust without leaving anything untouched, the tightness of her inner flesh only fueled me further. I grabbed hold of Bree and pulled her closer as I thrust harder into her.

Sweat broke out across my forehead as gritted teeth held back any sounds threatening to escape. I wanted her to reach another brink. When her screams filled the car again and she clung onto the seat belt for support, I gave into my end, filling her.

Her body collapsed onto mine and we stayed like that, unwilling to move just yet. But the desire to have her all to myself again was too strong to resist.

I pulled the seat close enough to reach the pedals and started up the car.

As she laid on me, I realized it wasn't the best circumstance, but I started driving while my cock was still within her. Feeling every inch inside. The ride stretched into an endless ten minutes until we arrived outside the mansion.

"We're home," I whispered.

TWENTY THREE

BREE

The cold air bit at my legs, slipping under the edge of his black sweater that only managed to warm my upper body. My arm still hurt from the fresh wound; I hadn't noticed until now that blood was still dripping down. I turned to look at him. His chestnut hair, icy blue eyes that saw too much, the sharp lines of his face that softened only when he smiled. His beard scratched against my cheek when we were close, I couldn't get enough of it. With him, everything else faded. How could something so real disappear in just a day?

They say love makes you lose yourself, your brain floats up into the clouds, forgetting everything that once seemed so important. Maybe that's true, or maybe I was just caught up in the way he made me feel. People say love weakens you, but I felt stronger than ever.

Mel was okay, Joe and Laura, were gone. I didn't ask why or how. Somehow, it was easier not to know. The silence left space to pretend.

He stepped closer, his arms sliding around me before I could react. He lifted me onto his back, making me yelp in surprise. His hand came down against my bare skin, spanking me.

"Ready, Mrs. Karlsson?" he teased, his voice light.

"Karlsson?" I chuckled. "Did you do something I don't remember?"

His laugh was warm, rolling through the cold as he carried me to the front door, opened it, and set me down. His hands cupped my face, his touch grounding me.

"Not yet," he said with a soft growl.

I wasn't afraid. I wasn't drowning in thoughts of what could go wrong or what had already happened. I just existed, here and now. My mind, usually dark and chaotic, felt quiet. Not empty, but peaceful. I wasn't just fine, I was okay. That alone felt so real.

I laughed under my breath, my fingers brushing against my lips as the memory of last night flickered through my mind. The way his body moved with mine, the way he left me trembling, wanting for more.

"You coming?" His voice pulled me back to the present. He was waiting near the staircase. When he caught me openly staring, he arched an eyebrow and walked toward me.

Before I could say anything, he scooped me up again, throwing me over his shoulder.

"You know I can walk, right?"

"I know," he said, laughing as he landed another smack on my ass.

He carried me up the stairs, the glass railings reflecting fragments of our steps as we moved. The black and white tiled floors in the hallway blurred together as we passed, hypnotizing me. The house was modern, and clean, but layered with something raw. Animal pelts draped over chairs, skulls, and old guns hung like forgotten memories on the walls.

At the end of the hall, a nearly invisible door blended seamlessly into the white walls. He pushed it open and stepped into a bedroom where a circular bed held a court in the middle, its frame made from polished marble as white as fresh snow that covered the ground outside. Windows stretched from floor to ceiling, circling the room, revealing an uninterrupted view of snow-covered meadows and dense woodlands.

"It's beautiful," I said quietly, my hand finding its place against his chest. "Your home is beautiful."

"Ours," he corrected, pulling me closer. His voice dropped as he whispered, "Our home is beautiful. Just like you."

His words wrapped around me, words I was not used to. If they could melt the snow outside, I would have let them melt me, too. He was so kind to me, despite the pain he carried. He still found ways to build something beautiful. And somehow, I was part of it.

But I knew his pain, and that kind of pain had carved itself into me so deeply that I couldn't separate it from who I was. But with him, this pain was bearable, real.

I was falling for him. For a man so cold, a man who lived his life in the dark but made space for me in his light. A man who killed for me. And I know, without question, I would let myself die for him, too.

He moved to a shelf by the wall, where an old radio was. As he turned the button, his voice crackled, and he stood there, listening.

"We can positively confirm that the primary suspect in the investigation is an ex-detective named Isak Storm."

The voice on the radio made my stomach drop.

I turned to him, his name already slipping out in a shaky breath. "Thor? What's going on?"

He didn't answer.

His hand shot out, twisting the radio knob to silence it. He stood there, shoulders low, jaw clenched, his silence pressing against my chest.

"Did you blame it on him?" I asked, my voice steadier than I felt.

He didn't look at me, didn't move. My heart was pounding, and I took a step closer, pushing him lightly. "Thor, did you?"

Still nothing.

"Answer me!" My voice cracked as I pushed him again, harder this time.

Finally, he lifted his head, meeting my eyes.

"I did. He pretended to be me to get close to you. Don't you think he deserves to pay for that?"

I froze.

I didn't even know how to respond.

He wasn't lying; I knew that much. But he wasn't telling the whole truth either.

Isak wasn't Snowman, Thor was. Thor knew it. I knew it. And still, he stood there, as though nothing about this situation was twisted or wrong.

"It's not right," I said, pushing him again. My hands trembled, but I didn't stop. "You can't just... you can't live with this, and you know it."

"Would you rather it be me?"

His voice rose, anger bleeding into each word he spat. "Is that what you want? To see me behind bars?"

"No!" My hands pressed flat against his chest, and I pushed again, tears stinging my eyes. "How could you even think of that?"

I kept pushing him, words tumbling out. "Do you think I could stand that? Watching you waste away because of this? Because of him?"

My fists beat against his chest now, anger rising inside me. He staggered back, and his back hit the wall with a dull thud.

Above him, a deer skull with sprawling antlers hung on the wall. The force of his body knocked it loose, and it fewn, landing hard against his leg. He shouted in pain, dropping to one knee. I rushed toward him, but he didn't look at me.

His eyes were locked on the skull, his chest heaving as he stared at it. His breathing slowed, then deepened, the sound growing heavier each second.

"Thor?" I said, kneeling next to him.

He didn't answer.

His fingers reached for the skull, shaking slightly as he picked it up.

"Thor, stop," I pleaded, but he wasn't listening. He was somewhere else.

Slowly, he pulled the antlers up to his face, twisting off the wood mount at the back. I watched, frozen, as he placed the skull over his head.

The empty lifeless sockets stared back at me.

"Thor?" My voice trembled.

I staggered to my feet. He turned to me, the antlers swaying as he moved.

Thor I knew was gone. All that was left was this... thing.

"Thor, please." My voice cracked, but he didn't respond.

He stepped forward, tilting his head like he was scanning me.

Then he laughed. It wasn't his laugh, this was deeper, rougher, and wrong in every way.

"Oh, birdie, birdie," he said, his voice a low rasp. "You're the one who won't leave my fucking mind, huh?"

I stumbled back, panicking.

He moved closer, closing the distance between us in seconds. His hand shot out, taking my arm and pulling me against him.

He leaned in, his mask with antlers hovering inches from my face, and his tongue dragged across my cheek, leaving a trail that made me shudder.

My stomach flipped, and I tried to twist away, but his hands tightened around me.

He leaned into my ear, growling. **"Run."**

This wasn't Snowman. This wasn't Thor. Someone else was in his body, someone I didn't recognize.

My heart raced as I pushed him hard, watching him stumble backward onto the bed.

I didn't wait to see if he got up. I just ran. My feet slid on the hallway tiles as I scrambled toward the stairs.

I could barely breathe.

My whole body felt like it was moving through molasses, but I forced myself forward. The mirrored glass staircase caught the low light and, I knew, this was the beginning of a nightmare. I grabbed the railing, my sweaty palms slipping as I ran, stumbling down.

At the last second, I made the mistake of looking back.

He was there.

The deer skull mask covered his face, those hollow eye sockets boring into me. His bare chest shimmered, every muscle tensed and alive under his skin. He still had the black jeans on from earlier, but now his hand gripped an axe.

A scream tore out of me, and I sprinted down the last few steps, my legs wobbling. It was useless, I hit the bottom, and his hand was already in my hair, yanking me back so hard I thought my neck might snap.

"It's my fucking turn now," he growled, pulling me closer until I could feel his breath against my ear. "You have no idea how long I've been waiting."

Panic took over. I didn't think, I just reacted. My elbow drove into his stomach with everything I had. His grip loosened, and I broke free, running toward the front door.

It was locked.

"No, no, no!" I clawed at the lock, my fingers trembling. I spun around, desperate, and there he was, laughing, enjoying the whole fucking thing.

He raised the axe, and it came down, slamming into the door behind me. I screamed again, but it didn't stop him. He just kept laughing.

This thing, whatever it was, didn't have a shred of humanity left. It felt like I was looking at some kind of revenant, something that had crawled out of the woods to hunt me.

I ran, slipping past the door and into the living room. My foot caught on the carpet, and I went down, the air knocked out of me.

I tried so hard to get up, but his hand closed around my ankle. He didn't just grab me, he dragged me. The carpet burned against my skin as I clawed at it, trying to hold on to anything. He didn't stop until we were back at the staircase.

The mirrored steps caught everything. His mask, his body, and me reflected in broken pieces.

"Birdie," he said, tilting his head. "What a cute little name. But you're not just cute, are you?"

I didn't answer. I couldn't. My throat was too tight.

"You like this, don't you?" he taunted, his tone almost playful. "Being chased. Tsk, tsk, tsk."

He shoved me further up the stairs. My body collapsed onto the cold mirror, I felt the glass dig into my palms as I tried to push myself upright.

Before I could move, he was on me, his full weight pressing me down. I couldn't breathe, couldn't think.

His mask was just a breath away from my own, his fingers tracing a slow path beneath my sweater, across my chest. Yet, there was no discomfort, no fear. I knew it was Thor, even if he wasn't fully aware of it at that moment.

He lifted my sweater over my head and used it to bind my hands above me. His face moved down, traveling from the rise of my breasts to the flat of my stomach, the silhouette of deer antlers framing my face.

Every brush of his skin against mine sent shivers rippling through me, but I didn't pull away. I craved for him. With one knee he nudged apart my thighs and bent his head lower still. My trousers lay in tatters around us, I was naked from earlier.

"Hold still," he commanded.

As I nodded, he widened the distance between my legs further apart. Turning my gaze to the reflective mirror of the railing next to me, I saw him dropping slowly towards me.

As his masked face hovered over mine, he lowered the antlers of his mask and glided on my clit with their tips. A soft moan escaped from between my lips as I sank lower onto him; this time feeling part of one horn slide inside me, locking me onto him.

The bone structure of the horn was shaped as an 'L', with a shorter side at the base that now pierced me, and an extended higher half with three more protrusions on top.

As he moved between my thighs, the horns grazed against my butt hole, probing.

He removed his mask, drawing nearer, the horns persisting within me, securing the mask onto me as he drove the horns deeper within. I completely surrendered myself to him. Both horns were lodged inside me; he was thrusting them further in and I craved for more.

"You're soaked," he said, retracting one of the horns from within me.

He freed my hands from the sweater and commanded, "Turn around and kneel."

I turned around, my palms resting on the middle step, while my knees found comfort on the step beneath it. I could feel how wet I was, I could feel how the drops fell onto the mirrored floor, and my legs were wide open for him, spine curved into an arch and I begged for more.

He broke both horns off the mask and moved closer, his face hovering above, lips parted, saliva sliding down to my backside, and he poked it with his finger before sliding his thumb inside. I sobbed, my knees buckled. He pulled out his finger and slowly stuck the horn inside, inch by inch.

He placed the other end of the horn against my clit, rapidly shifting it from side to side. My eyelids fell shut, teeth gnawing at my lower lip.

"Snowman, I need Snowman," I whimpered but was met with nothing more than a raw chuckle from behind.

"Sorry, birdie, you're stuck with me," he said as he lifted the antler, hooking me onto it and spiraling within me. I could feel every single twist and turn inside me.

Then he moved closer; his trousers hit the glass floor with a soft thud and one antler clinked against it. He tormented me with the tip of his cock, easing into me slowly as he simultaneously tugged at my backside with the antler. He thrust inside me so hard that it brought me to my knees, but his arms were around me, keeping me upright.

He pulled the antler out of me and threw it onto the steps, and with his hands spread my ass cheeks and thrust himself deeper and deeper into me. Each thrust became more intense until I fell down. He picked me up gently, guiding me before him until I found myself kneeling again.

"Open your mouth," he said as his hands gripped my hair, and I knew what was coming.

I looked at him with a fire in my eyes, parting my lips and allowing my tongue to pop out.

He leaned in, placing his cock into my waiting mouth, pushing it further in. His hands found the back of my head, gripping firmly as he drove himself deeper within me. The air escaped from my lungs, a gasping struggle for breath that seemed futile against his relentless pace. I felt my eyes blur, and my breath was gone, but he just continued, his palm delivering sharp slaps across my face while shouting, "BREATHE."

He continued to thrust inside, my throat aching from the constant pressure. In a moment, the only sounds permeating the air were my choked sobs. Then he released me, placing me back on the staircase. The chill of the stone steps seeped through my torn clothes as I sat there, clothes ripped and scattered around us.

Parting my legs once more, settling himself between them. He drew me closer and continued his pace.

I screamed again, every fiber of my being protesting in pain yet craving for more.

I was addicted.

To pain.

To him.

To every single version of him.

TWENTY FOUR

Snowman

"Snowman," she called. "I need Snowman. Please, Snowman, come to me."

The last hour was blank; no images, no sounds, no memories. I didn't know how I ended up in this room. Bree was on the bed, her arms clutching a blanket against her bare skin. Moonlight slipped through the curtains, casting her in a pale glow. My chest tightened. My head felt like it was packed with static.

I pressed my hands against my face, trying to ground myself.

"What happened?"

When I looked at her, she pulled the blanket tighter. I reached out, instinct taking over, but she flinched. Her reaction stopped me cold.

"Don't touch me," her voice was trembling.

Her words cut deep, but I couldn't stop myself. "Bree," I said softly. "What happened?"

She stayed silent for a moment, her eyes flicking to mine, then away. Finally, she inched closer, hesitant. Her hands, shaking, found my face. The touch was so light I barely felt it.

"Thor?" she whispered, her voice fragile.

I frowned. "Yeah, it's me. Who else would it be?"

She stared at me, her lips pressed into a thin line. Then, without warning, she wrapped her arms around me. Her body trembled against mine, and I froze, unsure of what to do. Her grip tightened like she was afraid I'd disappear.

"What happened?" I murmured again, the question catching in my throat.

She pulled back just enough to meet my eyes. Her lips parted, but the words seemed to stick. Finally, she said, "Did you know you have someone else? In you?"

I blinked. "What?"

Her fingers curled into the fabric of my shirt. "Not Snowman. Someone... someone else. You scared me."

My stomach dropped. The room felt like it was spinning. I'd always known something was wrong with me, I always knew I had a Snowman who could resurface at each moment. But this? Someone else? Someone who hurt her? The thought made my chest ache.

"Did I hurt you?"

She shook her head, but her eyes told a different story. They darted away, unable to meet mine. "You scared me, that's all," she whispered.

I didn't need her to say more. I knew. Deep down, I knew.

"Bree, I swear," I said, my voice cracking. I pressed a kiss to her forehead, trying to hold myself together. "I would never hurt you. Never."

Her shoulders shook as she covered her face with her hands.

"You had no control," she said through her fingers. "None."

"I'm sorry," I said, the words tumbling out in a rush. I kissed her forehead again, lingering as if it could erase everything. Then I stepped back.

"I can't..." My voice broke. "I can't stay."

She didn't stop me as I turned and walked to the door.

I couldn't face her, couldn't look at the bruises I knew I'd caused. The sight of her curled up on the bed, clutching that blanket like a lifeline, was enough to break me.

I needed to get out.

The hallway was dim, the tiles cool under my feet. My eyes blurred as I stumbled forward, my steps uneven. At the top of the stairs, I froze.

A broken deer skull lay on the floor, its jagged antlers glinting in the faint light. Around it were scraps of torn clothes. My stomach twisted. I held the railing to keep from collapsing.

A scream clawed its way out of my throat. It echoed through the house, bouncing off the walls. The door creaked open behind me, but I didn't turn around. I couldn't.

I staggered down the stairs, each step heavier than the last. At the bottom, I found a dark sweater crumpled on the floor. I pulled it on, the fabric scratching my skin, and stumbled out into the night. The cold air hit me like a slap, but I barely felt it.

The car was parked in the driveway, its windows fogged from the chill. I climbed in, gripping the wheel with my trembling hands. The engine roared to life, loud in the quiet night.

Without looking back, I drove away.

I didn't want to leave her. I never wanted it to end. But I needed to breathe. Just for a second, I needed to step back and clear my head. Something didn't sit right. Was the person she mentioned the same one Joe had called out in the barn? The thought gnawed at me, but the harder I tried to focus, the further it slipped away. My mind felt like it wasn't mine anymore.

Snowman, at least, I could control. Over the years, I'd learned how to reach him, leave notes, plant the right images, and guide his hand. But when I saw that new name tacked on the board at the station, somehow, it had to be connected.

It had to be.

The sharp buzz of my phone yanked me back to the moment. I fumbled for it, fingers stiff, and saw Eric's name flashing on the screen.

"What's going on?" I asked, trying to steady my voice.

"Lena," Eric's voice was shaky, his breath coming in short bursts. "Mom..." His words cracked, barely holding together. "Someone... someone burned the farm down."

My chest tightened.

"Do you know who?" I asked, my voice flat, almost cold.

He didn't answer right away. When he spoke again, his words were fragile, like they might shatter. "Lena's dead, Thor."

My world stopped. Everything went quiet. Just... nothing.

"No."

My voice was barely above a whisper. "That's impossible."

"Thor, I'm looking at her. I'm looking at her body."

The phone slipped out of my hand and fell onto the seat. I didn't reach for it. My hands found the wheel instead. The car swerved as I spun it around, tires screeching on the cold road ahead. I floored it, the needle climbing past 200 kilometers per hour, the engine roaring as the road blurred ahead of me.

I had to see it for myself. I couldn't believe it. Not her. Not like this.

How do you even begin to process losing someone? She was my mom, but she wasn't a perfect mother. She stood by me when I needed her most, silent when I begged for help without saying a word. She saved me in her way, but she also let me suffer. There was love there, but it was buried under so much anger, resentment, words we had never said.

And now she was gone.

"Fuck!" I yelled, slamming my hand against the steering wheel. The sting shot up my arm, but it wasn't enough to drown out the storm in my chest. I hit it again. And again.

I had just seen her. That morning, she'd been right there. How could this be real?

I blinked hard, my vision swimming. This wasn't just about her. It was everything. Everyone. People around me kept dying, slipping through my fingers no matter how hard I tried to hold on. I was always too late. Always too helpless.

"Fuck," I muttered this time.

Lena was gone.

And I couldn't save her.

The farm was gone. Nothing but gray ash stretched across the land. It was all gone. Only the stable stood intact, a few pigs wandered near, their snorts and shuffle the only sounds breaking the silence.

Erik sat on the wooden fence, staring at the pigs and what was left of the farm. He was still, sunglasses hiding his face, but I knew him well enough to read the slump in his shoulders. Erik never wore sunglasses. Not unless he was trying to hide the tears.

"Hey," I said quietly, walking over and sitting next to him on the fence.

He didn't look at me, just let out a small laugh. "Had to tell them not to touch the pigs. Told them I would shoot the first one who tried."

"Yeah," I said. "You should've just told them you're emotionally attached."

He huffed a laugh, shaking his head. "If they knew what those pigs ate... they would have backed away without me saying a word."

I raised an eyebrow. "No evidence yet in the pig shit?"

His smile fainted, "She burned alive, Thor."

I froze.

"Who did this?"

"They haven't told anyone yet, but I've got a bad feeling. I think... Mom was involved. Ingrid was Donna's cousin."

My stomach turned. "Are you saying Donna and Jan had something to do with this?"

"Yeah," he said, finally looking at me. His jaw was tight, his voice low. "Everyone knows Jan's been screwing Donna. They probably cooked this up together."

He rubbed the back of his neck. "And everyone knew why women went to Lena. She helped them, so they decided to burn a witch."

I let the words sink in, staring at the ashed ruins. "Do you know where they are?"

"No," he said. "And we can't risk it. Frida's all over everyone since Isak got arrested."

The snow under my boots crunched as I shifted. My hands were clenched into fists, nails biting into my palms.

"They'll be my last," I said. "I'm done after this. I almost hurt Bree..."

Erik turned sharply, his sunglasses slipping down his nose. "What the hell did you do?"

"I don't know," I said, my voice hollow. "I blacked out. Found the axe at the door. She said it wasn't the Snowman."

Erik exhaled, running a hand through his hair. "Maybe it was foreplay," he said, raising his hands and mimicking an exaggerated chopping motion.

"Not exactly her style."

"Good," he muttered, but the faint smile faded quickly. "Man, don't tell me there are fifty of you. I don't think I can handle that kind of crazy."

"Neither can I," I admitted.

He studied me for a moment before asking, "So, what's the plan? You're really gonna do it?"

I nodded, standing and brushing the snow off my pants. "Yeah. I'll burn them."

Erik stood too, slower like he was carrying a weight I couldn't see. "She wasn't a good mom," he said after a pause. "And I've never wanted to kill anyone before. But this time? I want to help."

I looked at him, then toward the car. "Let's go, then. The more, the merrier."

We started walking towards the car, the snow crunching under our boots in a steady rhythm. The air was cold enough to sting, but it didn't matter. Nothing mattered except what came next.

As the car rumbled to life and we pulled onto the icy road, I didn't look back at the farm. There was nothing left to see.

For a moment, I forgot about Bree. Forgot about everything. I let Snowman take over. I had to. If I didn't stay in that dark, ruthless place, I wouldn't have the nerve to do what needed to be done. Jan and Donna had to pay for what they did to my mother. No one else was going to make sure of that, just me.

We parked a block from Jan's house, but still from here, I could see through their front window. The lights inside were warm, Jan and Donna were dancing in the living room, their laughter was taunting me. My fists curled tight, nails digging into my palms. The sight of them, the way they looked so happy, so normal, made my stomach turn.

Erick leaned over. "You ready?"

I blinked and forced myself to focus. "Yeah."

I reached for the plastic mask on the dashboard and slid it over my face. The cool, hard plastic pressed against it like a second skin. The railway mirror caught my reflection, blank, cold, like the person I was before had disappeared. It was what I needed.

Snowman.

"You really had to pick the red mask?" I asked, glancing at Erick. He was tugging on a red ski mask with a dragon sticker across the front.

"It's Julia's," he said, not looking at me. "It was this or the pink one with a unicorn."

I snorted, shaking my head. "You'd pull off pink better, it goes with your eyes."

"What, are you the fashion police now?" he muttered, grabbing the door handle. He stopped, and looked back at me.

"You good?"

"Yeah," I said again, softer this time.

The truth was, I didn't know.

But it didn't matter.

I had to be.

We crouched through the wooden area, circling to the back of the house. Erik moved like he'd done this a hundred times before, and I was right behind him. When we reached the back door, he pulled a thin screw from his pocket and worked the lock. The faint click was barely louder than the rustle of leaves behind us. He opened the door slowly, motioning for me to follow.

The inside of the house smelled like cinnamon and pine, holiday cheer that had no place in my life. We moved through the dark hallway, staying close to the walls. The sound of Christmas music spilled out from the living room, along with bursts of laughter.

At the edge of the doorway, I stopped. Erick crouched beside me, gun in hand, waiting for the signal. I straightened my back, adjusted the mask one last time, and walked into the room.

The music kept playing. Jan and Donna were in their own little world, spinning and laughing, dancing. For a moment, I just stood there, watching them. Then I stepped forward, moving with the music, my boots tapping softly on the floor. They didn't notice at first. I raised my arms and spun around, dancing alongside them.

Donna saw me first, she froze, her face going pale. Jan followed her gaze and turned, his face shifting in fear.

I tilted my head.

"Don't stop on my account," I said.

Jan fumbled for the remote and turned off the music.

"Oh, fuck, that was my favorite part."

I reached into my pocket and pulled out the knife.

"Jingle bells," I sang softly to myself. "Jingle bells, jingle knife away," I spun around, twirling the blade in my hand. My tone, almost teasing, tore them apart, and I just took a step closer, singing, "Oh, what fun it is to ride the blade," I giggled.

"In a one-horse open... slayed." I spun again. "Dashing through the snow," I sang softly, "making Snowman go."

Taking a step forward, "To slash your throat," I whispered, drawing closer, lifting the knife in the air.

Donna grabbed Jan's arm, her fingers brushing against his shirt. He stepped in front of her, his hands up in a shaky attempt to calm her.

"You're supposed to be in prison," he shouted, his voice cracking.

I took a step closer. "The funny thing about bars--they don't hold as well when you don't exist."

From behind, I heard Erik shouting, "Why did you burn the farm?"

"Please," Donna whispered, her voice trembling. "We didn't..."

"Lies." His voice cut through the room as he stepped forward, the gun steady. "You burned the farm. Don't even try to deny it."

Jan backed up until his shoulders hit the wall. "We can talk about this," he said, desperate. "We can figure this out."

I stared at him, at the panic in his eyes. I could feel the rage rising, but it wasn't the wildfire I expected. It was cold, and sharp, like he didn't care at all.

I tilted my head, studying him. "Talk?" I said quietly. "Sure. Let's talk."

Erik pressed the gun into Jan's neck, and he flinched, his breath hitching so rapidly. "Ingrid left a diary," he started, words tumbling over each other. "It... it talked about the cult, the family, and Lena." He looked at Donna as if she might save him.

"We just went to talk to her, I swear. But she... she freaked out! She came at us, and Jan hit her, and she fell," she whispered.

Erik's eyes narrowed, the tension in his body coiling tighter.

"The fire," Jan said quickly, his voice rising, "it was an accident! That's all it was."

"No," I said, cutting through his excuses. "She was alive. You left her there. You let her burn."

Donna's lip quivered as she spoke, "If we'd known, we wouldn't—"

"You wouldn't do a damn thing," Erik snapped. "Because this is who you are. This is what you do." He was shaking now, his fury barely contained.

I could see it, he was about to break.

"Take a walk," I said, stepping toward him.

"But—"

"Now!"

Erik stared at me for a moment, his chest heaving, then turned and stormed out. The door slammed behind him, leaving nothing but silence.

They both turned to me, I could see a trace of hope in their eyes, but for nothing. I tilted my head toward the kitchen, and shouted, "Move."

Donna hesitated, but Jan was already shuffling toward the kitchen island, his knees trembling. As they sat down in the wooden chairs, I reached into Erik's bag and pulled out the duct tape. The ripping sound echoed the room as I taped their wrists and ankles to the chairs. It wasn't precise, but it held.

Jan looked up at me, his lip trembling. "Please," he started, but I cut him off.

I yanked his shirt, the fabric tearing easily in my hands, and I tied the strip across his mouth, muffling his voice. His breathing turned shallow, panicked.

I moved to the sink, filled a pot with water, and turned back to him.

"Where's the diary?" I asked, my voice flat.

Jan shook his head violently. "It burned on the farm!" he mumbled through the cloth.

I tipped the pot forward, water pouring over his face. He gasped and sputtered, his body jerking against the chair.

"Try again," I said, refilling the pot at the sink.

"I'm not lying!" he cried, struggling to breathe, his voice desperate.

"Sure," I muttered, dousing him again. His head snapped back as he choked, his chest rising and falling in sharp bursts as he gasped for air.

I turned to Donna, her eyes wide as I approached, "You?" I asked.

She shook her head quickly, her voice shaking. "Did you... did you kill my son?"

The question hung in the air for a moment without answer, her eyes following mine, looking for truth.

Then words came through, "I did," I said finally.

Her sobs broke free, and she collapsed against the tape, her whole body shook. I just watched her for a moment, detached. Her grief didn't move me, I just simply didn't care.

I turned to the stove, twisting the knob, the soft hiss of gas filled the room.

"No!" Donna's cries grew frantic. "Please! No!" She thrashed against the chair, the tape straining but holding still.

I didn't answer.

I let the gas spread, walking away, and when the sharp smell reached the tip of my nose I dipped into my pocket and pulled out a matchbox.

I lit a single match, watching the flame flicker, walking further away.

Her sobs turned to screams. "Please, please—don't!"

I didn't look back.

I tossed the match inside, the flame catching instantly, and I closed the door and walked away.

The fire spread fast, licking up the walls and consuming the whole house. Their screams filled the air, together with the crackle of flames.

I walked, the heat at my back, their voices fading in the fire. They were burning, their life belonged to the flame now.

Some part of me felt lighter.

Justice wasn't perfect.
But it was enough.

TWENTY FIVE

BREE

I DIDN'T KNOW WHAT day it was. I didn't know if I would stay here like this forever, or if he would come back. He hadn't spent the night. I was alone, bruised, and waiting for him within the cold walls of this house. I needed him. I needed him to come back and tell me that everything would be okay. I needed to hear his voice promising that no matter how hard it got, we would be okay.

But no matter how hard I tried to imagine a brighter outcome, the reality always dragged me deeper. It always seemed worse, no matter which ending I dared to hope for.

And it was breaking me.

Piece by piece, I was falling apart.

I sat at the bottom of the staircase, wrapped in his white shirt. It hung loose on me, oversized, but it had his scent, and that was enough to make me feel like he was still near. On my lap, I gathered the ripped parts of my clothes, picking them up piece by piece from the stairs. My fingers trembled as I fought back tears.

Not again. Please, not again.

My gaze drifted to the door. The axe was still lodged in it. I had always managed to imagine some kind of ending, to escape, but this time, my mind was blank. Should I just leave? Should I find my way to somewhere, anywhere, or should I wait?

If I waited too long, would I miss a chance to feel alive again? Even if I was broken, with the shadow of despair pressing against my brain, I still hoped for something more. I wanted to grow old, and gray. I wanted to tell someone that I had lived, that I had survived whatever this life had thrown at me.

And yet, here I was. Watching. Choosing him. Even when he walked away because cooling down was easier for him than facing me.

Then I heard the sound of a car pulling up in front of the house. My heart leaped before I could think. I sprang to my feet, the pieces of fabric slipping from my lap and scattering onto the floor. The sound was drowning out every single thought from before as I ran to the front door and opened it, throwing it wide.

I saw him.

He was in the car, staring at me through the windshield. His hands rested on the steering wheel, his eyes hesitant, like he wasn't sure if he wanted to get out. But I needed him to. I needed him to come to me, to wrap me in his arms, to make everything else disappear.

I needed him.

Without thinking, I rushed down the steps of the house, the door left swinging ajar behind me. The icy snow stung my bare feet, but I didn't stop. My heart thundered in my chest as I ran toward the car, toward him.

The door opened, and he stepped out. As he closed the distance between us, I didn't wait. I jumped into his arms, wrapping myself around him, my hands clasped tightly around his neck, my legs locking at his hips. I held on as if letting go would break me completely.

His hands pressed against my back, locking me as he carried me toward the house. Neither of us spoke. We didn't need to.

Everything we couldn't say was in that one embrace.

I needed him more than air, I needed him more than water, and he was the food that fueled my soul. Even though it hurt so damn much, I still wanted him. I wanted him more than life, I wanted him more than love, and he was the need that fueled my heart. Even when I broke apart, just seconds away from him, I knew I belonged—here, with him. In hell or heaven, I didn't care, as long as I was by his side.

The door clicked shut behind us. He lowered me to the floor, his face hovering above mine, his breath warm against my skin.

"I'm sorry I left," he finally murmured. "I never should have."

I silenced him with a kiss, my lips meeting his before he could say more. I stood on my tiptoes to reach him, my fingers tracing the back of his neck, grounding us together.

He pulled me closer, lifting me, his arms tightening as if he couldn't bear to let go. He stole my breath away, again.

"I know," I whispered against his lips. "It's okay."

His forehead pressed against mine, his skin brushing softly, his eyes searching mine. "I had a rough night," he whispered, his voice cracking. "All I want is to lie down with you and forget the rest of the world."

He set me gently on the floor, his hand still in mine as I tugged him toward the stairs. "Then let's forget the world," I said softly.

But he stopped.

His hand tightened around mine, and I turned around to face him.

"Lena died last night," he said. "And Laura is still missing." He swallowed hard. "If they look into it... if they find the farm and what's on it... this could all be the end."

His words hit me, leaving me frozen on the steps. My heart pounded, not just at the thought of what had happened, but at what might come next. Lena was gone. And Laura... the thought of her, out there somewhere, sent a chill through me colder than the snow outside.

Fear clawed at me, threatening to spill out, but I couldn't show it. I couldn't tell him that the thought of her return terrified me, thought of her chaos. She was my mom, but she was never real. Deep down, I was afraid. Afraid of what she would do if they found her alive. Afraid of what it would mean for us.

I didn't know Lena well, but I knew she cared about him. Even in her cold, distant way, she was still his mother. And in their own twisted, complicated way, they loved each other. My heart broke for him.

There were no tears in his eyes, the icy blue that usually sparkled had deepened, and darkened. They looked more like mine now, ocean blue, muted as if all the light in them had drowned. As if we both lost that spark for life, with nothing left to light it again.

Our eyes locked, two waves crashing into each other, drowning together, searching for something, anything, to cling to.

"I'm sorry about Lena," I said softly. "I never thought... I didn't expect her to leave so soon."

"Yeah," he murmured, his voice distant. "Me neither."

He stepped closer, brushing his lips against my forehead. "I'm going to take a shower," he said quietly. "If you want to eat, the fridge is full."

"Oh." The word fell out of me before I could stop it. I wasn't expecting that. I didn't want food, I wanted him. I wanted him to stay, to let me hold him, to let me help with the pain he was carrying. But I didn't push.

"Have a nice shower," I said instead.

He walked past me, his footsteps slow and disappeared up the stairs toward the bedroom.

I stayed where I was, standing in the hallway, staring at the space he just left. When I heard the soft click of the bedroom door closing, I felt pain swell in my chest.

I forced myself to move, turning back to the mess scattered around the room. The ripped clothes, the antlers, and one by one, I took them in my arms, and with my hands full, I walked into the kitchen.

I opened the trash bin and began to toss everything away. Each piece felt heavier than it should have, like I was discarding parts of myself.

I wanted him.

It had been thirty minutes. The longest thirty minutes of my life. Even though we were in the same house, it felt like we were worlds apart. I hadn't seen him, but I noticed the axe was gone from the door, and the guns that hung on the walls, were gone, too. From upstairs, I heard the metallic clicks of a chest being locked.

He was putting everything away.

He was afraid. Afraid of hurting me again.

Tears blurred my eyes as I stood there. He didn't understand. He thought the pain he caused would break me, but it didn't. It wasn't the pain that threatened to ruin me, it was the distance, that I was away from him.

Suddenly, the doorbell rang, startling me. I turned toward the sound, my breath catching as two blurred shadows moved behind the blurred glass pane beside the door.

I hesitated, then walked over and opened it.

Standing on the porch were two people. The woman was in her mid-thirties, with sharp whiskey-brown eyes and her dark hair tied in a ponytail. She wore a gray suit with a light blue shirt beneath it. Around her neck hung a badge, but not a detective one, but something else, something official. Her eyes cut through me, scanning me.

Beside her was a man. Isak.

"Hi, Bree," he said. "I see you're well."

I nodded, caught off guard, but before I could say a word, the woman spoke.

"May we come in?" Her voice was professional. "We're colleagues of Thor Karlsson. This is his house, isn't it?"

I nodded again, stepping aside. "Yes," I said softly.

As they entered, I closed the door behind them. My mind raced, wondering what this was about, but before I could call for Thor, he appeared.

He stood at the top of the staircase, dressed in a black shirt and matching trousers. His hair was swept back, though a few strands fell loosely onto his forehead. His blue eyes were icy again.

"Frida. Isak. What a surprise."

He walked down the stairs, casually rolling up his sleeves.

"Yes," Frida said, her eyes shifting between me and him. "I could say the same thing."

I moved to the staircase as Thor reached the bottom. He stood beside me, his hand brushing lightly against my back.

"Why are you here?" Thor asked. "I called Johansson. Told him I was taking some vacation days."

Frida's lips twitched, almost amused. "We're not here about that."

Thor's jaw tightened slightly. "Then why?"

"We're here for Bree," Isak said.

I instinctively stepped back, my body behind Thor's.

Frida chuckled, "Oh, we're not here to take you," she said. "We just came to pass on a message. Your mother," she paused, "your real mother, Victoria Muller, wants to know when you'll come back."

"Come back?" I asked, stepping out from behind Thor, my arms stiff at my sides. "I don't want to go back."

"No one's forcing you," she said, smiling. "But you'll have to contact her eventually. You need to claim your legal name."

I turned to Thor, my eyes silently pleading. **Make them go away**. I didn't want to leave. Not him. Not this life. I wasn't her daughter; I was Bree. I'd always been just Bree.

"Okay then," she said lightly, "why don't you make us some tea? We'll have a little chat with Detective Karlsson while we wait."

The false sweetness in her voice boiled against me, but I nodded, my feet dragging me to the kitchen. I had no intention of making tea, I slipped around the corner, pressing myself against the wall to listen instead.

"We found Laura's body. She drowned in the river, but there were... irregularities. Bruises, cuts, signs she might have been tortured before she ran."

Thor stiffened, his arms folding across his chest. Isak reached into his pocket and handed over something small and metallic.

"We found this in her coat," he said.

Thor's brows furrowed as he held the badge up to the light. "My badge?"

"Yes," she said. Her arms mirrored Thor's, crossing. "We were wondering how it got there, especially since you never reported it missing."

Panic surged through me, I couldn't let them accuse Thor, not for this, and before I could think twice, I stepped back into the room.

"It was me," I blurted, my voice shaking but loud enough to stop the conversation. "I gave it to her."

Thor turned as I pressed on, moving closer. "The water is boiling," I added quickly, pointing toward the kitchen, buying myself a moment. "Thor left the badge there when they came to ask about the missing woman. Mel and I both saw it."

Frida blinked, caught off guard. "Oh," she said, recovering. She turned back to Thor. "Well, you still should have reported it."

"I am on holiday. I planned to report it as soon as I return." His tone hardened. "But tell me, why is Isak here?"

"My shoe size is a 39," Isak interrupted, his voice flat, deflecting the question.

Thor chuckled, "You know what they say about small feet..."

I bit back a laugh, brushing my fingers across my lips. "So," I said, shifting the tension. "Still want that tea?"

"No," Isak snapped, glaring. "We're good."

Frida cleared her throat, regaining composure. "We'll be in touch," she said, already heading toward the door, but soon her eyes moved to the jagged cut near the frame. "What happened here?"

"Star Wars duel," I said, unable to stop the grin spreading across my face. "It turns me on." A blush crept up my cheeks, betraying me.

Thor's lips twitched, barely suppressing a laugh as he looked at me.

Frida raised an eyebrow. "Huh," she muttered. "Well, have a nice day."

As soon as the door clicked shut, Thor turned to me. His hand slid to the back of my neck, and he drew me to him. His lips claimed mine, the kiss deepening, his tongue exploring my mouth in hunger. Before I could catch my breath, he lifted me, pulling me against him as he carried me to the kitchen. The faint crunch of tires on gravel faded as the car drove away, leaving us in silence inside.

He set me down on the kitchen counter, the fridge humming softly beside us. His lips hovered over mine as he whispered, "You didn't have to cover for me."

"I know," I murmured, a sly smile tugging at my lips. "But I wanted them gone, so I could have you all to myself."

"Hmmm," he growled softly. "I love the thought of that."

His hand found its way back to my neck, pulling me closer as he kissed me again, slower this time, savoring every second of it.

Then he pulled away, the heat of his eyes never leaving mine as he turned to the fridge. Opening the lower drawer, he let the cold air out from the freezer and pulled out a plastic container. He placed it beside me on the counter, slowly, almost teasing.

"You know," he began, "when I first met you, I would wake up in the mornings and find these popsicles in the fridge."

I tilted my head "Ice cream?" I asked, grinning.

"Nah," he said, shaking his head as he took out one of the popsicles.

It was small, milky white, no more than four inches. His grin stretched from ear to ear as he held it up. "Guess again."

I slapped a hand over my mouth as I realized. "You're not telling me you... oh my God, Thor! That's messed up!"

He laughed, his eyes crinkling at the corners. "I think I was saving it for... situations like this," he said. His hands found my knees, parting them gently, his touch sending shivers down my spine.

I swallowed hard, fully aware of where that popsicle was made of his cum and ice. I curved my spine, widened the gap between my thighs, and leaned against the cool tiles of the kitchen wall. He held the popsicle so near now that I could sense the frosty chill from the ice grazing my skin, and then he pressed it against my clit, making a shiver course through me.

"Fuck," it came out of me.

"Have you ever got burned by snow?" he asked, his eyes locked onto me, "I did, it's cold."

He gently pushed it in, I could feel the ice melting inside me, my inner muscles clenching around it. As he drove it further into me, I surrendered, allowing it to dissolve. My eyes fluttered open, my hands finding their way to his shoulders, fingers digging into his skin.

His fingers wrapped around the stick once more and he thrust it deeper as it continued melting within me.

The dissolved ice dripped under me, making its way under my ass cheeks. His hand shifted again, taking the plastic stick that was left from the popsicle of his cum. All the ice was inside me, melting without the stick, I felt like my brain was freezing along with the ice inside me.

He threw the stick next to me, and drew me closer, unzipping his trousers.

"Can you feel the burn?" he asked.

I was speechless, I had no words, I just nodded.

I could feel the ice dissolving within me, leaving only his cold cum. My neck arched to the back, a moan escaping my lips as shivers moved down my spine. He drew me nearer, his lips locking mine. And with one single thrust, he entered me. I was so tight I felt each inch of him inside, to the point that it hurt. A scream tore from my throat, my body arching as he kept thrusting inside me.

He moaned against my neck, his hands roamed beneath my shirt, finding my breasts. He tore the buttons apart, and shirt opened, leaving me naked before him. My legs wrapped around him, drawing him closer, and allowing him to move in sync with me.

My hand went down to touch myself, rubbing my clit as he continued to thrust inside me. My back arched and eyes locked onto his, my mouth fell open in a silent cry for him while biting down on my lower lip.

A smirk graced his face as he drove deeper within me. With each thrust, I could sense him deeper inside. The thought of his cock growing inside me was taking my breath away, and just as I was about to come, he joined me. His name escaped my lips in a cry, "Thor."

He came within me, his warmth mingling with the icy aftershocks still rippling through me. It was as if I had fucked with both; Snowman and Thor, ice and fire both inside me. A smile tugged at my lips as I wrapped my arms around his neck, locking eyes with him while he whispered, "How is it to be fucked by Snowman?"

I chuckled, "cold."

"Luckily you have us both."

And I did, I had all his personalities.

It wasn't funny, but I laughed.

And I know you would too—anyone would. I had a man who would kill for me, a man who would chase me with an axe, a man who would burn the world for me and melt the coldest heart for mine. He was everything I could dream of, and I got all that in one man. How lucky was I?

TWENTY SIX

Snowman

JANUARY, 2017

> "If you continue to carry the brick from your past, you will end up building the same house."
> — Unknown.

BREE WAS AT HOME. Over the past two weeks, she had grown closer to Julia, Erik's wife. For Bree, this had started to feel normal, but for me, it was anything but. None of this was normal. Watching her with their daughter, the way she smiled at that child tied knots in my stomach. It was the kind of smile that hinted at a wish she hadn't said but knew she wanted, a wish for something I couldn't give her. Something I didn't want to share.

I hated myself for that. For not being enough. For not being able to offer her the life she deserved, a life I knew she needed, a life I couldn't touch.

Now, I sat in the office, the hum of people moving through the halls, their faces blurred, expressionless, as they passed by. Today was my last day here. Isak was excited about it, of course. In just a week, he had clawed his way into the chief's chair after Jan Johansson's body turned up cold. The department called it an accident. They didn't know the truth.

They couldn't.

The moment Isak's promotion became official, I handed in my badge. No ceremony. No fanfare. Just paperwork now. I was ready to let it go.

Life has a way of stealing dreams out from under you, and there's nothing you can do about it. You just stand there, helpless, watching as the wind scatters the pieces that were never yours to reach.

Frida left yesterday. I could see in her eyes how the unanswered questions still haunted her, how close she came to uncovering the truth about the Snowman. If it hadn't been for Mel backing up my story about the badge, she would have caught me. I could feel it all tightening around me, every thread pulling back into the same relentless puzzle. But I was done. I had decided to move on.

I was 34. No plans, no future. All I knew was that I needed Bree.

THOR, 8 YEARS OLD

Today, I found out I was going to have a sister. Mom was pregnant. Erik and I were upstairs in the kitchen, playing with little boats in the sink, letting the water carry them in the circles. But downstairs, their voices rose crashing against our little game.

We tried not to listen, but the words came through the walls, impossible to ignore.

"You are not going to have that child," Father said. "Get rid of it."

"But..." Mom's voice trembled. "It's a girl."

"That's exactly why!" he roared. "I can't have girls around my sons. They need strength, not her crying and whining."

"What if I don't?" she asked, and at that moment, her voice cracked. She wanted this baby. Maybe more than she wanted us.

"Then I will throw her to the pigs," he snarled. "You end it now, or I will end it later."

Erik and I didn't look at each other. We didn't speak. But even as we pretended to play, tears slid down our cheeks, silent as the little waves lapping in the sink. We wanted her, this sister we never met, never even seen. We wanted to play with her and share our toys. We wanted Mom to be happy for once, truly happy. She never was.

We heard the door slam a few minutes later. Dad left without a goodbye.

Mom climbed the stairs soon after, her steps dragging. She didn't say anything when she walked in. She just sat on the sofa, clutching a pink baby blanket in her hands, her body trembling as silent sobs shook her.

Erik and I rushed to her side, pressing ourselves against her. She wrapped her arms around us tightly, as if we might slip away too, and her cries became louder.

Between her sobs, she choked out the words that shattered everything. "We won't have a baby girl, boys."

Then, she slid down onto her knees in front of us, taking our hands as tears ran down her face.

She whispered, "The world breaks little girls so little boys can live."

We didn't understand. But we leaned into her, wrapping our arms around her as best we could.

PRESENT DAY

I got home, groceries in my hands, balancing the bags awkwardly as I nudged the door open. Tonight, I wanted to cook for her. Something special. But as I stepped inside, something felt off. The house was quiet, too quiet.

"Bree?" I called out, my voice bouncing off the walls. I set the bags down on the cold tile, my chest tightening. No answer.

I walked through the kitchen, peering around the corner. Nothing.

I checked the living room, but it was empty too. My steps quickened.

"Bree!" I shouted, louder this time.

I sprinted up the stairs, my pulse hammering in my ears. I threw open the bedroom door. It was empty, just like the rest of the house. Panic shot through me as I called her name again, my voice cracking.

"Bree!"

Finally, a soft reply came from the bathroom. "In here."

Relief crashed into me as I rushed to the door.

I pushed it open, expecting, I don't know what. But there she was, kneeling on the floor, her back to me, holding something in her hands.

"Bree?"

I dropped down beside her, wrapping my arms around her, and pulling her close. She didn't resist, but whatever she was holding slipped from her hand, landing on the tiles with a soft clatter.

I looked down and froze. It was a pregnancy test.

Heart pounding, I reached for it, turning it over in my hands. My eyes landed on two pink lines. The room seemed to tilt.

"What the fuck is this?"

She exhaled softly. "Thor, it's obvious, isn't it?"

"No," I snapped, shaking my head. "No, Bree, it's fucking not!"

Her eyes lifted to meet mine. Calm. Too calm.

"I'm pregnant."

She stood and turned to the sink to wash her hands as if this was just another moment in her day.

I stumbled to my feet. "Bree... how?"

"We can't... I mean..."

She turned, "Really, Thor? You want me to diagram it for you? We even played with your cum. What part of this isn't clear?"

I stared at her, my throat dry. "We can't do this," I said, my voice breaking. "Bree, we can't."

"But we can," she said. "And we will. There's no going back."

Her words sank into me like a stone, dragging me down, my chest tightened as flashes of a future I wasn't ready for raced through my mind. A child. Me, a father. It didn't feel real, it felt like a bad joke.

"Bree," I whispered, swallowing hard, "this is insane. Call me selfish, but isn't it crazy to have a child? Me? As a father?"

Her eyes softened for just a moment, a single tear slipping down her cheek. "We can do this," she said quietly.

But I didn't. I couldn't.

I turned and left the bathroom, the test still clutched in my hand, and I collapsed onto the bed, burying my face in my hands.

My breath came fast, shallow. "You need to see a doctor. You need to... you need to end this."

I heard her sharp breath, and then she was storming out of the bathroom, her face wet with tears. "Are you serious right now?" she shouted. "No. Absolutely not."

"Bree." I stood, walking toward her, trying to keep my voice steady. "What if... What if something happens? What if I hurt you? Or the baby?" My hands hovered near her shoulders, unsure if I should reach for her.

She shoved my hands away. "Don't touch me!" Her voice cracked, but her anger burned through it.

"What if he or she..." I paused, my throat tightening. "What if they end up like me? What if I ruin them, Bree?" My hands finally fell onto her shoulders, desperate to make her understand. "I don't want to hurt you. I don't want to hurt them."

"What if something happens to you, and I'm left alone with a baby? What kind of life could I even give them?"

Her voice wavered as she looked up at me, her eyes already shining with tears.

I pulled her closer, my arms tightening around her. "I can't even take care of myself," I said quietly. "Let alone a baby."

"But you're taking care of me," she whispered. I could feel her shaking, each sob breaking against me.

"That's different," I said.

I hated seeing her cry. It ripped something open inside me every time. But the thought of bringing a child into this mess terrified me. If it was a boy, what if he grew up like the worst men I had known? What if he hurt people, and turned into someone like Josh or Vic? And if it was a girl... God, what if the same things happened to her that happened to Bree? What if I couldn't protect her? What if she ended up with someone like me? A man too broken to love her right, someone who would turn her pain into addiction so he can enjoy.

I couldn't take that risk. It was too much. But as much as it terrified me, I knew this wasn't just my choice to make. She had a say in this too, even if it tore us apart.

For the first time, I felt a tear slip down my cheek. My voice cracked as I said, "Go to the doctor." I stepped back, my hands falling to my sides. "If you want to keep it, I'll leave. If you don't...I'll stay."

Her face crumpled, and she collapsed into me again, her sobs hitting like punches I couldn't dodge.

"Your choice," I whispered, steadying her before letting her go.

She looked at me through the tears, "I fucking hate you, Thor Karlsson," she sobbed.

Her words hit harder than I expected, but I didn't stop. I turned and walked toward the door, every step pulling me further from her, from us, from everything.

"I hate you!" she screamed behind me, her voice shaking.

It cut through me, but I didn't turn back. I couldn't.

When I hit the cold air outside, I stumbled onto the snowy stairs, sinking as my breath came in gasps. I looked at my hands, at the scar across my palm. My father gave me that scar the first time he sent me alone into the woods.

"Fuck."

My hands clenched into fists.

I couldn't do it. I couldn't bring a child into this world, not like this. Not with all the pain I carried, not with all the things I'd seen. I couldn't risk becoming my father. I couldn't be the reason another person ended up broken.

And her...she deserved more. More than me. More than this life I couldn't give her.

I was a monster, and monsters like me didn't deserve to be fathers, but angels like her deserved every chance to be mothers.

TWENTY SEVEN

BREE

I SAT ON THE cold stone steps outside, picking at the edge of my sleeve, while inside, he moved around with a glass of whiskey in his hand. Thor called Erik to take me to the doctor and said he would wait for my decision. But I hadn't given him one yet. The truth was, I didn't know. I didn't want to live with him, but I wasn't sure I could live without him either.

The sound of tires crunching over snow broke through the quiet, and I looked up to see Erik's black car pulling up. I stood slowly, brushing my hands over my legs, and I walked toward the car, but when I opened the door, it wasn't Erik behind the wheel. It was Julia.

"Get in," she said, her voice light, but her eyes sharp. Her long brown hair fell loose around her shoulders, and she gave me a small smile that didn't reach her eyes.

She knew.

I hesitated, then climbed in, and as soon as I buckled my seatbelt, she pressed on the gas.

"Erik told me what happened," she said.

I kept my eyes on the road ahead, the lines on the asphalt blurring in the headlights.

"Do you even want this baby?" she asked. "Or is this just a baby fever ever since you met Aurora?"

Her words hit hard, and I stiffened. Aurora. Her baby. Her life. I swallowed and shrugged. "I want him," I whispered.

"That's not an answer."

I didn't respond. I didn't know how to. I pressed my hands against my thighs, staring out the window, watching as the woods outside sped past.

"Bree, you're nineteen," she said. "You haven't had a chance to live yet. And Thor, he lived too much, he has seen more than anyone should."

I turned to her, my heart pounding. "What do you mean?"

Her lips pressed into a thin line as if deciding how much to say. Finally, she let out a small sigh. "He had a girlfriend once," she said. "He lost her."

That landed like a punch to the stomach. "I didn't know," I murmured.

"Not many do. And there's more to it. We still don't know if she... if she did it herself, or if he—" She stopped and shook her head. "It doesn't matter. What matters is, that Thor cares about you. He really does. But too much of that kind of care, Bree, it can smother you."

I turned to face her, "What are you trying to say?"

"I'm saying, you need to figure out if you're choosing this for yourself, or if it's what you really want. Because if you're not sure, Bree, he'll drag you down with him. Not because he wants to, but because that's all he knows."

"If you decide to keep this baby, run. Change your name, your address, everything. Just run."

"But—"

"Thor's a good guy, but there's something dark inside him. If that dark resurfaces, he'll find you. And when he does..." She hesitated, her gaze heavy. "You can say goodbye to your life."

I froze, my hand drifted to my stomach, trembling as it rested there. Tears stung my eyes. "What if I lose the baby?" I whispered, my voice breaking.

"You won't. I can see it in your eyes. You already love this child."

The words lodged in my throat. "What if I lose him?" My voice cracked, and before I could stop it, the tears came, spilling down my face.

"You already lost him," she said, her hand settling gently on my thigh. "But you can do this. You're stronger than you think."

My shoulders shook as I tried to hold back the sobs. "I can't," I choked out. "I just can't."

"You can," she said, her voice pulling me back. "And you will."

Soon she turned the wheel and pulled the car in front of a small house. A woman stood on the porch, waiting. Her long gray hair curled softly at the ends, and her face was wrinkled with worry. But it was her eyes that caught me, there was something familiar about them. My breath caught in my chest.

"That's her, isn't it?"

Julia nodded. "Erik called her. Thought you might need someone here for... when you decide..."

My chest tightened. "How did you even know?" My voice cracked. "I don't even know what I want!"

"Bree, come on." Julia gave me a smile. "It's obvious. We just didn't know how Thor would take it." Her expression turned serious. "Talk to her. Then I'll take you to him."

"I don't know if I can." My eyes stayed fixed on the woman, the distance between us suddenly too much and too close all at once.

"You can. You've got this."

I opened the car door, and stepped closer to the house, the woman's arms opened slightly. I wasn't ready for this. My feet felt like lead, and I stopped a few steps away, frozen.

Julia brushed past me, her hand grazing mine, she turned as she walked, giving me a quick wink as if to say, You'll be fine.

"Hi," the woman said.

"Hi," I murmured.

"How are you?"

"I'm okay," I said, my words felt empty. "You?"

"Okay," she said, though her tears betrayed her. "Erik told me you go by Bree now. But your real name is Zara."

"My name is Bree," I said, cutting her off. I couldn't explain why, but hearing her say my real name felt like a slap.

"Okay," she said. "Bree. It's nice to meet you."

She was trying so hard, but I couldn't meet her halfway. Not yet.

"Listen," I said, forcing the words out before I could lose my nerve. "I'm not going to pretend you don't know my story. And I'm not going to act like everything's fine. It's not." I looked her in the eye. "All I can give you right now is this... I'm going to be okay, but I need time."

She nodded, a tear slipping down her cheek. "That's okay," she said softly. "Take all the time you need."

"It is," I said, my own tears threatened again. "It is."

Her hand came up to wipe a stray tear from my face. "You have your father's eyes," she said, "He was a good man."

"Was?" I asked, my heart tightening.

She looked down. "He died a few years ago. It's just me now."

Another tear slid down my cheek. The truth hit me hard. I would never have a real father. Joe took that from me. Anger simmered inside, but instead of letting it take over, I just folded into her arms. My walls broke, and I let the sobs spill out.

"To be honest," I mumbled through the tears, "my life is really shitty right now, and I just... I need someone to hug."

Her arms wrapped around me tighter, warming me. "I'll always be here to hug you," she said softly. "I've waited fifteen years for this." She was crying now, her tears soaking into my shoulder. "My baby girl," she whispered, her voice breaking, "you're here."

"I am," I said, then, with a shaky breath, I added, "And... you're going to be a grandma."

She pulled back just enough to look at me, her eyes red from tears. "I know," she said, her lips trembling into a smile. She wiped at her face and then mine, brushing away the tears. "And you're going to be amazing."

"Am I?" I asked, my voice cracking.

"Yes." She nodded, smiling like it was the most obvious thing in the world. "You will."

Before I could say anything else, she pulled me back into another hug. I let myself sink into it, and over her shoulder, my eyes drifted to the house. Julia and Erik were on the balcony, watching us. Their faces were framed by the warm light spilling out from inside, they looked perfect, but I knew it was a lie.

I didn't know their whole story, and no one ever told the full truth about love or life. Not really. I could guess that what they had wasn't the picture they showed us, and I had seen it all before.

Still, I couldn't help but wish. I wished for a better life, one that didn't come in broken pieces. I wanted more. I needed more. And in that moment, I knew what I had to do.

This baby.

No matter how many times I have told myself I was enough, no matter how many times I put everyone else's needs ahead of my own, this time was different, this time, I had no choice.

This time, it had to be me.

For you, my baby, just for you.

TWENTY EIGHT

BREE

The door was wide open when I arrived. Stepping inside, I noticed two suitcases sitting by the hallway table, neatly placed as if they were waiting for something or someone. I looked around, my breath catching, but the house was still.

He wasn't here.

A strange pressure built in my chest, suffocating me. My heart pounded, each beat sharper than the last. My hands trembled, and I blinked rapidly, trying to clear my blurred vision. I reached out instinctively, hoping for something solid to hold on to, but my fingers found nothing but empty space.

That's when I saw a letter on the marble-topped table. My legs felt unsteady as I moved closer, I picked it up, the paper shaking in my grip as my tears began to fall. The first words, scrawled in his handwriting, hit me like a whisper I wasn't ready to hear:

"To Bree."

> "I will never be the man you deserve, even if you think I already am.
>
> Lena once told me, "The world breaks little girls so little boys can live." I didn't understand what she meant until I found out you were pregnant. I was raised to be one of those little boys, shaped by selfishness and entitlement. And maybe that's why I held on to you so tightly, never giving you the chance to leave. Maybe I thought if I kept you close enough, I could keep myself from falling apart.
>
> When I walked into the bathroom and saw you holding that test, I knew. I knew you'd keep the baby. I knew you'd make a choice I wasn't ready to make. And I knew I'd hurt you when I told you I couldn't stay to raise this child with you. But I swear, it's because I believed it was for the best, for both of you.
>
> If you have a boy, promise me you'll teach him to be the kind of man who lifts little girls up, not tears them down. Teach him to fight for them, to change the world for them. And if you have a girl, teach her to own her place in the world. Show her

> how to stand tall and hold her ground, so no one, not any little boy, can take it from her.
>
> Lena was right, the world does break little girls, but sometimes, it breaks little boys too.
>
> If there were another universe, I would call you again, just to hear your voice. I would hold on tighter on number one and love you better, never let go. But this isn't that universe.
>
> You'll always be my number one, Birdie. Always have been. Always will be.
>
> Love,
>
> Thor"

I sank to my knees, the letter crumpling in my hand, its edges digging into my skin. My chest tightened, and a scream ripped out of me. Pain shot through me, so sharp, and I doubled over, my forehead brushing the floor.

The door flew open, and Julia and Victoria rushed in. Their voices overlapped, worried, and unsure, but I couldn't make out what they were saying. They tried to lift me, their hands under my arms, pulling gently, but my body wouldn't move.

I just stayed there.

I patted my pocket, frantic.

Empty.

Panic spiked, and I shouted. "Phone! I need a phone!"

Julia fumbled through her purse and handed me hers. My fingers trembled as I grabbed it, the plastic warm from her hand. I brought it close, the numbers swimming before me.

I pressed one.

Nothing happened.

I pressed it again.

A faint beep, barely a sound.

Tears blurred the screen. My breath hitched as I jabbed at the number, again and again, the same response each time.

He wasn't here.

Julia crouched next to me, her voice low as she spoke. "Bree, stop. Leave him alone. He doesn't want—"

"No!" I cut her off, clutching the phone tighter. "He'll answer. He has to."

My voice cracked, and I pressed the number again.

Julia sighed, pulling the phone from my hands, standing up as I screamed. My voice felt like it was tearing me apart from the inside, spilling out into the room where no one could help.

I slumped forward, my body shaking. I curled my fingers on the floor, the pain swept me under again.

He was gone.

It wasn't my phone.
He wasn't her number one.
He wasn't mine anymore, either.
He left... me.

TWENTY NINE

BREE

NOVEMBER, 2019

"Bree!"

The shout pulled me from my thoughts. I looked up, pushing my blonde hair off my shoulder as I peered around the coffee machine. My coworker Nea was wrestling with a basket full of coffee bean bags, having wrapped her arms around it as if it weighed a ton. Her voice pitches higher with urgency as she yells again, "Bree! A little help here?"

I hurried over, sliding around the counter. Her face was scrunched with effort, and the basket wobbled precariously in her grip. Before she could cry out again, I grabbed one side. Together, we wrestled it onto the bar. It hit the surface with a dull thud, and Nea let out an exaggerated groan, her hands flying to her hips as she stood straight.

"You know," I teased, brushing my hands off, "you could've asked for help earlier."

"It's six in the morning," she said, fighting off a yawn. "I'm half-asleep."

"Clearly," I said, raising an eyebrow.

She gave me a saucy wink. "Besides, I forgot you were here."

"Nea," I laughed, shaking my head as I walked back to the coffee machine. "Sometimes I swear you've got early-onset dementia."

She laughed loudly and uninhibitedly, the kind of laugh that could wake the birds. She tapped the side of her head with mock seriousness. "You're probably right. I should check on my last two brain cells before they die."

I tossed a cleaning cloth at her, smirking. "Oh, stop it."

The loud tick of the clock announced six a.m. sharp. The sun had not been bold enough yet to cast its light upon us, and the café was wrapped in the dark. This was my haven—mornings like this. All the nightmares that haunted my nights felt so small under the glowing lights of this warm café. And when sleep at least decided to be a foe, I knew I would be in peace here.

The jingle above the door yanked me back to the here and now. Cold air swirled in, touching my skin, and on its heels came the scent of winter: sharp, clear cold and the earthly, homelike smell of wood.

I turned toward the sound of the door, my gaze rising from the counter to the man who'd just walked in. A black coat clung to the lines of his tall frame. The quiet intensity of him came with him into the air, like a whispered promise, as he turned toward me. Café light caught against his face, and my breath hitched. His eyes as icy as the frost locked onto mine, piercing, freezing me to a spot. His gaze was sharp, hard to forget, and my heart stumbled in my chest as recognition struck.

"Bree?" he whispered low and raspy as if wrenched from him.

He seemed to look as shocked as I felt; his exhalation froze in the cold air between us. It had been far too long, far too bloody long since I'd last seen him. Even through a cold swirl, stirring around, I felt the warmth inside, melt something frozen in me that was there for far too long.

I walked toward him, my steps slow, I didn't say a word. There was nothing left to say. The pain wasn't sharp anymore, just a faint ache I had learned to carry, but my heart still held the same fractured pieces I picked on that day when he walked away.

He sat at the table, his shoulders slightly hunched. I stopped just short, my fingers brushing the edge of the table, gripping it to steady myself.

"What can I get you?"

His eyes lifted to mine, his face unreadable at first. Then his gaze dropped to my hands, lingering there.

Was he searching for a ring? There wasn't one. Not since him. Not ever.

"How are you?" he asked, his voice careful, his fists pressing together on his lap.

"I'm good," I said, tilting my head slightly, keeping my tone cool, detached. "You?"

He hesitated, the movement of his throat betraying the words he was struggling to find. Finally, he said, "Can I have an espresso, please?"

I nodded and turned away quickly before the tears in my eyes could spill over. His silence had told me everything I needed to know. He was still the same Thor I remembered. The one who tried so hard to hide his cracks but never could when I was around. And now, sitting there, the pieces were slipping through his fingers all over again.

"You okay?" Nea asked in a hushed tone, glancing over at him.

I nodded, swallowing the lump in my throat, but I didn't speak. I let the tears fall silently instead. Let the memories wash over me like they always did. Like they always would.

The bell above the door jingled again, startling me back into the present. I turned, and there was my mother, carrying my daughter.

"Mama!" her tiny voice rang out, her hands reaching for me. She wore her favorite pink sweater, her teddy bear tucked under her arm, her blond curls bouncing as she squirmed in my mother's arms. Her eyes, icy blue eyes, met mine, and my heart clenched.

His eyes.

I took her in my arms, pressing her close as she giggled against my neck, her small fingers tangling in my hair like they always did.

When I looked back at him, his face had changed. His breaths were shallow, his eyes locked on her. He didn't say anything at first, but I could see unspoken questions. His mask was slipping, no matter how hard he tried to hold it in place.

I walked toward him, each step breaking me apart, and when I reached the table, I pulled out the chair and sat across from him.

"What's her name?" he finally asked.

"Snow," I said softly, my chest tightening with every word. "Her name is Snow."

A tear slipped down his cheek, his jaw clenched tight. Before I could say anything, he stood up, his fist slamming the table. The sound made Snow cry, her wail cutting through the room as he turned and rushed to the door. I watched through the window as he stopped outside, bent over, his hands on his knees, trying to hold himself together. But I could see it—he couldn't. He was breaking apart.

And quietly, so was I.

He left again, and it felt like my heart broke all over again.

I turned back to Snow, pulling her into my arms, her cries shaking her small body. I held her close and whispered, "Shh, mommy's here. Shh, baby."

"Is scary man gone?" she whispered against my chest, her tiny voice muffled as I pressed my palm against her head.

"Aha," I managed to say, but nothing else would come. My chest felt tight, words stuck in my throat.

How could I tell her?

How could I tell her that the scary man was her dada? The man I told her stories about every night before bed? How could I tell her that when he finally saw her, after all this time, he walked away instead of holding her? How could I tell her he wouldn't be there for her first day of school, for all the milestones that mattered?

He wasn't there when she took her first steps, or when she fell and scraped her knee. He didn't see me bandage it while she clung to me, while her cheeks drowned in tears. He wasn't there for her first word that wasn't "mama" or "dada," just a curious little "hi." He missed all of it. Her cries, her laughter, her playing "mom and dad" even though she didn't really have one.

He missed her first day of kindergarten, the excitement in her eyes, the way she lit up meeting other kids. He didn't hear everyone say how kind, how wonderful she was.

And I hated him for it. Not because he left me, but because he left her. He chose to leave her.

But what broke me even more was knowing that if he tried, if he even made the smallest effort, I'd let him back in. I'd let him break me all over again. I forgot too often that she was the one who saved me after he walked away. She was the one in my arms on nights when I cried for him. She was the one who gave me a reason to keep going. She gave me hope, gave me life.

And yet, I named her after the man who chose to leave us both behind.

Snow.

THIRTY

Snowman

IF A SINGLE LOOK could break a man, theirs would be the one. If a single sound could rip the soul clean out, it would be her cries.

I sat on the bench outside the café where she worked. I knew it well—it was mine. I knew she struggled after me, and it was tearing me apart to watch her from a distance.

She didn't know I was still around. That I cried when she cried. I smiled faintly when she laughed as if her happiness still had the power to reach me. She didn't know I stayed away because losing her made me lose myself.

She didn't know that I kept waiting. Watching her stare at her phone, like she was trying to work up the courage to press that number one on speed dial. I waited every time, hoping—foolishly—that she'd call. But the call never came.

I told myself I let her go. But deep down, I knew I never really did. And now, when I thought I was ready to let her see me again, I couldn't move. I couldn't face her.

If she knew my side of the story if she knew how much I waited for her, how I chained myself to the guilt every time she crossed my mind. How I made sure HE never knew where she was.

I lost myself when I lost you, Bree.

If only you knew how many nights I looked up at the stars, wondering if they'd ever align again. Wondering if they'd bring us back together. Wondering what if.

What if I'd just stayed? Would you still be here? Would she?

But this isn't my story to get a happy ending. It's yours.

Forgive me.

I sat on the bench outside her house, the icy wood biting through my jeans. The window light flickered off, leaving the house dark and still. I stayed, staring up at her window, hoping for just a shadow, a sign of her. Even a silhouette.

But there was nothing.

My jaw tightened, frustration knotting in my chest.

Another day lost. Another day without her.

A soft tap on my shoulder snapped me out of my thoughts.

"Why are you here?"

I turned, startled.

She stood behind me, her red pajamas poking out from under a long, heavy coat. It barely shielded her from the cold, and she was shivering. Her arms were crossed tightly over her chest, her eyes red and swollen, like she'd been crying for hours.

"Bree?"

"Why are you here?" she asked again, her voice sharp but trembling. "What are you trying to do?"

I opened my mouth, but the words caught.

What was I trying to do?

"Speak, Thor." Her voice cracked, her hands balling into fists. "Please."

I stood, the coffee I'd been holding slipping from my hand, the dark liquid spilling over the snow like ink.

"Bree," I started, stepping toward her.

She didn't move, didn't flinch. But her eyes brimmed with fresh tears. "Why are you here now? After everything?"

I hesitated, my breath hitching. "I—"

Before I could finish, she let out a bitter laugh, wiping her eyes roughly with the back of her hand. "You don't even know, do you? You just show up, expecting... I don't even know what."

"I needed to see you," I said, my voice low.

Her eyebrows furrowed, and her lip quivered. "You needed to see me?" Her voice rose. "What about when I needed you? What about when your daughter needed you?"

"Bree, I—"

"Don't." Her voice cracked, and she turned away, her shoulders shaking. "Don't stand here in the cold and pretend like this fixes anything."

I reached out, grabbing her arm gently. She froze but didn't pull away. Not yet.

"I love you," I said, the words spilling out before I could stop them. "I love you, Bree. I always have."

She shook her head, a small, bitter sound escaping her lips. "You don't get to say that. Not now. Not when I was finally learning how to forget you."

I stepped closer, trying to catch her eyes, but she wouldn't look at me. "I left because I thought it was the only way to protect you. To protect both of you."

Her laugh was sharp and hollow. "Protect me? That's what you're calling it?"

"Yes," I said, my voice firming. "I left because Frida knows. She knows it was me."

That made her stop. She turned to face me, "You're lying."

"I thought leaving would fix it. I thought it would make it better for you, for her. But it didn't. It only made things worse."

Her expression softened for just a moment, but then she shook her head, walking away. "You were never here, Thor. Not really. If you were, you'd know her name."

"Snow Tora," I said quietly.

Bree stopped, her back stiffening.

"I know she named her teddy Bambi because she loves the story. I know you tell her about me before bed, even when you don't want to. I know you give her your phone when she's scared and tell her to press one to call me, even though you don't believe I'll answer."

Tears spilled down her cheeks as she turned away again, her shoulders heaving. I didn't move, didn't try to stop her this time. I just stood there in the cold.

"I'm sorry," I said softly, but I wasn't sure if she even heard me.

She crumpled to the floor, her knees hitting the snow.

"I did," I said. It felt like the truth was choking me. "Every time."

Her head snapped up, her eyes blazing.

"Fuck you!" she screamed. "You saw me struggling every goddamn day! Every single fucking day, and you just stood there. Watching from a distance. Fuck you, Thor!"

I took a step toward her, my heart pounding, but she thrust her hand up, stopping me in my tracks.

"No!" she yelled. "Don't come any closer."

"Bree," I whispered, pleading with her, but she wouldn't even look at me.

"It's worse," she said, her voice quieter now, trembling. "It's worse knowing you were here the whole time. Knowing you were close enough to help but didn't. That's worse than you leaving. Twice. And not looking back."

"What do you want me to do?"

"Tell me. Please."

"Call Frida," she said. "Call her right now and tell her where you are. Tell her you would rather rot in jail than keep hiding from your own daughter."

My chest tightened, and I stared at her, frozen. "Bree, I—"

"Do it!" she shouted, her chin lifting defiantly. "One call, Thor. That's all I'm asking."

I swallowed hard, my hands clammy as I pulled my phone from my pocket.

My fingers trembled as I dialed, and the ringing on the other end seemed impossibly loud. The operator's voice finally broke through the silence. "122, what's your emergency?"

I hesitated for a moment, then forced the words out. "I've killed people."

The line went quiet. Bree froze, her eyes widening as her hands flew to her mouth.

"Eighteen men," I continued, my voice steady even though my whole body felt like it was breaking apart. "And ten women. I... I cut them. Used their parts to build snowmen." My breath caught, and I looked at Bree, her tears were now streaming freely. "I did it to mock them. To mock their lives."

The operator's breath hitched. Still, I pressed on. "And Jan Johansson," I said. "The chief of police. He and his lover, Donna. I burned them alive. Buried their sons, Josh and Vic, because they abused the woman I love."

The operator finally found her voice. "What's your name, sir?" she asked, her tone unsteady.

"Snowman," I said, staring straight at Bree. "Thor Karlsson."

"Where are you now?" she asked, but before I could answer, Bree lunged forward, grabbing the phone from my hand and ending the call.

Her palm cracked across my cheek before I could react, the slap ringing on my skin, leaving nothing but a red trail behind.

"You idiot!" she cried. "Why would you do that?"

"You told me to call," I said, shrugging.

I have nothing left to lose.

Her face crumpled, and then she grabbed me, pulling me close. Her lips met mine in a desperate, angry kiss, her hands gripping my jacket like she was holding on to life. "Run, Thor," she whispered against my mouth, her voice breaking. "Please. Run."

I shook my head, cupping her face in my hands. My thumbs brushed the tears from her cheeks as I kissed her again, softer this time, leaving clues in her mouth.

"No more running," I whispered, my breath mingling with hers. "Not anymore."

The sound of sirens pierced the air, growing louder with every second. Red and blue lights flashed around us. Commands were shouted, and the crunch of boots on snow drew closer.

We didn't stop. We didn't care. We just held on, kissing like the world was ending. Maybe it was.

They tore me away from her, their hands rough as they pulled me back and cuffed me. Bree stood there, her arms hanging limply at her sides, tears streaming down her face.

I smiled at her, as they dragged me away. "See you around, birdie," I said softly.

She didn't respond, just stood there, watching as they led me out into the cold.

Snowtime.

They could stop Thor, but they couldn't stop The Phantom.

EPILOGUE
THE PHANTOM

THE WORLD SPUN. My eyes fluttered, shutting and opening seconds apart. Their screams echoed in fragments; gurgling, strained, parting with the final goodbye to life. And me? I could still taste the metallic tang of their throats on my tongue.

In thirty seconds, it was over. The spinning stopped, and the car door creaked open. All I could see was snow, the empty road, and the silence hanging in the air.

They were gone.

I clenched my fist, snapping the bone in my finger to get free from the handcuffs. The crack was sharp, just a short pain slice, but I didn't stop. The cold steel slipped from my wrists as I forced them apart, and I jumped out of the car.

The car lay crumpled against the bark of a tree, its front twisted around it. Bodies had been flung out; one of them split clean apart, shredded by the collision. I couldn't stop myself. A laugh ripped from my throat as I turned away and walked on.

I spun once, checking if it was all just a bad dream, then kept moving.

In front of me came a road sign, its letters marking the stretch as **D8**. I crossed it, my boots crunching on the frosted road, and the forest rose alongside the road.

Familiar. Too familiar.

The snow fell in lazy, thin at first, then thickening as it was closer to the ground. The flakes touched my face as I stepped off the road and into the woods.

Crunch. Crunch. Crunch.

Each step felt familiar, pulling me deeper into the dark. I knew this place.

Eight steps to the thick pine tree. Another ten to the rock with the small, jagged cut running across its surface. I knelt, ignoring the frozen earth against my hands as I dug through the frozen dirt.

There it was—a box, buried just deep enough to stay hidden from everyone, yet shallow enough for me to find.

Inside: a mask, an axe, and a gun. A slip of paper, too, with numbers of a location, a safe house. A place where I could disappear.

I took the mask in my hand. White plastic was cold and stained with dried blood, split into halves: one side white, the other dark red. I didn't flinch. I didn't care. I slipped it on.

It wasn't just a mask. It was a reminder.

I stood slowly, my breath blurring the cold air. The axe was tight in my hand, the gun steadily tucked against my back.

I wasn't Thor Karlsson anymore. That man was gone, a ghost trapped in the past.

I was something else now. A shadow. A ghost. A phantom of what I once was.

And this time, no one could bring me back. No one could make me kneel.

"Every snowflake falls exactly where it's meant to. Even me," I said, my voice lost to the woods as I leaned against the rock.

Memories flashed behind my eyes, like snapshots from an old Polaroid camera. Each image dragged me back to where it all began. Back to the moment I first became who I am now.

The Phantom.

NOVEMBER, 2009

Lana Dahl. The new girl in town.

She always wore tight jeans and a black coat, her hair slicked back into a ponytail that framed her pale face, making it look alive, almost glowing. And those whiskey eyes—God, they made me drunk every time she passed by.

She spent her afternoons outside her house, playing with her younger sister, and building snowmen. But hers were different. She didn't use branches for arms, she'd stick empty gloves in their place. She didn't bother with coal for a smile, either. Instead, she stitched threads into wide grins, like they'd painted their lips with lipstick. And the finishing touch? A pot for a hat.

To someone like me, those snowmen were masterpieces. To someone like her, they were just another game.

I stood on the sidewalk, watching from a distance. She was laughing.

I couldn't help but chuckle, too. Then she turned, her eyes locking onto mine.

"Hey, stranger!" she called out, a teasing grin on her lips. "Do you want to build a snowman?"

I didn't answer. How could I? But something about her pulled me in. Step by step, I walked toward her house, the freshly fallen snow crunching under my boots.

"How do you like it?" she asked, gesturing to the snowman.

"It feels... incomplete," I said back.

She laughed, her sister giggling beside her as they stepped back to let me approach the snowman. Her sister stumbled, falling into the snow.

"Are you okay?" Lana asked, rushing to her side. Her sister winced, holding up her hand. A thin red line ran across her palm, just a scrape from a hidden rock beneath the snow.

Lana frowned but didn't panic. Instead, she gently held her sister's hand and pressed the injured palm to the snowman's chest.

"Better?" she asked.

When her sister pulled her hand back, the bloody imprint was left behind, then she turned to me.

"How about now, stranger? What do you think?"

"Perfect," I said, unable to look away from it.

Her sister tilted her head, studying me. "What's your name? You're always around, like a ghost."

"The Phantom," Lana said, smirking before I could answer. "He's the one who comes at night and takes people who ask too many questions."

Her sister huffed, shaking her head. "You two are weird," she mumbled, trudging off toward the house, leaving Lana and me alone in the snow.

I laughed softly. "She's not wrong," I said, looking at her.

That was the beginning.

After that day, we never parted. She was my Snow, and I was her Phantom. She was my light; I was her dark. My first girlfriend. The first person I let into my heart.

She was the first to know the truth.

That I wasn't whole. That I was split into eight fractured parts, each one surfacing when the world went dark. And yet, she accepted every part of me. Every single one.

She brought me back each time I fell, every time my masks threatened to pull me under. She took my hand and held on tighter than anyone ever had.

Until the day came when I couldn't bring her back.

Not anymore.

PRESENT DAY

A tear slid down my cheek as the wail of sirens echoed in the distance. Without a second thought, I ran deeper into the woods, leaving everything, and everyone behind.

I used to love. I was loved.

And now, somehow, I've found that again.

I love, and I am loved.

But I won't let what happened in the past repeat itself. Not to Bree. Never to Bree.

I'll stop it. Whatever it takes. Even if I have to hunt down every last member of The Family, past, present, or the ones yet to come.

I'm free now. And it's my turn to chase.

One by one, I'll find them.

It's fucking time.

Acknowledgements

I want to extend my deepest thanks to all my BETA readers and friends who stood by me through every mistake, tear, and laugh on this journey. I couldn't have done it without you. Thank you, guys, from the bottom of my heart.

A special thank you to my personal, personal assistants, Elizabeth and Molly, who were there for me, constantly encouraging me to keep writing. Your support has meant the world.

And finally, to all my readers who have been with me since day one, I'm incredibly thankful for each and every one of you.

Let this man with an axe be the one who takes your heart.

Love you all,

A.eM.

Made in the USA
Coppell, TX
03 February 2025

45140951R00238